STANDOFF ON THE PRAIRIE

"I'm sorry you feel that way," Seaforth said. "The only way I can figure to settle this is for my men and me to take your herd." The man shrugged. "It's only fair."

"You're not takin' our herd."

"Are you going to stop us?" Seaforth asked.

"We are."

"In case you can't add," Seaforth said to Chance, "you're outnumbered two-to-one."

"There's a rifle pointed right at you, Major," Jake said. "If you and your men try anythin', you'll be the first to die."

RALPH COMPTON

BIG JAKE'S LAST DRIVE

A RALPH COMPTON WESTERN BY

ROBERT J. RANDISI

BERKLEY
New York

BERKLEY
An imprint of Penguin Random House LLC
penguinrandomhouse.com

BERKLEY and the BERKLEY & B colophon
are registered trademarks of Penguin Random House LLC.

ISBN: 9780593102244

First Edition: June 2020

Printed in the United States of America
3   5   7   9   10   8   6   4   2

Cover art by Steve Atkinson
Book design by George Towne

This is a work of fiction. Names, characters, places, and incidents either are the product
of the author's imagination or are used fictitiously, and any resemblance to actual persons,
living or dead, business establishments, events, or locales is entirely coincidental.

THE IMMORTAL COWBOY

This is respectfully dedicated to the "American Cowboy." His was the saga sparked by the turmoil that followed the Civil War, and the passing of more than a century has by no means diminished the flame.

———◆———

True, the old days and the old ways are but treasured memories, and the old trails have grown dim with the ravages of time, but the spirit of the cowboy lives on.

———◆———

In my travels—to Texas, Oklahoma, Kansas, Nebraska, Colorado, Wyoming, New Mexico, and Arizona—I always find something that reminds me of the Old West. While I am walking these plains and mountains for the first time, there is this feeling that a part of me is eternal, that I have known these old trails before. I believe it is the undying spirit of the frontier calling me, through the mind's eye, to step back into time. What is the appeal of the Old West of the American frontier?

———◆———

It has been epitomized by some as the dark and bloody period in American history. Its heroes—Crockett, Bowie, Hickok, Earp—have been reviled and criticized. Yet the Old West lives on, larger than life.

———◆———

It has become a symbol of freedom, when there was always another mountain to climb and another river to cross; when a dispute between two men was settled not with expensive lawyers, but with fists, knives, or guns. Barbaric? Maybe. But some things never change. When the cowboy rode into the pages of American history, he left behind a legacy that lives within the hearts of us all.

—*Ralph Compton*

CHAPTER ONE

The death rattle could be heard very clearly for the Texas trail drive by the 1880s. And more clearly than ever for Big Jake Motley.

Motley considered himself a broken-down old bronc buster and cowboy at fifty-five years old. And not only was he broken down, but the Big M spread that had owned for over twenty-five years was also on its last legs. His acreage had been whittled down over the years by new outfits encroaching from both sides, either claiming land that he had mistakenly not filed deeds for, or buying large slices at a time when he had to sell parcels off to stay in business.

The main problem for Big Jake was that while he had always been a fine cowboy, he was a bad businessman. And where he once drove five to six thousand head of cattle from Texas to Kansas City, he was now down to his last six hundred head. And, terrible businessman that he was, he currently found himself with no hands for the drive. This meant riding into Brownsville, and other, smaller towns, to find men for hire.

And they would have to be men willing to work for a lot less than was usual. In addition, he wasn't going to be able to pay them until the drive was done and he was paid himself.

On this night he sat on his porch, smoking his pipe and staring out at what was left of his Big M spread. Usually, he enjoyed the feel of the Texas breeze on his face, the scent in his nostrils, but tonight it felt stagnant, and smelled of defeat.

He had managed to find a buyer for the ranch; the transaction would be completed just prior to Big Jake's last drive. Once he and his men left with those last six hundred cows, he'd have no place to come back to. His life as a cattle rancher would be over, and Big Jake Motley did not know what his future held.

But he was sure of one thing. For this final drive he needed two men to help him assemble a crew. One of them he'd hopefully find in Brownsville, but the other was out there . . . somewhere . . . for him to locate.

The first man was his old partner, Chance McCandless. They were the same age, and McCandless had given up trail drives long ago. But Big Jake needed a man he could trust. He didn't want anything to go wrong, and for that he needed an experienced, dependable trail boss— and that was Chance McCandless.

The second man he needed would act as his top hand, a position he had held many times before for Jake, but certainly not lately. He was José Luis Diego— his name was much longer than that, but Jake had never been able to remember it all. In the end, Jake had always called him, simply, Taco.

Taco was one of the more valuable things Big Jake had lost over the years. He wasn't sure what the Mex was doing these days, or where he was doing it, but he was hopeful that Taco would be willing and able to join him on this last venture.

He puffed on his pipe and continued to stare at what was certainly one of the last sunsets he'd see over the Big M, hoping that Chance and Taco would be able to help him through his last drive.

CHANCE MCCANDLESS STARED at the cards in his hands. He had aces and eights. If he wasn't mistaken, this was a bad omen, the hand Bill Hickok had been holding when he was shot to death from behind.

But McCandless didn't believe in other people's bad luck. He'd had plenty of his own, over the years, both good and bad. Now in his fifties, he had fallen on hard times. This was the reason he had recently been living across the Rio Grande from Brownsville, Texas, in Matamoros, Mexico. Most of his days were spent trying to turn what little money he had into more, playing poker. There weren't many other ways for a broken-down ex-cowboy to make money. He couldn't see himself clerking in a store, or swamping out a saloon.

"It's to you, señor," Hector Martinez said to him.

Martinez had dealt the hand and was the only player left after the other three—all also Mexicans—had dropped out. The Mexicans in Matamoros enjoyed attempting to take the gringo's money.

Martinez had opened and drawn three cards. McCandless had been dealt the aces and eights, and had drawn one. He could have stood pat, trying to bluff the others into thinking he had a perfect hand already. Instead, he had made the one-card draw in an attempt to improve, and failed. Now he had to decide whether or not Martinez had improved. Having drawn three cards, the Mexican had better odds for improving his hand than McCandless did. At that moment, he could have been sitting on three-of-a-kind. But McCandless had too much money invested in the pot to fold. He even considered raising, but instead just said, "I call."

Martinez laid his cards on the table with a big smile, revealing black rotted teeth surrounded by two gold ones.

"Three tens, señor." He held up three fingers. *"Tres."*

McCandless tossed his aces and eights on the table.

"Ah, señor," Martinez said, "such a unlucky hand."

"Yes," McCandless said, standing and giving his last ten dollars a wistful look as Martinez raked in the pot, "yes, it is."

As he left the cantina, Martinez called out, "Come back when you have more money, gringo."

Their laughter echoed in his head long after he left the building. He had to find something soon, or he would likely starve—or end up swamping a saloon for drinks and hard-boiled eggs.

IN THE MORNING Big Jake rose and prepared himself a meager breakfast. While his wife was alive breakfast was a celebration. Abby would cover the table with platters of food—eggs, bacon, potatoes, some days flapjacks and biscuits—and very often they'd have some hands eat with them, or Chance and Taco. But since her death ten years ago, Big Jake's meals had become more and more simple, and private. In fact, he could even trace the downward spiral of his life and ranch as having picked up speed at that point. He had pretty much been going downhill, toward an abyss, daily. Hopefully, she was waiting for him on the other side.

But living his life was ingrained in him, and giving up had never been an option. Hence the sale of the ranch and the planned last trail drive. When all of that was finally done, this part of his life would be as well, and he would be free to move on.

After breakfast he went outside and walked to the barn. Inside, where there were once thirty or forty horses, there were now two—one to pull his buckboard, and one saddle mount. That was another thing new hands would have to deal with: supplying their own mounts.

He walked his horse out and saddled it next to the empty corral; the dirt floor had long since ceased to be kicked up by hooves. The wind had blown away any remnants of tracks long ago, and there was now a smooth surface of undisturbed dirt.

Big Jake mounted his nine-year-old steeldust. He could tell that he would also need to get himself a new mount for the trail drive. He just hoped his old bones would be able to stand the rigors of such a ride. It had been years since he had gone on a drive himself, leaving it to younger men to get the herd where it needed to go, allowing his top hand or foreman to pick up the payments, and trusting them to bring it back.

His last good foreman had been Jessup Coleman, a man he employed and trusted for sixteen years, until he died in the saddle one day. The doctor said his heart simply gave out and that, for a man not yet fifty, he had the constitution of someone much older.

"He literally worked himself to death," the doctor told Jake, who knew the implication was that he had driven his foreman to death.

Since then he'd had several foremen and top hands, until they each moved on to greener pastures.

Chance McCandless had once told Jake, "You're lettin' this place die beneath you, Jake, and you with it." That was when Chance left, saying, "I ain't gonna watch you do it, and I ain't gonna wither away with you." He only hoped his old friend would sign back on when he heard what the plan was.

But before he could sign Chance McCandless up for the drive, he had to find him. And the same was true for Taco. Once both men were with him, he knew he would be able to pick up the rest that were needed. But that all had to happen soon, as the cattle were ready to go, and he needed to get them to market in top condition if he hoped to get the best price.

So first things first, a ride into Brownsville to see if anyone there had seen Chance McCandless recently.

B ROWNSVILLE HAD A colorful history. The town was the site of the first battle of the Mexican-American War, and the final battle of the Civil War. Yet with its storied past, it had yet to grow beyond its existence as a border town. Directly across the Rio Grande was Matamoros, Mexico's own version of Brownsville. It, too, had been the site of many battles of different wars, ranging from the Mexican Revolution, to the Texas Revolution, the Civil War, and the French Intervention.

As Big Jake Motley rode into Brownsville he drew the eyes of the locals, who had not seen him in town in some time. He even had a deal with the mercantile to deliver supplies to him every month so he wouldn't have to come to town. Once respected by the citizens of Brownsville, he was now nothing more than a curiosity to them.

Jake did not exchange looks, nods, or pleasantries with any of the people he rode past. He simply kept his eyes looking straight ahead. His wife, Abby, had been the one who made the friends, and invited people to the ranch, and when she died that had all simply stopped. Oh, some of his neighbors had made attempts to keep in touch, but it soon became apparent that Big Jake Motley couldn't be bothered, so folks just gave up.

Now here he was, riding right down Brownsville's main street, big as life.

He knew what they were thinking.

For the love of God, why?

CHAPTER TWO

Big Jake rode into Brownsville with definite destinations in mind. There were two people he was sure would know where he could find Chance McCandless.

First he reined in his horse in front of the sheriff's office. He had known Sheriff Ogden Smith—who folks called O.G.—ever since he first assumed the job twelve years before, while the Big M was still a going concern.

He looped the horse's reins around a hitching post, stepped up onto the boardwalk, and entered the sheriff's office.

O. G. Smith looked up from his desk with his customary scowl, but brightened when he saw who was coming in the door.

"Well, sonofabitch," O.G. said, "what the hell are you doin' off the reservation?"

The lawman was ten years younger and half a head taller than Jake. The scowl he wore had arrived during his first year in office, and grown increasingly worse year after year. These days it was enough to make people knock at his door before entering—except for old friends. But Jake could see O.G.'s taste for vivid colors in clothes hadn't changed. The blue of his shirt was enough to hurt the eyes, along with the red bandanna around his neck. Abby had tried her best for years, but could never break Jake of his habit of wearing brown.

He stood up, came out from behind his desk, and shook Jake's hand. It had been a while since Jake had felt that vise-like grip. He pulled his hand away and flexed his fingers.

"Take it easy, O.G.," he said. "I'm an old man with brittle bones."

"Well then, sit them bones down and tell me what brings you to town," O.G. said, returning to his chair. It creaked beneath his weight, but held.

"I'm lookin' for—"

"What the hell is wrong with my manners?" O.G. suddenly exploded, coming out of his chair again. "Want some coffee?"

"Sure, why not?"

"Don't know what's wrong with me," O.G. said, walking to the potbellied stove in the corner and pouring two mugs of coffee. "It's probably because I get no visitors in here."

He walked back, handed Jake a cup, and then sat back down, putting his cup on the desk.

It had been a while since Jake had sampled O.G.'s coffee. He sipped it and grimaced.

"You've gotten better," he said.

"That's good to hear," O.G. said. "I couldn't be sure because I'm the only one who drinks it. Okay, okay, I won't interrupt you again. What's on your mind?"

"I'm looking for Chance."

"McCandless?"

"Yes."

"Well," O.G. said, "you are comin' out into the open, aren't you? What do you need with Chance?"

"I'm mounting a trail drive, and I need him to come along."

"Come along?" O.G. said. "Does that mean you're goin', too?"

"Yes, it does."

"What about your old bones?"

"It's my last drive," Jake said. "The last one ever from the Big M. I ain't about to miss it."

"Yeah, but . . . Chance? Neither one of you is exactly in shape for a drive to . . . where? Not Kansas City."

"No," Jake said, "I know those days are over. Barbed wire and territorial ranchers now make it impossible to get to Kansas City. But there's still a route we can take."

"Where to?"

"Dodge City," Jake said.

"Dodge's heyday is long over, Jake—"

"I know that, O.G.," Jake said. "That sort of makes two of us. But there's still a railroad there."

"Aren't the splenic fever quarantines still going to be in force?" O.G. asked.

"They can check all they want, my cattle don't and won't have anthrax."

"I hope you're right."

"So," Jake said, "what about Chance. Has he been around?"

"Not in Brownsville," O.G. said. "Not that I've heard, anyway."

"Well," Jake said, putting the coffee cup down on the desk, "you were just my first stop."

"Right," O.G. said, "you'll probably be better off checkin' with bartenders."

"I'll get to that," Jake said, standing. "After I talk with Doc Volo."

"The doc," O.G. said. "That makes sense. He knows Chance pretty well."

"He should," Jake said. "He's taken enough iron out of his body over the years."

"Out of everyone's," O.G. said. "Jesus, he was here before any of us."

"Thanks for the coffee," Jake said, and headed for the door.

"Let me know if you find him!" O.G. called out as Jake left.

D OCTOR ETHAN VOLO had taken iron out of the bodies of men who were involved in some of those historic battles, particularly during the Civil War. After the war he decided to stay on in Brownsville, and was already there when Jake Motley bought the Big M. He had managed to keep Abby alive during her first pregnancy, when she lost the baby. He had also been at her bedside ten years ago, but could do nothing to keep her from dying when a high fever ravaged her body. To this day they still had no idea what the illness actually was, or what had brought it on. Maybe that fact fed the guilt Big Jake continued to feel about his wife's death.

Volo's office was two streets away from the sheriff's, so Jake walked his horse over there. While on foot he had actually received several head nods from citizens who recognized him. Grudgingly, he returned them, whether or not he recognized the person.

In front of Doc's he tied off his horse again and went inside.

There were no patients waiting in the office's outer room, but he could hear voices from the doctor's exam room. Rather than interrupt someone's doctor visit, he waited until the door opened and Volo walked over with a woman and a five- or six-year-old boy whose arm was in a sling.

"Now remember," Volo said in a voice thick with phlegm, "no more trees—at least none that are bigger than you. Understand, Toby?"

"Yes, sir."

As the boy and his mother left Volo looked over at Big Jake and said, "Well, hot damn. What're you doin' in town?"

"Just had a question to ask you, Doc," Jake said.

"Well, ask it," Volo said, taking off his wire-framed glasses and rubbing his faded blue eyes. "I got other patients comin' in."

"Have you seen Chance McCandless lately?"

"Chance," Volo said, replacing his glasses so that they sat down on the edge of his bulbous nose. "Another ghost from the past, huh?"

"Is it?" Jake asked.

"You and Chance . . . those were the days, huh, Jake?" Volo asked.

"Yeah, they were, Doc," Big Jake said. "And they're gone, but I think I'm gonna look to capture them one last time."

"Is that right?" Volo asked. "I heard you were sellin'."

"Not sellin'," Jake said. "Sold. But I got one last trail drive in me."

"You think so?" Volo asked. "You think those old bones of yours are gonna stand for it?"

"They better."

"I only got two words for you, Jake," Doc said. "Jess Coleman."

"Don't go there, Doc," Jake warned.

Volo put his hands up in surrender.

"Fine, you want Chance?" Volo asked. "Try across the border."

"How far across?" Jake asked.

"Right across," Doc said. "Matamoros. But I hear he's in a bad way."

"Physically?" Jake asked. "Or financially?"

"Every way possible," Volo said. "If you're gonna try to drive a herd east with you and Chance at the head of it, good luck."

"I ain't no idiot, Doc. I know I'm gonna need plenty of luck," Big Jake said, with a shrug. "But I gotta do this. I got nothin' left."

"Whose fault is that, Jake?" Volo said. "If Abby could see how you gave up after her death—"

"Thanks for the information, Doc," Jake said, and stormed out of the office without letting the old sawbones finish his thought.

Doc volo sat at his desk, took his glasses off again, and rubbed his eyes. There was a time he felt that both Jake and Chance were his friends. That was a long time ago. The death of Abby Motley seemed to have ended it all. Volo didn't know if Jake was even aware that his best friend had been in love with his wife. Her passing had destroyed two men in one fell swoop. Maybe those two men really did need one last trail drive to either bring them back to life, or just end it all on a high note.

Big jake motley untied his horse from the hitching post and mounted up. He sure as hell didn't need Doc Volo's two-word reminder about his foreman who had died in the saddle. Truth be told, Jessup Coleman probably wouldn't have wanted to die any other way than in the saddle, with his boots on. And if Jake Motley's bones gave out on him between Brownsville and

Dodge City, so be it. That would be better than dying while sitting on his porch, smoking his pipe and staring out over what was left of his former empire.

Maybe this was what he had in mind for this last drive, to finish it with his last breath, while offering Chance McCandless the same opportunity.

He directed his mount out of Brownsville and headed for the Rio Grande.

CHAPTER THREE

Matamoros had seen more battles than Brownsville, yet for a town with that lively a history, "sleepy" was still the only way to describe it as Big Jake rode in. Of course, that could simply have been because he arrived at siesta time. Mexican towns had a habit of suddenly coming awake, only to settle down once again at siesta time.

While Jake had the sheriff and the doctor to question in Brownsville about Chance McCandless's location, he had no such contacts across the border. For a man who lived on the Rio Grande, he could count the times he had crossed it on the fingers of one hand. Jake was a Texan through and through, and didn't leave home unless he had to.

As he rode down Matamoros's main street he drew none of the attention he had drawn across the border. It was not unusual for gringos to ride into town, looking for cheap tequila or even cheaper señoritas.

Jake had no choice. His best chance of locating Chance was to talk to bartenders. While the storekeepers and business owners loved it when gringos came to town, the same could not be said for the local *alguacile*—the sheriffs in sleepy towns liked their towns to stay that way. Liquored-up gringos only meant trouble. And while Chance McCandless might very well be in a local *cárcel,* Jake would save looking in the jail for after he talked to all the bartenders.

There was no law governing the business hours of the cantinas in Mexico, so they were pretty much all open. At the first cantina he took two sips of a warm beer and asked the bartender if he had seen a big gringo lately.

"Many gringos come in here, señor," the man said.

"You'd remember this one," Jake said. "He's a tall man, with big hands and ears."

"Ah, sí, the big ear gringo," the bartender said. "I have seen him."

"Do you know where he is now?"

"I am sorry, señor, no," the bartender said. "Perhaps one of the other cantinas?"

"Yeah," Jake said, "I'll check. Gracias."

"De nada, señor."

Jake left, walked his horse to the next cantina, just doors away. He got much the same result; yes, they had seen the gringo with the big ears; no, they did not know where he was now.

The third cantina he entered was larger, and had a poker game going on at one table. It also had a pretty Mexican girl working the floor, at the moment watching the game. Her peasant blouse was well off her smooth shoulders, which were partially covered by her long, black hair.

Jake went to the bar and ordered another *cerveza*, his third of the morning. Luckily, they were all warm and he wasn't drinking much of them.

When the bartender delivered his beer he asked the same question—gringo with the big ears.

"Sí, he has been in here, señor, but not for some time," the man said. "Perhaps—"

"I know," Jake said, "one of the other cantinas. Gracias."

Jake turned to head for the door, but at that moment a Mexican in a faded red shirt stood up from the poker table.

"Señor," he called. He waved Jake over, saying, *"Por favor."*

Jake walked over and asked, "What's on your mind?"

"Señor, you are looking for the gringo with the big ears?" the man asked, with a big smile.

"I am," Jake said. "Have you seen him?"

"Sí, señor," the man said, sitting back down, "but not since he lost the last of his money with aces and eights. A very bad hand." The man shook his head sadly as another Mexican sitting across from him dealt out the next hand. The pretty girl stood with her hand on the man's shoulder. She seemed more interested in him than the game.

"You wouldn't happen to know where he is now, would you?" Jake asked.

"I do, sí, señor. And I will tell you because perhaps you will give him some money so he can get back into our game, eh?"

"That's a possibility."

"Ah, *muy bien.* There is a cantina at the very edge of town, señor; just keep going until you reach the end—presto, there it is!"

"He's there?" Jake asked.

"The bartender will know where he is, sí. But a word of advice, señor. Do not drink the *cerveza* there." He made a face. *"Muy malo!* Very bad!"

"Thanks for the warnin'," Jake said, "and the tip."

"De nada, señor," the man said. "Tell your amigo a chair is always open for him."

Jake couldn't imagine that Chance's poker playing had gotten any better over the years, so he knew why the Mexicans wanted him to come back.

The last thing he would ever do was give Chance McCandless money to play poker.

JAKE FOLLOWED THE bartender's directions and walked directly to the far end of town. The very last building there, which looked as if a stiff breeze would blow it away, was a cantina.

He secured his horse out front and entered. As he walked to the small bar the wooden floor sounded hollow beneath his bootheels.

There was only one other patron in the place, a man with his head down on a table, a sombrero covering it. But he could tell that it wasn't Chance McCandless.

"Ah, señor," the rotund bartender said, "you are perhaps thirsty?"

"I was warned about your beer," Jake admitted.

The man smiled, revealing one gold tooth among the yellow.

"That is because they are jealous, señor. Do you know why?"

"No, tell me why."

"Because my *cerveza* is the only cold *cerveza* in town."

"Well," Jake said, "in that case, I'll have one."

"Muy bien, señor.*"* The bartender drew the beer and set it in front of Jake, beads of cold plain on the side.

Jake lifted it, sipped, and nodded approvingly.

"I can see why they're jealous," he said.

"Sí, señor," the man said. "Please, spread the word."

Jake knew he wasn't going to be in Matamoros long enough to do the man any good, but he said, "I'll do that. Now maybe you can help me."

"Sí, señor. I will try."

"I'm looking for a friend of mine," Jake said, "a gringo with big ears. I heard that he might be here."

"Oh, sí, señor," the bartender said, happily, "your amigo, he is here."

Jake looked around.

"Where?"

"He is in the back, señor," the man said, "Asleep. I let him sleep there and he swamps out the cantina for me at night."

Jake cringed at the thought of Chance swamping out a saloon just for a place to sleep. He had no idea his friend had fallen this far.

"Can I go back there?"

"Oh, sí, señor," the bartender said. "He must wake so he will be ready for the next siesta."

"I'll tell him."

Jake drank half his cold beer, then left it on the bar and walked to the back. There was a curtained doorway to the back area, which he assumed was for storage. As he entered he saw that he was right. There were sacks and boxes and crates all around. For a moment he couldn't locate Chance, but then he saw him, lying on some sacks he had used to make a mattress.

He walked over and looked down at his old friend. The ears were the same, but everything else seemed different. He was lying there slack-jawed, his shirt hanging out of his pants, more belly beneath it than there used to be, and the smell of liquor in the air came from more than just all the bottles on the shelves around them.

"Chance."

He didn't move.

"Come on, Chance."

He nudged the man, who still didn't move. He leaned in close to make sure his old friend was breathing.

A quick look around the room didn't reveal anything he could use to wake him. Dousing him with whiskey wasn't going to help. But then he found himself looking out the back window, and saw something useful. He opened the back door, then went to Chance, grabbed him by one leg, and dragged him off the sacks. He then pulled the unconscious man across the floor—with difficulty, since he was so heavy—and out the door. Even dragging him over the hardscrabble dirt, raising dust clouds the entire way, didn't wake him up.

But when he reached his goal, Jake—with great difficulty—managed to get Chance up and over the side, into the horse trough full of water.

If Chance McCandless had not awakened he surely would have drowned. But he did come awake, and began struggling and sputtering, trying to figure out what was happening while also fighting to get out of the trough.

Finally, he simply sat up and looked around, saw and recognized Motley. He stared at him with what seemed like great effort, scowling.

"Jake?"

"Hello, Chance."

"What the hell—"

"Are you awake?"

"Goddammit, Jake, I'm awake and wet. What the hell did you do?"

"I had to do somethin'," Jake said. "You were dead to the world."

"I was asleep!"

"You were unconscious," Jake said, "in an alcoholic stupor."

"I was asleep." He used his big hands to wipe his face. "This water is filthy."

"Then let's get you out of there, Chance," Jake offered.

He extended his hand to the bigger man, and helped

him step out. From there Chance lowered his big keister to the edge of the trough. He took some deep breaths, rubbed his face again with his hands, and then stared at Jake without scowling.

"It's good to see you, Big Jake."

CHAPTER FOUR

J AKE HELPED CHANCE to his feet, through the back
door and storeroom, and into the cantina.

"Ah, señor, you woke him," the bartender said.

"It wasn't easy, but yes," Jake said, helping Chance
to sit at a table. The man at the other table still had his
head down on his arms.

"Drinks, señor?" the barman asked.

"Yes," Jake said. "Coffee, black."

"Sí, señor," the man said. *"Inmediatamente!"*

Jake sat across from Chance, who was now shivering.

"We'll get some coffee into you," Jake said, "and
then get you into some dry clothes. You do have some
dry clothes, don't you?"

"Th-things have been a little l-lean lately," Chance
said. "I'm wearin' my only clothes."

"Well, there's gotta be a store in town. We'll get you
somethin'."

The bartender came over with a pot of coffee and two
mugs. He poured them each full, and set them down.

"Thanks, Manny," Chance said.

"De nada, Señor *Orejas Grandes*."

As Manny went back to the bar Jake asked Chance, "What did he call you?"

"Señor Big Ears," Chance said.

"Oh," Jake said. "Of course."

Chance greedily drank down half of the hot coffee and set the mug down on the table. For a moment, at least, the shivering stopped.

"Jake," Chance said, "what the hell are you doin' out of Texas?"

"I'm not that far outside of Texas," Jake said. "But I came here lookin' for you."

"It's been years," Chance said.

"Nearly eight."

"Well," Chance said, "I hope the last eight years have been kinder to you than they've been to me."

"I'm not here to compare hardships, Chance," Jake said, "I'm here to give us both a second chance."

"To do what?" Chance asked.

"To live again," Jake said, "Or die doin' what we love to do."

"Which is?"

"A trail drive."

Chance stared at his friend.

"Trail drives are dead," he said. "The trails are blocked, quarantines are up—"

"We can make it," Jake said.

"To where?"

"Dodge City."

Now Chance looked shocked.

"Dodge is dead."

"There's still a railroad there," Jake said. "Look, I've got six hundred head left. I want to get them to market. It's my last drive."

"And the Big M?"

"I sold it."

Chance sat back in his chair.

"Sold it?"

"Let's face it, Chance," Jake said. "All these years I been a shit businessman. But I've always been a good cowboy. I probably shoulda spent the past twenty-five years bein' somebody else's top hand."

"Fine time to realize somethin' like that," Chance said. "Okay, lemme get this straight. You're gonna drive these cows to Dodge City yourself?"

"Right."

"And you want me to come with you?"

"Right again."

"Who else do you have?"

"Right now . . . nobody."

"No one?" Chance asked. "What happened to all your hands?"

"I had a few that helped me get the herd into Candy Box Canyon," he said, "but when they found out I couldn't pay them until after the drive, they left."

"So you and me—two broken-down old cowpokes— and six hundred head?"

"We'll come up with more men."

"How?"

"Well . . . I was hopin' you'd be able to tell me that."

Chance drank some coffee, then poured more while he thought.

"This is crazy to even think about," he said, finally.

"Would you rather swamp saloons in a Mexican town?" Jake asked. "I'll give you a percentage. Then we just need half a dozen other cowboys."

"Half a dozen men who won't mind bein' paid after the drive," Chance said.

"That's right."

"I ain't been on a horse in a dog's age, Jake," Chance admitted.

"Ridin' ain't somethin' you forget, Chance."

Chance studied his friend's face.

"By God, you're really serious."

"I am."

"And crazy."

"As a scalded cat."

Chance rubbed his face vigorously with both hands, then said, "We're gonna need Taco."

BIG JAKE MOTLEY had enough money on him to get Chance a bath and some new clothes. Once that was done, they went back to the little cantina that served the only cold beer in Matamoros.

"Tequila, Señor *Orejas Grandes*?" Manolito the bartender asked.

"Just a beer, Manny," Chance said.

"The same," Jake said.

"Sí, señores."

Jake looked around the little cantina, saw that there was still only one other customer, the man with his head down on his arms.

"Who's that?" he asked Manny, when he served their beers.

"Oh, señor, that is Desiderio."

"Does he spend his days that way?" Jake asked.

"Oh no, señor," Manny said, "only when his heart, she is broken."

"And how often does that happen?"

Smiling broadly, Manny said, "Señor, Desi falls in love and has his heart broken every week."

"And when Desi's heart ain't broken," Jake asked, "what's he do?"

"Ah, Desi is a *vaquero*, señor."

Jake and Chance exchanged a glance. Jake noticed that his friend's glassy eyes had cleared some with the half a beer he drank. He just had to keep Chance away from tequila for a while.

"Is he a good cowboy?" Jake asked.

"Oh, sí, señor," Manny said. "*Muy bien!* But you must keep him from falling in love."

"Should be easy on a drive, right?" Jake asked Chance.

"I would think so," Chance said.

The two men picked up their beers, walked over, and sat on either side of Desiderio, the *vaquero*.

The sad-eyed Desiderio raised his head. Once he saw that neither of them was armed he was not alarmed at their appearance at his table.

"Señores," he said. "I can help you?"

"Maybe," Jake said, "we can help each other."

"Oh? How may we do that, señor?"

"I understand you're a *vaquero*?"

"Sí, señor, I am."

"On what ranch are you workin'?" Jake asked.

"Alas, señor, I am without employment," Desiderio said, "but that does not matter, as my heart is broken. I cannot work when the woman I love does not love me back."

"Well," Chance said, "wouldn't you like to get out of this town, so you don't see her every day?"

"Oh, sí, señor," Desiderio said, "that would be ideal, but alas, no one is hiring."

"Well now," Jake said, "I think that's where I can help you."

BIG JAKE MOTLEY felt that his ride across the Rio Grande to Matamoros had been a lucrative one. He came away with Chance McCandless as his foreman, and Desiderio as one of his cowboys.

However, he wasn't quite ready to leave yet.

"We need Taco," he said.

"Manolito will make you tacos," Desiderio said.

"No," Chance clarified, "we're lookin' for a man named Taco."

"Ah, Taco," Desiderio said. "Sí."

"Do you know him?" Jake asked.

"Sí, señor," Desiderio said, "he is my cousin." Then his eyes widened and he smiled. "Ah, you are that Señor Jake!"

"He spoke of me?"

"Oh sí, señor, many times," Desi said. "And you are Señor Chance!"

"I am."

"Sí, sí," Desi said, "he told me of many adventures you had together. Oh, this is wonderful." He seemed to be very animated for the first time since they had awakened him. "Now I, too, will have wondrous adventures with Señores Jake and Chance."

"That may be true," Jake said, "but we also need your cousin Taco."

"Oh, sí, sí, señor," Desi said. "I know where my cousin is. I will take you to him."

"Is he here, in Matamoros?" Jake asked.

"No, señor, but he is nearby. I will take you!" Desi said, happily.

"Do we need horses?" Jake asked.

"Sí, señor, but I have my own."

Jake looked at Chance.

"No extra shirt, no horse," he said, with a shrug.

"That figures," Jake responded.

CHAPTER FIVE

J AKE MOTLEY'S FUNDS were earmarked for all his trail drive expenses. That included three horses per man and the chuckwagon. He expected each man to supply his own bedroll, rifle, and rope. So buying Chance McCandless a horse in Matamoros just went on the list. But the bath and clothes for his friend came from his own pocket.

Once he had bought Chance a horse—a decent five-year-old bay mare who looked solid enough for a trail drive—they followed Desi to the place where he said they would find his cousin Taco.

Taco's real name was much too long for Jake to ever pronounce, so years ago the Mexican just told Jake he could call him Taco, as many of his own family members did.

"Is that your favorite thing to eat?" Jake had asked him.

"No, señor," Taco said, "but I did not want my family to start calling me Enchilada."

Desi took them about twenty miles outside of Matamoros, deeper into Mexico, which made Jake a bit uncomfortable. If he was going to be this far from the Rio Grande, he preferred it be on a trail drive.

They reined in their horses in front of a large, two-story structure with boarded-up windows. There was a front porch, but nothing on it, no furniture, and certainly no people. The front door was weather-beaten and faded.

"Do you know what this place is?" Jake asked Chance.

"Yeah," he said, "it's Lady Conchita's Whorehouse."

"I ain't goin' in there," Jake said, appalled.

"We'll send Desi in to get him to come out," Chance said.

"Conchita's," Desi said, spreading his arms and smiling.

"Damn," Jake said, "according to what Manny said, if we send Desi in there he's gonna fall in love and be useless to us."

"Okay, and you're not goin' in there because then you'll go to hell."

"If Abby knew I even stepped foot in a whorehouse—" Jake started.

"Relax, Jake," Chance said. He'd forgotten what a prude his old friend was about some things, especially whores. Not that he had never been with one. In his youth, Jake Motley had probably patronized every whorehouse in South Texas. But marrying Abby Cummings, a devout churchgoing woman, had changed him drastically.

Chance dismounted and handed Jake the reins of his horse.

"I will come with you, señor," Desi said enthusiastically.

"No!" Jake snapped. "Stay out here with me, Desi. Chance will get Taco and bring him out."

"Does he have a favorite girl?" Chance asked.

"Oh, you do not understand, señor," Desi said. "Taco is not a customer, he is employed here. He keeps the girls safe."

"That sounds more like the Taco I remember," Jake said. He had been harboring some disappointment that they had to go to a whorehouse to find his old friend. But hearing that the Mexican was there safe-guarding the girls, and not sampling them, made him feel better.

"Well," Chance said in a self-deprecating manner, "let's hope when these whores get a gander at this old cowpoke, they let me leave."

"Just go in and bring Taco out here," Jake said. "He belongs on a horse on a drive with us, not in there."

"Well, he better join us for the love of it," Chance pointed out, "because he ain't gonna do it for what you'll be payin' him."

Chance went up onto the porch and knocked on the faded, peeling door. He expected it to be opened by a scantily clad girl, but it was Taco himself who opened it.

"Señor Chance!" the little Mexican said in surprise.

The two men had formed a bond of friendship long ago, one that could not be circumvented by the dispar-ity in their size. Next to Chance, Taco looked like a twelve-year-old boy, but smiled broadly and the two old friends shared an awkward hug.

"What brings you here, mi amigo?" Taco asked. As usual, the silver buttons were gleaming on his vest, and the gold from his teeth shining. He did not look like he had aged a day, wearing his years much better than Chance and Jake were. He also had a pistol tucked into his belt, which was something Chance was not used to seeing. Usually the three of them carried only rifles. None of them had any illusions about being a *pistolero*.

"I'm here with our old friend Big Jake," Chance said, pointing.

"Ah, I see . . . and is that my cousin Desi?"

"Yes, he's joinin' us," Chance said.

"Joining you to do what, amigo?"

"Drive a herd to Dodge City, Taco," Chance said. "It's Big Jake's last drive. He's sold his ranch."

"Ah, well," Taco said, pounding his chest, "Desi is a very good *vaquero*, but he is not Taco. You will need me, señor."

"That's exactly what we were thinkin'," Chance said. "Do you have a horse?"

"Sí, in the back." Taco stepped out onto the porch and closed the door behind him, thus also closing out his life in a whorehouse.

"Don't you need to tell them you're leavin'?" Chance asked.

"Oh, señor," Taco said, waving a hand, "when they see I am gone they will know I have left."

"And don't you want to know what you're to be paid?"

"Señor," he said, taken aback by the question, "you and Señor Jake are my amigos. Whatever you pay me will be fair. It will take me but a moment to get my horse."

While Taco hurried to the rear of the house, Chance joined Jake and Desi. He accepted his reins back and mounted up.

"Where's he goin'?" Jake asked.

"To get his horse."

Taco appeared moments later, riding a rangy paint, as usual. If Jake and Chance didn't know better they would have thought it was the same horse the Mexican always rode.

"Desi, *primo*," he cried out, "*cómo estás?*"

"*Bien, Taco, muy bien.*"

"Señor Jake," Taco said, riding up to the man and shaking his hand, "*el ultimo viaje*, eh?"

"Taco," Jake said, "you know I don't talk Mex."

"The last drive, señor," Taco translated. "It is sad, no?"

"It could be sad, Taco," Jake said, "or it could be a new beginning."

"At our age, señor?" Taco said, smiling. "Surely you are joking."

"Did Chance tell you what I'm payin'?" Jake asked. "And when?"

"Ah, señor, that does not matter," Taco said. "How could I not go on my good friend's last drive, eh?" He waved a dismissive hand. "Whatever you pay me will be fine."

"Well," Jake said, "we need at least four more men, and they're not gonna feel the same."

"Do you wish me to suggest some *vaqueros*, señor?" Taco asked.

"No," Jake said, "I want to go back to Texas and find them. I'm gonna be hearin' enough Mex talk between you and your cousin."

"Ah, but señor," Desi said, "Spanish is the language of God."

Chance watched Jake closely. His friend had come to a parting of ways with God when his wife died. At that point he stopped going to church, observing Catholic holidays, and even started eating meat on Fridays.

"You talk to God, Desi," Jake said. "I'd rather talk to my cows."

Big Jake turned his horse and started riding back to Matamoros, and the Rio Grande.

Desi looked at his cousin and asked, *"Que dijo?"*

"It is not what you said, *mi primo*," Taco replied, "but who you said it to. Come," he said as Chance followed Jake, "I will explain on the way."

CHAPTER SIX

CHANCE MCCANDLESS AND Taco were saddened by the state they found the Big M in. They both remembered it as a huge, sprawling empire. The two-story house itself was in need of paint and repairs, as were the barn and the corral.

Desi, who had never seen the ranch before, was impressed, but Taco waved away any approving comments from his cousin before he could utter them.

"Chance, you can stay in the house," Jake said as they dismounted, "Taco, you can show your cousin to the bunkhouse, where the two of you will stay. Hopefully, it'll only take a matter of days for us to find our additional hands."

"And the herd, it is safe?" Taco asked.

"It's in Candy Box Canyon, and I blocked the mouth with a gate of sorts. They should be fine there until we go and collect them."

"Señores," Taco said, "we will take your horses to the barn."

"Thanks, Taco."

Jake and Chance handed over the reins of their animals. On the walk to the corral Taco explained to Desi why he should not rave about the ranch.

"But, cousin," Desi said, puzzled, "I have never seen such a place . . ."

AFTER CHANCE DROPPED his rifle and new saddle-bags off in his room, he came back downstairs and found Jake sitting at a desk in front of a window. The inside of the house was not in the same state of disrepair that the outside was. It looked the way it had the day Abby died. She had done all the decorating, had directed the building of some of the furniture, bought some of the other pieces, and it looked as if Jake had not changed a thing. Chance had to admit that he felt right at home being back in that house.

"Paperwork was never your strong point," he observed, sitting across from his friend.

"You don't have to tell me that," Jake said. "That was why I had Abby do the numbers. When she died the paper just took over."

"And now?" Chance asked.

"Now I've got to make it work," Jake said. "I need to buy the horses we're gonna need for the *remuda*, outfit the chuckwagon—"

"You buyin' a chuckwagon and an equipment wagon?"

"No, we're just gonna have a chuckwagon, and I'm hopin' to find a cook who has his own. We can load it with food and supplies rather than using two wagons. We're only gonna have six men and the cook."

"Six? You said we needed four more."

"I was thinkin' about that on the ride back from Mexico. I think two more waddies is all we need, and I'd like them to be young and white." "Waddy" was cowboy slang for a hired hand.

"You should be able to find two like that in Browns-ville," Chance said.

"I hope so."

"How much are you gonna pay?"

"I'll offer the two new waddies twenty-five a week. Desi and Taco I'll give forty. You'll get fifty, although I'd like to give you more."

"You said somethin' about a percentage."

"That, too, but I wanna pay you—"

"I'll just take the percentage, Jake," Chance said. "Just worry about payin' the boys."

"Okay, Chance, we'll do it that way."

"How many horses you wanna have along?"

"Three horses a man, I think."

"Six hands, that's eighteen. The four of us have our own, so you have to buy fourteen. You got the money for those horses and the supplies?"

Jake sat back in his chair.

"I've gotta go to the bank and meet my buyer. He'll pay me for the ranch, then I'll pay the bank what I owe in mortgage and loans. What's left over should cover the bills for this drive."

"How much are you lookin' to sell the herd for?"

"I'm hoping for at least fifteen dollars a head. We're startin' with six hundred head, and I'm gonna try not to lose too many of those along the way."

"Gotta lose some," Chance pointed out. "Even if it's just the ones we eat."

"I'm countin' on you and Taco to watch out for the herd, and watch over the other hands."

"Want me to come to town with you?" Chance asked.

"Might as well," he said. "We'll take Taco and Desi, too. We can all eat, find our last two hands, buy the supplies and horses, and go to the bank. But that'll all be tomorrow."

"And what about the cook and chuckwagon?" Chance asked.

"I've got a coupla ideas," Jake said. "Maybe you do, too?"

"I can think of a few names, hopefully they're still around."

"We'll find out tomorrow."

"What about eatin' tonight?" Chance asked. "You gonna cook?"

Jake made a face and said, "I was kinda hopin' you would."

"Let's see if either one of our Mexican *vaqueros* can ride a stove."

As IT TURNED out, Desi could cook. He looked at what Jake had in his root cellar and managed to make a meal out of it for the four of them.

"That was pretty good, Desi," Chance said, sitting back in his chair. "Maybe we should make you the cook on the drive."

"Oh, señor," Desi said, "I appreciate the offer, but Desi is a *vaquero*, not a cook."

"That's okay, Desi," Jake said. "I'm lookin' for a cook who has his own chuckwagon. It'll cut down on my expenses."

"Oh, but señor, I know just the person," Desi said, looking at Taco. "Cousin, what about Carlito?"

"Who's Carlito?" Jake asked.

"Another cousin," Taco said thoughtfully. "Sí, he might be your man."

Jake wasn't sure he wanted another Mexican on the drive, let alone making him the cook.

"Can he cook American?" Jake asked.

"Sí, he can cook anythin', señor," Desi said.

Jake looked to the older cousin, Taco, for the final word.

"Would he do it, Taco? And does he have his own wagon?"

"Sí, señor," Taco said, "you would only need to buy the supplies."

"Okay," Jake said, "Chance and me, we're goin' into Brownsville tomorrow to find two more hands and do some other business. How far would you have to ride back into Mexico to get your cousin?"

"Not far, señor," Taco said. "We could all be back here by tomorrow night—with the wagon."

Jake looked at Chance.

"Sounds doable, Jake," he said. "And when we hire two more waddies from Brownsville, we'll still out-number these Mex rascals."

"All right, then," Jake said, "let's do it."

"Sí, señor," Desi said, standing. "And I will clean up here."

"Let it go, Desi," Jake said. "Chance and me'll clean up. You and Taco turn in. I want you to get an early start tomorrow mornin'."

"As you wish, jefe," Desi said.

Taco and Desi left the house to go back to the bunk-house. Jake and Chance cleaned off the table, but left the dishes piled in the kitchen. They went back to the table to share some coffee.

"It's a small price to pay," Chance said, "havin' a Mexican cook, if he's got his own chuckwagon."

"I shoulda asked Taco if we had to buy him a team of mules to pull it."

"Seems to me a fella who's got his own wagon would also have his own team."

"Sounds right," Jake said.

"You wanna split up tomorrow?" Chance asked.

"You go to the bank, and I'll go and look at some horses?"

"We might as well split the chores," Jake said. "Then we can look for two hands together."

"I'll ask the hostler at the livery if he knows anybody lookin' for work," Chance suggested.

"Good idea. If not him, then some bartender is gonna know."

Chance sat back in his chair and looked around the dining room. There was a large cabinet filled with china he knew Abby loved, and they were seated at a long dining room table she had had delivered from St. Louis.

"Whadaya gonna do with all this stuff?" he asked. "The furniture and all."

Jake hesitated before answering. He wasn't sure how his friend would take what he was about to say.

"I'm sellin' the place as is, Chance," he said finally.

"All Abby's stuff?" Chance asked.

"The buyer's young wife loves it all," Jake said, "and I agreed to just leave it be. I mean, what the hell would I do with all of it if I don't have a house to put it in?"

"I guess you got a point," Chance said.

"I'm convinced she wouldn't mind," Jake said.

"I think you're right," Chance said. "Why not let some other young bride enjoy it all."

Jake noticed his friend's eyes still roaming around the room.

"You wanna sweeten that coffee with a little whiskey?" he asked.

"I do," Chance said, licking his lips, "but . . ."

"It's okay," Jake said. He got up, went to the front room, took a bottle of whiskey out of his desk drawer, and carried it back to the dining room.

"Tonight we can have it," he said, pouring some into

each of their coffee cups, "but once we start the drive, no whiskey for anybody."

"That sounds fair," Chance said.

So fair, in fact, that once the coffee was gone, they continued to pour whiskey into their cups.

"I think that's enough," Jake finally said. "Let's turn in, and clean the kitchen tomorrow before we go to town."

Chance gave the half-full whiskey bottle a wistful look before Jake whisked it away and put it back in his desk drawer—which he locked.

CHAPTER SEVEN

IN THE MORNING Jake rose before Chance, went into the kitchen, and cleaned it, because Abby would have turned over in her grave if he didn't. When somebody knocked on the door it turned out to be Taco and Desi, to tell him they were heading out.

"I'm glad you stopped here first," Jake said. "I don't need to buy your cousin a team of mules, do I?"

"He will have his own, jefe," Desi assured him.

"And are you sure he'll come along?" Jake asked.

"It is either that," Taco said, "or stay home with his fat wife and ten children."

"He will come," Desi said, and both cousins laughed.

As they turned and left, Jake closed the front doors, and Chance came down the stairs.

"Who was that?"

"Taco and Desi," Jake said. "They're on their way."

Chance was scowling and squinting, probably both because of a headache.

"We got any coffee?"

"I thought we'd have breakfast in town," Jake said. "Whadaya say?"

"Let's get a move on," Chance replied. "I need coffee."

They went to the barn, saddled up, and headed to Brownsville.

B IG JAKE MOTLEY and Chance McCandless riding back into Brownsville was enough to draw looks on the street. For Jake, it was his second day in town. For Chance, his first day in years. These two men were well known on sight in Brownsville, but no one was thrilled to see them, just curious. What were they doing in town after all this time? And why were they together again when everyone knew that Chance had left the Big M?

Jake reined in his horse in front of the bank, followed by Chance.

"Let's get breakfast across the street," Jake said, "then you can go down to the livery stable on Market Street. He'll have the best horses."

They walked across the street to the Borderline Café and entered. Many of the tables were occupied, and the patrons looked up from their plates to see who was coming in. When they saw Jake and Chance, some of them stared, some quickly looked away.

"What's your reputation in town, these days?" Chance asked.

"I'm crotchety," Jake said, "and not lookin' to make any new friends."

"I can tell."

"What about you?"

"I've been across the border for so long, I don't think these people know me anymore."

"You're bein' modest."

A tall man with a dirty white apron came over and said, "Mr. Motley, Mr. McCandless, it's been a long time."

"You still serve food, don'tcha?" Jake asked.

"Oh yes, sir."

"Well then, we'll take a table with a little privacy."

"Sure, sure, gents," the man said. "This way."

"I see what you mean," Chance said as they followed the waiter. "Crotchety."

They sat at a table that had only one other occupied table near it. The two men there looked over, recognized the pair, and then put their heads together.

Jake and Chance gave their order to the waiter before he withdrew. They wanted their food and coffee quickly.

"I knew I hadn't been here in a while, but when's the last time you were in town?"

"I was here yesterday," Jake said, "but before that . . . I don't know. Months."

"These folks seem real curious about us," Chance said.

"I . . . sort of withdrew after Abby died," Jake said. "Stayed to myself."

"I remember."

"Well, you didn't stay around very long."

"If I had," Chance said, "we woulda killed each other, Jake. We needed that time apart."

"And now we need this last drive," Jake said.

"When it's over," Chance said, "we'll know how much we needed it. I told you, I ain't been ridin' much lately. My butt's already sore from bein' in the saddle yesterday and today."

"You'll get your seat back, Chance."

"What about you?" Chance asked. "You been ridin'?"

"Yeah," Jake said, "I had to ride to get that herd

together. I couldn't trust the men I had. About the only thing good about them was they could do what they were told, but I couldn't trust them to work on their own."

"Okay, but ridin' on your land is a lot different from ridin' to Dodge."

"We're gonna find out just how much we can take," Jake said.

The waiter came, then, with their plates and coffee. Chance greedily drank his first cup and poured another. Only then did he take his first bite of eggs. Jake noticed his friend was sweating.

"How bad is it, Chance?"

"What?"

"How bad was the drinkin'?" Jake asked. "When I found you . . . was that usual?"

"It was pretty bad," Chance said, "but don't worry. I'll be okay. I just gotta get through these next few days."

Jake was hoping he hadn't made a mistake by pulling his old friend in on this job. The drinking, the shape he was in, Chance could end up being a problem rather than a help. But in their prime, Jake had never known a more reliable man in the saddle. He just hoped they both had this one last drive in them.

He stopped worrying about it and began to eat.

AFTER BREAKFAST THEY paid their bill and stepped outside, ignoring the curious looks. Jake hadn't realized what a stranger he'd become in town until now. The bank, right across the street, had opened for business.

"My buyer should be in there, waitin' for me," Jake said.

"The deal is made, right?" Chance asked. "It's just a matter of paperwork?"

"Yeah," Jake said, "but you know how I am about paperwork."

"Just sign on the dotted line, Jake," Chance said, "and get it over with."

"Good advice," Jake said. "Get us some good horses, Chance, at a fair price. Then come and get me. By then I should have the cash."

"I'll do that," Chance said. "See you in a while."

Chance headed off down the street to the livery while Jake crossed to the bank.

THE BUYER WAS waiting in the bank manager's office when Jake arrived.

"Come on in, Jake," Ben Caplock, the manager, said. "Everything's ready for your signature."

Jake followed the well-dressed, barrel-chested manager into his office. There was one other man there, his buyer, Edwin Forest. The manager closed the door.

"We'll have plenty of privacy," he said, sitting behind his desk.

Jake sat next to the buyer, asking, "Your wife's not here?"

The man looked at him and smiled. His Eastern-cut suit was out of place here in the West, but the young man had assured Jake that he and his wife were committed to becoming Westerners.

"Laura's quite excited about this, and is already shopping for items that she wants to add to what's already in the house. I don't quite understand it, but . . ." He shrugged.

"I'm sure you're also committed to making the necessary repairs to the property," the manager said.

"Oh, indeed," Forest said, "but I am more concerned with the outside. The inside will be entirely up to her."

"I know what that's like," Jake assured him.

Forest smiled. He and his wife were more than twenty years younger than Jake. They might even have been the age Jake and Abby were when they built the Big M.

"Here are the papers," Ben Caplock said, pushing the documents over to Jake's side of the desk. "Mr. Forest has already signed."

Jake leaned forward, saw the younger man's flourishing signature on all the papers.

Caplock held up another slip of paper.

"You sign and this bank draft is yours," he said.

"Have you already taken what I owe your bank?" Jake asked.

"Not at all," Caplock said. "This is the entire amount Mr. Forest is paying you for your ranch. When you and he have completed your transaction, you and I can discuss ours."

Jake nodded, leaned forward, picked up the pen, dipped it into the ink, and signed in three places.

"I'll take those," Caplock said, retrieving the documents, "and this is yours." He handed Jake the bank draft.

Jake accepted it and nodded his approval when he saw the amount.

Edwin Forest stood up and extended his hand to Jake.

"Thank you for this, Mr. Motley," he said as they shook. "You've made my wife a very happy woman."

"I'm glad."

"I hope you don't mind, but my first act as new owner will be to change the name of the ranch."

"That's your right."

Forest turned and shook hands with the bank manager, who handed him a copy of the documents.

"We will make sure the rest of these are filed properly," he said.

"Thank you."

Forest started for the door.

"If you don't mind . . ." Jake said.

"Yes?" Forest turned at the door.

"What will you be naming the ranch?"

Forest smiled.

"We're simply going to call it 'Laura.' It has a Southern feel to it, doesn't it?"

"But . . . you're not Southern," Jake said.

"Laura is," Forest said. "Her family is from Atlanta. Thank you again, gents."

"I'll walk you out," Caplock said, rising and quickly walking to the door. "I'll be right back, Jake." Both men left.

CHAPTER EIGHT

A S CAPLOCK REENTERED his office moments later, he was surprised to see Jake Motley still sitting there with the bank draft in his hands, staring.

"That's a lot of money, Jake," Caplock said.

"Yeah, it is, Ben," Jake said. "Too bad I can't keep it all."

"But you can," Caplock said, seating himself behind his desk. "You don't need to cover all your debts now. You can make payments—"

"I've been makin' payments for years," Jake said. "I'm tired of it. Besides, I don't have any idea if I'm gonna be comin' back from this trail drive."

"You expect to die?"

"I might," Jake said. "I'm a worn-out old cuss. I might die on the trail. But even if I don't, what reason would I have to come back here?"

"I understand," Caplock said. "No home, no family, and . . ."

". . . no friends, I know," Jake said.

"You had friends here, Jake," Caplock said, "once."

"Abby had friends," Jake said. "I was . . . tolerated."

"Now, Jake—"

Jake held the bank draft out to Caplock.

"Take what I owe and I'll have the rest back in cash," Jake said. "I've got some purchases to make."

"Well then," Caplock said, "I better get to it." He stood up. "Wait here."

W HEN CAPLOCK RETURNED he was carrying a canvas bag with the bank's logo on it. He set it down on the desk in front of Jake, and then sat back down.

"There's your cash," he said. "Still quite a bit of money. Why don't you just . . . live on it?"

"I'm not livin', Ben," Jake said. "I'm just existin'. I need this trail drive to . . . wake me up. Then, if I live through it, I can decide what I'm gonna do with the rest of my life."

"With the money you get from selling your cattle."

"Yes."

"Which may not be as much as you have right here," the bank manager pointed out.

"I know that."

Caplock sat back in his chair, ran one hand through his shock of white hair.

"All right," he said. "I suppose you've made up your mind."

"I have." Jake picked up the bag of cash and stood.

"Aren't you going to count it?"

"I trust you, Ben," Jake said. "After all, you trusted me every time I came to you for a loan."

Caplock stood up and extended his hand. Jake shook it.

"Good luck, Jake," he said. "I hope you find what you're looking for."

"So do I, Ben," Jake said, "so do I."

* * *

CHANCE WAS WAITING when Jake stepped outside the bank.

"All done?" he asked.

"Done."

"That the money?"

"What's left of it."

"Well, I got the horses picked out," Chance said. "You wanna go over and settle up?"

"I do." What Jake really wanted was a drink. But he didn't want Chance to have one. "Let's go."

They walked to the livery, where the hostler was waiting for them.

"All the horses are in the corral," he said. "Four colts, four geldings."

"I just feel better with all male—" Chance started to explain to Jake, but his friend cut him off.

"You don't have to explain. I told you to pick them out." He looked at the hostler. "How much?"

"A hundred a head," the man said.

"We're takin' eight of 'em off your hands," Chance said. "How about eighty?"

The hostler looked at Chance and said, "Ninety."

"Ninety it is," Jake said. He took the money out of the bag and handed it to the man. "We'll come for them at the end of the day."

"They'll be ready," the hostler said, "with bridles."

"Come on," Jake said to Chance, "let's find those other two hands."

"Your friend told me what you're lookin' for," the hostler said. "Try the Oakwood Saloon. There's some young fellas there who came into town a couple of days ago. They're lookin' for work. I don't know if a trail drive is what they had in mind, but . . ." He shrugged.

"Thanks," Jake said. "We'll try it."

They left the livery, stopped just outside.

"Did you see the way he was lookin' at that bag?" Chance said, indicating the money.

"Yeah," Jake said. "I guess we better get rid of it. It's too damn obvious."

"And let's do it before we talk to anybody else," Chance suggested.

THEY WENT BACK to where they had left their horses, in front of the bank, and quickly transferred the money to their saddlebags. Jake put equal portions on his horse and Chance's.

"All right," he said, "let's try that saloon."

"You think we can trust him not to set us up?" Chance asked.

"Well, he didn't know about the bag until we got there. He hasn't had time."

"Just in case," Chance said, "I guess we better start carryin' our rifles."

They mounted up and rode to the Oakwood Saloon, which was on the other side of town. When they dismounted in front they saw five horses standing there. Two looked fit, three looked done in. They took their rifles and saddlebags into the saloon with them.

They went directly to the bar and ordered two beers. The bartender was a stranger to them, which they preferred. No need to exchange any kind of false pleasantries. There were other men at the bar, and some at tables, but they assumed that the table of five in the rear should be their concern. The men were young, white, and playing poker for matchsticks.

When they had their beers they both walked over to the poker table and watched a few hands. Finally, one of the young men looked up at them.

"You old-timers are interested in watchin' a poker

game for matchstick stakes?" He laughed. "Not much to do in this town, is there?"

"Actually," Jake said, "we're not as interested in watchin' as we are in the stakes."

"Matchsticks?" the young man said, again.

"That kinda shows me that you boys might be needin' some money," Jake said.

One of the others asked, "You wanna put money up against matchsticks?"

"We were thinkin' more about jobs," Chance said. "You fellas lookin' for a job?"

"That depends," the first one said. "What kinda job?"

"A trail drive," Jake said.

"A what?" a third man asked. "We didn't think there was any more of them."

"Just one. Mine," Jake said.

"And who are you?" the first one asked.

"My name's Jake Motley. I own the Big M, outside of town."

"Big Jake Motley," Chance added.

"Big Jake, huh?" the second one said. "I was thinkin' maybe you was Charlie Goodnight hisself, plannin' one last drive."

"We don't know you," the first man said.

"That's fine," Jake said. "At least you know who Charlie Goodnight was."

Goodnight had not only blazed the Goodnight trail for future trail drives, he was also the inventor of the chuckwagon.

"Any of you boys ever work cows?" Chance asked.

"I have," the first one said. "Ain't you, Curly?"

"Yeah, I have," Curly, the second man, said, "but I was fourteen at the time."

"How old would you boys be now?" Chance asked.

"Twenty," the first one said.

"Nineteen," Curly said.

The other three were frowning at their cards, showing no interest in the conversation.

"Are all you boys together?" Jake asked.

"Naw," Curly said, "me an' Dundee, here, we rode in here together. We met these three just outside of town."

Dundee, the first man, looked up at Jake and Chance.

"How much you payin'?" he asked.

"Well, that's the thing," Jake said. "Twenty-five dollars a week, but I can't pay until we get where we're goin' and I sell the herd."

"Aw, geez—" Curly said, but Dundee cut him off.

"And where are you goin'?" he asked.

"Dodge City."

"Dodge, huh?" Dundee said. "I ain't never been to Dodge, and there ain't much to do around here."

"Are you thinkin' about this?" Curly asked his friend.

"Sure, why not?" Dundee asked. He looked at Jake again. "Sweeten your pitch, Big Jake, and let's see if we can make a deal."

"We're only drivin' six hundred head," Jake said. "There'll be six of us, and a good cook. You'll eat well . . ." Jake thought a moment, then added, ". . . and I'll give you each your first twenty-five dollars up front."

Dundee looked across the table at his friend.

"Which of those horses out front are yours?" Chance asked.

"The dun and the mustang."

Jake and Chance exchanged a glance. Those were the two that looked fit.

"I'm supplying two more horses each," Jake said.

"You gonna trust we can do the job without seein' what we can do first?" Dundee asked.

"You're young," Jake said. "If you can't do the job, we'll teach ya. By the time you get to Dodge, you'll be honest-to-God cowpunchers."

Dundee looked at Curly.

"I say yeah, Curly. What about you?"

Curly thought a moment, then looked down at the matchsticks on the table and said, "Yeah, why not." He turned toward Jake. "But we get our twenty-five now."

"Wait a second," Chance said. Then, to Jake, "Lemme talk to ya, a minute."

They walked back to the bar.

"If you give these young yahoos twenty-five dollars each now, you'll never see 'em again."

"Naw," Jake said. "I think they're in. They're both young and fit, and that's what we need."

He dug into his saddlebag, came out with fifty dollars. At least the five youngsters didn't see him do that, didn't know they had two saddlebags full of money.

They walked back to the poker table and Jake dropped the money on the table.

"There's your twenty-five each," he said. "Be out at the Big M tomorrow morning at eight. Anybody in town can tell you how to get there. You wearin' sidearms?"

"Yeah, we are."

"Well, put 'em in your saddlebags. I don't want pistols around the herd. Too much of a chance one will go off and cause a stampede."

"What about rifles?" Curly asked.

"We'll all have rifles, but keep it in your scabbard. Bring your own ammunition, canteen, and bedroll. Everything else will be in our supply wagon."

Dundee picked up his twenty-five dollars.

"We'll be there," he said.

"We got Mexicans on our crew," Chance said. "You got a problem with that?"

"Not if they do their jobs," Curly said.

"Everybody's gonna do their job," Jake said. "You wanna know anythin' about me, ask around. But if you decide not to ride with us, I'd appreciate it if you come out and tell me why."

"We'll be there," Curly said, repeating Dundee's words.

"And if you got it," Chance said, "bring a second shirt."

Jake put his hand out and shook with each young man.

"See you in the mornin'," he said.

As he and Chance left he heard Curly say, "I bet five matchsticks."

Outside Chance said, "I hope we didn't just waste fifty dollars."

"Let's go over to the mercantile," Jake said. "We still got some supplies to pick up."

CHAPTER NINE

T HEY PICKED UP a variety of supplies at the mercantile, whatever they thought Taco and Desi's cousin
would not already have in his wagon. Then they went
back to the livery to get their eight horses. While there,
they also rented a buckboard to take their supplies
back to the ranch. When they left town they had seven
of their *remuda* tied to the back—with one pulling the
buckboard—along with Chance's mount, since he was
driving the buckboard.

Chance had muttered all afternoon about paying
the two young cowboys twenty-five dollars in advance.
He was convinced they would never see them again.

"And you," he added to Jake as they rode back to
the ranch, "you crotchety old cuss, you believe 'em
when they say they'll be there."

"I think they were interested in goin' to Dodge
City," Jake said.

"Well, that Dundee was, but the other one? Curly?
I don't know about him."

"He'll go where Dundee goes," Jake said. "You know what your problem is?"

"What?"

"They reminded you of us."

"What?"

"That's right," Jake said. "You're seein' you and me at that age all over again."

"Aw, Jesus, you're crazy," Chance said. "For one thing, I ain't never played poker for matchsticks."

"That's about the only difference," Jake said. "That Curly, he follows Dundee around like you used to follow me."

"I used to follow you?" Chance exploded. "Now I know you're crazy. Hey, where you goin'?"

Jake rode up ahead of the buckboard, which was dragging a lot of horse weight behind it. Chance was still shouting at him . . .

THEY PULLED TO a stop in front of the barn and, as they climbed down, untied the horses and walked them into the corral. Chance was still muttering. Jake was starting to think his friend needed a drink, but he didn't want to give it to him. He had hoped that the one beer they had in the saloon would hold him over.

"Me follow you, that's a laugh," Chance grumbled as they closed the gate of the corral.

"I think you need some coffee," Jake said.

"I think you're right," Chance said. "And you got anythin' to eat?"

"I don't know," Jake said. "Desi mighta cleaned out my cellar last night."

"Guess we shoulda eaten somethin' in town before we left," Chance complained.

"Well," Jake said as they walked the horse and

buckboard into the barn and started to unhitch the animal, "maybe our new cook'll have somethin' in his wagon."

"That's a thought," Chance said. "We'll get to sample his cookin' before we hit the trail with 'im."

They walked the unhitched horse into the corral with the others, then unsaddled their mounts and put them into their stalls. After rubbing them down and making sure they had feed, they also put some food out for the corralled horses before finally walking to the house.

Instead of going inside, they each sat down in a chair on the porch.

"How come you ain't got a rockin' chair out here?" Chance asked. "I always saw you in my head sittin' in a rockin' chair."

"Now who's crazy?" Jake asked. "I wouldn't be caught dead in a rockin' chair."

They sat in silence for a few minutes, during which Chance rolled a cigarette and lit it.

"Want me to roll you one?" he asked.

"No, thanks."

More silence, and then Jake spoke.

"Abby bought me one."

"One what?"

"Rockin' chair!"

"She did? When?"

"The year before . . . when I turned forty-five."

"I was still here," Chance said. "How come I didn't know that?"

"Because I sent it back," Jake said. "She had it delivered from Denver, but what was she thinkin'? I wasn't ready for no rockin' chair. I returned it and got the money back."

"How did she react?"

"How did she react to everythin'?" Jake asked.
"She laughed."

Chance knew what he meant. Abby Motley went through life with that smile on her face, and he knew that she died with that smile there, because Jake had been sitting next to the bed, holding her hand when she went.

"Well," Chance said, "if you had a rockin' chair I think I'd be sittin' in it right now."

"What time is it?" Jake asked.

Chance took a pocket watch out of his vest and peered at it.

"Almost suppertime," he said, putting it back.

"You hear that?"

"Hear what?" Chance asked.

"Listen."

They both listened, and heard the sound of metal on metal.

"Wow, I ain't heard that sound in a long time," Chance said, "Pots and pans in the back of a chuck-wagon."

As they listened the sound came closer and closer, then they recognized Taco, riding in ahead of his cousin's wagon.

"Hola, jefe," he called out. "We are here!"

"I can hear it," Jake said, standing up. "Where's Desi?"

"Ridin' with the wagon," Taco said. "Do you want it to stop right here?"

"No," Jake said. "Put it in the barn and we'll have a look, there."

"And meet your cousin," Chance said, also standing.

"Sí, señores."

Taco turned and rode back to catch the wagon before it approached the house. As they watched, it came into view, with Desi alongside. Taco pointed, and the wagon changed direction and went right into the barn, its pots-and-pans serenade coming to an end.

Jake and Chance walked to the barn, entered as Desi was dismounting and another man was jumping down from the wagon. The three men began to chatter in Spanish.

"Whoa, whoa, whoa," Chance said. "Stop all the Mex talk. We can't understand a word yer sayin'."

"Oh, excuse us, Señor Chance," Taco said. "We are excited to be here."

The wagon looked loaded, pots and pans actually hanging off the outside.

"Señores," Desi said, "this is our cousin, Carlito."

Carlito smiled broadly and shook their hands. He was even smaller in stature than Taco, but with the same large smile. He appeared to be between the age of Desi (twenties) and Taco (forties).

"*Con mucho gusto*, señores," Carlito said, also shaking Chance's hand. "I am very much lookin' forward to this venture."

"Well, *con much gusto*, too, Carlito," Chance said. "but do you think you could cook somethin' for us tonight? We're starved."

"As are we, señores," Carlito said. "Come, I will prepare a feast."

He got in his wagon and started handing out supplies to each man to carry into the house.

"If you cook all this, Carlito, will you have enough for the drive?" Jake asked.

"Oh, señor," Carlito said, "I have stocked up very well, but we will also be able to acquire supplies along the way, no?"

"Yeah, we will," Jake assured him.

"Then *muy bien*, señor," Carlito said. "Tonight we eat well."

And they all made their way to the house, each laden with his own donation to the upcoming feast . . .

. . . AND A FEAST it was.

Carlito proved his skill with pots and pans, and with beef and vegetables as well. He also prepared biscuits and tortillas. The meal was a combination of American and Mexican, as if he were auditioning for the job.

And if he were auditioning for the job, he passed with flying colors.

The icing on the cake was freshly prepared flan and strong coffee.

"If you can do this on the trail, Carlito," Chance said, "we're all gonna arrive in Dodge City much fatter than when we left here."

"Do not worry, señor," Carlito said. "You will be eating very well."

"Did you find your extra hands, jefe?" Taco asked Jake.

"We did," Jake said.

"Maybe," Chance said. "If they show up in the mornin'."

"At eight we're gonna ride out to the herd," Jake told them all. "If all's well with them, we'll get 'em movin'."

"Why would they not be well?" Desi asked.

"I'm just sayin'," Jake said, "I ain't been out there in a few days."

"If I know you, jefe," Taco said, "your herd is clean of disease, and fit for the drive."

"Let's hope you're right, Taco," Jake said. "I ain't what I used to be."

"Do not worry, jefe," Taco said, "it will all come back to you."

"I hope you're right."

Jake looked across the table at Chance, who was frowning into his coffee cup. He needed a drink.

"All right," Jake said, "Taco and Desi, you can show your cousin where he can sleep tonight."

"Sí, jefe," Desi said, standing up.

"And the kitchen, señor?" Carlito asked.

"Don't worry about it," Jake said. "I'll clean it in the mornin', before we leave."

"Sí, jefe," Carlito said, and followed his cousins out.

The coffeepot was still on the table, and still half full.

"More coffee, Chance?" Jake asked.

"I don't think—"

"With a touch of sweetener?"

"Oh, Jesus, yes," Chance said.

Jake got the whiskey bottle from his desk, poured the coffee, and added the whiskey.

"That's it," he said as Chance lifted the cup to his mouth, "that's the last one."

Chance looked at him over the rim of the cup and said, "Until Dodge."

"Until Dodge," Jake agreed.

Chance drank it down and set the cup on the table.

"Not another drink until the job is done, Jake," he promised. "I swear."

"I believe ya, Chance." He finished his. "The same goes for me, and for every man. No whiskey on the drive."

"Don't do that on my account," Chance said.

"I'm not, I just don't want any mistakes because of drunkenness."

"Better make your new boys aware of that," Chance said, getting to his feet.

"Oh, I will."

As Chance left the dining room he said over his shoulder, "If they show up."

CHAPTER TEN

JAKE CAME OUT the front door the next morning at seven forty-five after cleaning the kitchen. He knew it wasn't as good as it would have been if Abby had cleaned it, but that was always the case.

She came to him in dreams, sometimes, smiling and touching his face. However, last night he had had no dreams at all—at least, none he could remember.

Chance was already there, sitting in a chair with his rifle across his legs. Next to the chair, on the deck, were his saddlebags.

Jake sat next to him, set his saddlebags down, and laid his rifle across his legs.

"They're not here," Chance said. "If they don't get here, we'll be short."

"We'll do what we have to do," Jake said.

"The four of us? Driving six hundred head?"

"We'll stick Carlito on a horse."

"He's a cook," Chance said.

"They still have time," Jake said.

Chance took out his watch.

"Ten minutes."

"We'll wait."

While they were waiting both Taco and Desi came riding over, leading both Chance's and Jake's saddled mounts. They stopped in front of the porch.

"Step down," Jake said. "We're still waitin' for our new hands."

They both dismounted and stepped up onto the porch.

"What about Carlito?" Chance asked.

"He is almost ready," Desi said.

At that moment they heard the pots-and-pans jangle as the chuckwagon pulled out of the barn and approached the house with a four-mule team.

"We are ready," Carlito said happily.

"Five minutes," Chance said.

At that moment the sound of horses came to them from nearby. Then two riders appeared from the other side of the barn. Jake and Chance both grabbed their saddlebags and stood up as they approached.

"You just made it," Chance said.

"I had to convince my buddy that we really wanted to do this," Dundee said, with a grin.

"We're ready to go," Curly said. "What's first?"

"Let's get that *remuda* out of the corral," Jake said. "Then we'll head for the herd."

J AKE AND CHANCE led the rest to Candy Box Canyon, where Jake had secured the herd. As they approached they could hear the cows bawling.

"They're hungry," Chance said.

"They can graze when we let them out," Jake said. "It'll take time to get them all ready."

Chance looked around, saw mostly bare ground.

"There's not much to graze on here," he said.

"They'll find whatever there is," Jake assured his friend. "They'll suck it dry before we leave. Within a few miles there'll be some more."

The other riders came up alongside them. Carlito's chuckwagon pulled up behind them, with the *remuda* tied to the back.

"Okay," Jake said, "let's get that herd out of there."

He and Chance opened the makeshift gate he had fashioned to keep the herd in, and they entered, moving among the cattle. Behind them Desi and Taco also came in, with Dundee. Curly had orders to remain on the outside.

"Once we get 'em movin'," Jake shouted, "Taco, you and Desi leave the canyon and start directin' them."

"Sí, jefe," Taco called back.

They began to move the herd outside of the box canyon . . .

O NCE THE ENTIRE herd was milling about outside, Jake, Chance, and their hands started them moving forward.

The chuckwagon led the way, as it would be doing for the length of the drive. It would be up to Carlito to find the places where they would camp each night, after about fifteen miles of traveling per day. At that rate it would take them about two months to reach Dodge City, barring any difficulties.

It was decided that Curly would be the wrangler, in charge of the *remuda*. That meant he would ride close behind the chuckwagon, leading the horses and making sure nothing happened to them. He would also saddle and unsaddle horses when the others needed to change mounts, which could happen three to four times a day.

Jake decided the first day he would ride point, Taco,

Desi, and Dundee flank, and Chance would ride drag.
For a larger herd—say two to three thousand head—he
would have had at least ten men per thousand. Many
of them would be flanking the herd on either side, with
at least two riding drag. But with six hundred head he
chose to believe that one man could ride drag, and decided that they would alternate that position, since that
man would eat most of the dust that day. With two men
on one flank, and only one on the other, Jake figured
he would occasionally leave the point and assist on the
flank. He might have added Curly to the flank, but
didn't want to take a chance on anything happening to
any of the extra horses. They needed those remounts
in order to keep moving.

The first day was interesting; as they left Brownsville behind them, Jake was able to judge the abilities
of the men he had never traveled with before—Desi,
Carlito, Dundee, and Curly. Desi seemed to be as adept at flanking as his cousin Taco was. Dundee was not
as adept, but seemed to be a fast learner. As for Curly,
it seemed Jake had made the right decision to use him
as the wrangler. He was good with the horses.

The only way to judge Carlito was going to depend
first on where he chose to camp for the night and, second, how their first meal was.

On that first day he was also judging his own fitness
and abilities. He certainly hadn't forgotten how to
drive a herd, but felt himself growing weary much too
soon. That would be due to his age, and to the fact that
he hadn't been on a drive in quite a while.

He assumed that Chance would be having the same
feelings, but he wouldn't know until they spoke that
night. In the morning he would decide who was going
to ride drag the second day, as he would do every
morning thereafter . . .

* * *

As JAKE LOOKED up ahead he saw Curly riding toward him. When the young man reached him he turned his horse and rode alongside.

"Just wanted to let you know Carlito found a place to camp. He's already settin' up. It's just over this ridge."

"Got it," Jake said. "We'll stop the herd here. Get back to the *remuda*, make sure they're secure."

"Already done, boss," Curly said, but then spurred his horse on and rode off to join Carlito.

Jake turned his horse so he could ride back and inform the others.

Once THEY HAD camped and unsaddled their mounts, they all gathered around the campfire for Carlito's supper. It was succulent meat and tortilla, something simple for the first night.

"After we've eaten I'll want two men to watch the herd," Jake said. "And then two men will relieve them after four hours. You can decide among yourselves who goes first and who goes second."

"Desi and I will go first," Taco said.

"Then Curly and me, we'll go second," Dundee said.

"I can go—" Chance said, but Jake cut him off.

"I want you in camp."

"What for?"

"To discuss tomorrow."

"What about—" Chance started, but he saw the look on Jake's face and stopped.

After they finished eating, Desi and Taco saddled fresh mounts and rode out to keep watch over the herd. Dundee and Curly turned in so they would be relatively fresh when it was their turn. Carlito cleaned up, but left a pot of coffee on the fire, then went inside his wagon to sleep.

That left Jake and Chance around the fire.

"What's this about tomorrow?" Chance asked.

"Nothin'," Jake said. "I just wanted to talk."

"About what?"

"About whether or not you're feelin' the way I am."

"Which is?"

"Old and out of shape."

"Oh, yeah."

"Then there's no reason for either of us to stand watch over the herd when we could be sleepin'," Jake said.

"Is that how it's gonna be the whole way?" Chance asked. " 'Cause we'll have to explain that."

"No," Jake said, "just till you and me, we get our sea legs under us."

"Sea legs?"

"It's a sailor's term—"

"I know what it is, Jake," Chance said. "I was just wonderin' how an old cowpoke like you knew."

"Hey, this old cowpoke has done some readin' over the past few years," Jake said.

"Readin'? You?"

"I know, it's hard to believe even for me," Jake said. "I never thought I'd be able to sit still long enough to read a book."

Jake poured Chance another cup of coffee, noticed his friend's hand was shaking. It could have been because he was craving a drink, but Jake was also feeling kind of shaky after the day's ride, so he decided to give Chance the benefit of the doubt.

"Why don't you turn in after that cup?" Jake suggested. "I'll keep an eye out here for a bit."

"I think I'll do just that," Chance said. "I'll open my

bedroll under the chuckwagon. And you better rest your old bones, too, old-timer."

"Right after this cup," Jake said.

So the two old cowpokes sat and sipped and listened to the sounds the herd made at night.

CHAPTER ELEVEN

THE FIRST WEEK went without incident.
    They all got into a rhythm with each other, do-
ing their jobs well whether they were riding flank or
drag, standing their watches over the herd at night,
bringing stragglers back into the fold. They lost a few
head to injury, but Carlito turned them into meals, and
kept proving his worth not only as a cook, but as a
scout for their campsites.

Curly proved his worth as wrangler, keeping the *remuda* in good condition, having a fresh mount ready
for each rider when they needed one.

The work was grueling, there was no doubt, but Jake
and Chance found themselves dealing with it in better
and better fashion following each day. Even when the
youngsters, Dundee and Curly, complained at night
about how tired they were, they only received sympathy
from Desi and Taco.

Desi was an experienced *vaquero*, but still found the
work taxing. Taco had not been on a drive in some
time, and his body seemed to be protesting each night.

"You are both older than I," he said to Jake and Chance one night. "How is it I am more worn out than you, señores?"

"Don't worry, Taco," Jake replied. "We're feelin' every mile of it. But for me, I've been off the trail for so long this is really like comin' home."

"Our bodies are gettin' used to it," Chance said. "I didn't think I'd take to the saddle again, but I have, even at this age."

"Well," Dundee said, from across the fire, "I don't know if my body's ever gonna be the same again."

"Don't worry," Jake said, "you'll get used to it. I tell ya what. Chance and I will take a watch on the herd tonight."

"Sure," Chance said. "That'll give you time for some much-needed rest, but believe me, after a few weeks on the trail, you'll start to feel better."

"I hope so," Dundee said. "My body's never hurt this much before."

"Well," Jake said, "finish eatin' and get some rest."

They all applied themselves to Carlito's latest concoction of meats known as SOB stew, with beans that he called pecos strawberries and biscuits that were known as sourdough bullets.

After supper, Dundee groaned and turned in, while Curly offered to stand first watch with Desi. They seemed to be the two who were in the best condition.

Jake and Chance drank some more of Carlito's thick, black coffee while both the cook and Taco turned in.

"You know this ain't gonna last, don't you?" Chance said.

Jake knew exactly what Chance meant.

"These younger men are gonna start feelin' it less, while we start feelin' it more," Jake admitted.

"I think it's just that we missed this," Chance said.

"Once we're used to it again, all those old aches and pains are gonna set back in."

"Maybe not as bad, though," Jake said. "We're gonna need to find some balance between how we felt in the beginning, how we feel now, and how we're gonna feel later."

"These kids are gonna be used to it, and our bones are gonna be achin'," Chance said. "But I gotta admit, right now I feel younger than I have in years. I'm not even cravin' a drink."

"That's good," Jake said. "Hopefully, it'll stay that way for you."

"Desi and Curly are doin' fine," Chance said.

"Well, Desi's an experienced cowboy, and Curly's the youngest. Taco's been guarding whores for too long, but he'll come around."

"And Dundee's young enough to bear these first aches and pains," Chance said. "I think we've got a good crew here, Jake. Carlito is sure livin' up to his part of the deal. His food is great."

"We'll have to check with him and see how his supplies are doin'," Jake said. "We should be outside of Three Rivers in a couple of days. We can pick up more supplies there."

"Good idea," Chance said. "Let's check with him in the mornin'."

"Let's get some sleep now. Remember, we volunteered to take a watch."

VOLUNTEERING TURNED OUT to be a bad idea.

Sitting in the saddle for four hours, hardly moving, turned out to be more taxing than four hours in the saddle on the trail. By the time the smell of Carlito's bacon—"chuckwagon chicken"—came to them, announcing breakfast, their backs were aching. Chance's butt was also sore, indicating he hadn't gotten as much of his "seat" back as he thought.

At breakfast Dundee was more bright-eyed and bushy-tailed, ready for the day.

"I appreciate the extra rest you fellas gave me," he said to Jake and Chance. "Thanks."

"Don't get used to it," Chance said sullenly. "It ain't gonna happen again."

"Yeah, well," Dundee said, "I'll be okay after this."

"Since you're feelin' so much better," Jake said, "you take drag today."

Riding drag was usually more of a punishment on the trail than anything else. But Dundee said, "Sure, okay."

"I'll get the horses ready," Curly said, after he finished his breakfast.

"I will help," Desi said. The two men seemed to be getting along pretty good.

Taco quietly had a second helping of bacon and coffee.

"Carlito," Jake said, "how are supplies?"

"We can use some more bacon and beans, señor," he said, "but we could get by if we had to."

"Chance and me were thinkin' about stoppin' near Three Rivers tomorrow night. Then we could go in the next mornin' and pick up some things."

"Sí, señor," Carlito said, "I will make a list."

"You could come in with us," Chance suggested.

"Sí, señor, I will do that," the cook said, "but I will still make a list."

"Fine," Jake said.

Taco finished his breakfast and helped Carlito load the chuckwagon. By then Curly came over, leading the horses, and they all mounted up. Carlito climbed up onto the seat of the wagon and snapped his reins at his mules to get them started. Curly followed with the *remuda*.

Jake, Chance, Taco, Desi, and Dundee rode out to the herd, took up their positions, and got the cows moving.

T HE NEXT TWO days proved a little more difficult.
     For one thing they came to a rather wide stream. It didn't help that it had started to rain, with loud claps of thunder and blinding bursts of lightning.
     The cattle got skittish with the thunder and lightning, and the men had to do what they could to keep them from panicking. Jake still felt he had enough men to drive this herd, but if a stampede occurred there would be a problem.
     With all the rain, the stream was deeper than usual, with water that was flowing fairly quickly. Some of the cattle didn't seem to want to cross, and even the horses showed some resistance. In the end they had to drive the herd into the water, where they had no choice but to continue on to the other side or drown. The men had to swim across, holding on to their horses' reins at the same time, almost towing the animals behind them. Everybody needed a rest by the time they got the entire herd across, but Jake decided to keep them moving. Once they camped for the night the men could all dry off by a fire and get some coffee into them. The herd could huddle together for warmth from the cool night air, until their coats dried.

B Y THE SECOND night, with all the rain and reluctance, they were not as close to Three Rivers as they would have liked to be.
     "So we cannot ride in for supplies?" Carlito asked, during supper.
     "We should keep the herd movin'," Jake said. "By midday we might be close enough."

"We could keep them moving while the two of you go into town, jefe," Taco offered. "When you are finished you can catch up to us."

"That won't work," Jake said. "There'll only be four of you, and one of you would have to drive Carlito's chuckwagon."

"I thought he'd take the wagon into town with you," Dundee commented.

"That would slow us down," Jake said. "We just wanna ride in quick and pick up some supplies, then get back on the trail."

"Señores," Carlito said, "I could give you my list, then I can continue to drive the wagon while the others drive the herd."

"Yeah," Curly said, "the four of us can handle it. I can pitch in and hitch the *remuda* to the back of the wagon for a few miles."

Chance looked at the sky.

"Looks like the storm's passed, Jake," he said. "They could probably handle it."

"I tell you what, Chance," Jake said. "Why don't you stay with them? I'll take Dundee with me. Together we could carry the supplies back on our horses, and you could make sure there's no trouble while I'm gone."

Chance frowned, but said, "Yeah, okay, I could do that."

"Good," Jake said. "Dundee and me, we'll stick with the herd until we're close enough to Three Rivers to ride in easy."

"Fine," Chance said, and they all went back to eating.

AFTER DESI AND Taco rode out to watch the herd, Carlito cleaned up and turned in along with Curly and Dundee. Jake and Chance sat at the fire as they had been doing, drinking some coffee before retiring.

"So, you don't want me to ride into town 'cause you're afraid I'll drink?" Chance asked sullenly.

"What?" Jake asked. "Where'd you get that idea, Chance?"

"Then why are you takin' Dundee instead of me?" Chance asked.

"I told you," Jake said. "I'd feel better if you were with the herd. I think they can handle it with you directin' them. Dundee and me, we'll be back quick."

"After a few drinks?"

"I'm not havin' any drinks, Chance," Jake said. "Remember, we said not till after the herd's delivered."

"But you'll let the kid have a drink, won't ya?" Chance demanded.

"I toldja from the beginning," Jake said. "I don't want anybody gettin' liquored up. What's bringin' this up?" he asked.

"Nothin'," Chance said. "Nothin' at all. Let's just ferget I said anythin'." He dumped the remnants of his coffee into the fire. "I'm turnin' in."

Jake watched his friend go, wondering if Chance was having more trouble staying off the whiskey than he had first thought. Maybe it was a good idea, after all, not to take him into town, where there would be temptation.

A FTER JAKE AND Dundee left, Chance McCandless decided this was his opportunity to show his friend Big Jake that he was as reliable as ever.

The night before, the thirst for whiskey had crept up on him, just when he thought it was all gone. Then, when Jake decided to take Dundee to town with him and not Chance, he had almost exploded. But he slept good and woke feeling refreshed. The coffee and breakfast had gone down well, and he was looking forward to Jake leaving for a while.

Once they were gone he called the others around him.

"Jake's gotta feel that this ain't all on him, boys," he said. "So we gotta show him that drivin' this herd ain't a hardship."

"Sí, Señor Chance," Taco said. "We can do that."

"Desi, you take drag," Chance said. "I'll take point. That leaves flank to you guys." Taco and Curly both nodded. "I'll help out when I have to."

"Sounds good to me," Curly said.

"Tie the *remuda* to the back of Carlito's wagon, Curly," Chance said. "Carlito, if you start draggin', don't worry about it and don't fight it. We'll make up the time when Jake gets back."

"Sí, *patrón*," Carlito said. Chance felt good about the "*patrón*" since they'd been calling Jake "jefe" all along. It showed that he had some authority.

"All right," he said, "let's get it done!"

CHAPTER TWELVE

JAKE WAS WORRIED about Chance.

For two weeks now he seemed to be doing okay, but last night had come as a surprise. He had the feeling that the urge for whiskey had snuck back up on his friend, which almost pushed him over the edge. Then, when Jake told him to stay with the herd and not come to town, that almost did it.

But this morning seemed different. Chance seemed renewed somehow, and Jake was happy for this opportunity to leave him in charge, and show that he trusted him. During past trail drives, even though the herds had belonged to Big Jake, he had always felt that he and Chance were equals.

He wanted that feeling back again.

THEY REINED THEIR horses in just outside of Three Rivers.

"Have you ever been here before?" Dundee asked.

"No," Jake said. "You?"

"No," Dundee said. "It looks . . . peaceful."

"Yeah, it does."

"How many people did that sign say there was?"

They had passed a signpost a few miles back that stated Three Rivers, pop. 255.

"Two hundred and fifty-five," Jake said.

"Not bad," Dundee said. "Not big, but not bad."

"You could fit ten of these towns in Brownsville," Jake pointed out.

"Yeah, well, there still wasn't very much to do in Brownsville, which is why me and Curly are on this drive in the first place."

"Well," Jake said, "they're bound to have a general store of some kind, which is all we really need. Let's go and get this done."

They rode on.

THE STREET WAS quiet, just a few people walking or sweeping. The buildings looked old and weathered, but solid. They spotted a barbershop and bathhouse, a couple of saloons, a hardware store, and, finally, what they wanted, a mercantile.

"There we go," Jake said.

They reined to a stop right in front and dismounted.

"You got Carlito's list?" Dundee asked while tying off his horse.

"Right here," Jake said, patting his shirt pocket. He looped his horse's reins around the hitching rail and stepped up onto the boardwalk with his saddlebags. He left his rifle on his saddle. Now that they were in a town, he wished he had brought his pistol, but it was back at camp.

Dundee tossed his saddlebags over his shoulder, grabbed his rifle, and followed.

As they walked in they found the store small, and

empty but for a clerk behind a counter, wearing a white apron and a worried look on his young face.

"We need a few things," Jake said.

"S-sorry," the clerk said, "we're all out."

"Out of what?" Dundee asked.

"Everythin'!" the clerk said.

Jake and Dundee exchanged a glance, then looked around at the supplies on shelves around them.

"I've got a list," Jake said, taking it from his pocket and putting it down on the counter. "I'd like it filled."

"I c-can't, mister," the clerk said. "I'd really like to, but—"

"I can see some of the items I need," Jake said.

"S-sorry, but—"

"You know what?" Jake said. "We'll just grab 'em ourselves."

He and Dundee began to take things off the shelves, mostly canned goods, and some spices Carlito had written down.

"Please, sirs," the clerk said, "you don't understand—"

Jake turned on the young man angrily.

"What don't we understand?"

"These supplies," the clerk said, "they're . . . spoken for."

"Spoken for?" Dundee asked. "The whole store?"

"The whole town."

Jake put some more cans on the countertop.

"Okay, so somebody owns the town," he said. "They're not gonna miss a few cans of peaches. Tally this up."

Dundee came over, stood next to Jake, and put his armload down.

"Bacon," he said.

"Right," Jake said. "We need twenty pounds of bacon. And put it in gunnysacks with the rest of this stuff."

"Mister—"

"Do it now, son!" Jake said. "I got a herd to get back to."

As the clerk tallied things up and stuffed them into sacks, Jake and Dundee also filled their saddlebags. The last thing the clerk stuck in one of the sacks was the bacon.

"How much?" Jake asked.

The clerk showed Jake the total for all the supplies he had written down. His handwriting was shaky at best.

"Here," Jake said, dropping some money on the counter, "this should cover it."

"When they find out you took their stuff—"

"I don't have time to hear about some gunslicks who think they own a town," Jake snapped. "If they wanna know who took their supplies, you tell 'em Big Jake Motley was here. You got that?"

"I g-got it."

"Come on!" Jake said to Dundee.

At the last minute, before going out the door, Dundee stuck his hand in a glass jar and took out a few pieces of licorice. He tossed a coin onto the counter so they couldn't be accused of stealing anything.

With their saddlebags bulging, and two burlap sacks, they left the store and went to their horses. They tossed their saddlebags over their mounts and tied the sacks to the saddle horns, then mounted up.

"You think we're askin' for trouble?" Dundee asked.

"Probably," Jake said.

"Then why didn't we just leave?"

"Because this is what bein' old and crotchety gets ya," Jake told the younger man. "You might wanna work on this not happening to you."

"I will," Dundee said, "if we live through this."

They turned their mounts and rode out of town.

* * *

OUTSIDE OF TOWN, they stopped by the signpost.
"You think there was really two hundred and fifty-five people in that town?"

"I don't see why not," Jake sad. "It just seemed like nobody wanted to be on the street."

"They must've been hidin' from us," Dundee said, with a shrug.

"From us?"

"Or from trouble," Dundee said. "Who do you think that clerk was talkin' about?"

"Probably some rich rancher in the area," Jake said. "Or like I said, some cheap gunnies that think it's fun to control a town."

"You sound like you don't like rich ranchers."

"I hate em!"

"But . . . weren't you a rich rancher, once?"

Jake ignored the comment. He was too busy noticing how smooth and unpitted the main street was.

"Whoever it is claims to own this town," he observed, "keeps a neat, tidy street."

"I noticed that when we rode in," Dundee said. "It must not have rained here."

"Maybe," Jake said, "the same people who own the supplies and the town won't allow it to."

Dundee gave Jake a sideways look, to make sure he was kidding.

CHAPTER THIRTEEN

S EAFORTH BAILEY ENJOYED calling his men "raiders."
But he didn't like the sound of "Bailey's Raiders," so he went with "Seaforth's Raiders."

The raiders were born during the Civil War, fashioned after both Mosby's Raiders (sometimes called "Rangers") and Quantrill's Raiders. In point of fact, Seaforth Bailey had not been accepted into Quantrill's band, and so decided to start his own. Only his did not have the desired effect on the war effort that the more infamous Mosby and Quantrill groups had. The war ended without anyone paying the least bit of attention to Seaforth's Raiders.

But Seaforth didn't give up. Over the ensuing years he tried to keep his raiders together, dropping those men who did not fit, adding men who did, and trying to find an area where they could virtually rule.

At forty-five, after years of trying and failing, Seaforth and his raiders found the little town of Three

Rivers, and that became their bailiwick. They were literally big fish in a little pond.

This was the situation Jake and Dundee rode into . . .

SEAFORTH—WHO HAD promoted himself from ser-geant to major after the war—led his raiders into Three Rivers hours after Big Jake Motley and Dundee had left. The group of twelve reined in their horses in front of the mercantile, and Seaforth went inside. Be-cause he had laid claim to everything in the store, he immediately noticed the things that were missing.

"Edgar," he said to the clerk, and that was all he had to say.

"I'm sorry, Major Bailey," Edgar said, "there was nothin' I could do. They just took the stuff."

"My stuff?" Seaforth demanded. "My peaches, my beans?"

"Yes, sir."

Then Seaforth's gaze fell on the licorice jar.

"My licorice!" he exploded.

"Yes, s-sir," Edgar said, "a-and . . . b-bacon."

Seaforth, a large man, reached across the counter, grabbed Edgar by the shirtfront, and pulled him half-way over.

"Who were they?"

"I—I don't know, sir," Edgar blabbered. "I dunno, honest. One of 'em, he said his name was, uh, B-Big Jake Motley."

"Big Jake, huh?" Seaforth repeated. "And what were they doin'?"

"They, uh, they said somethin' about a trail drive."

"You must be hard of hearin', Edgar," Seaforth said, "there ain't no more trail drives."

"Well, most of the things they bought was for a ch-ch-chuckwagon," he stammered.

Seaforth thought that over for a moment.

"And where's this herd supposed to be?" he demanded.

"I-I heard 'em talkin' that they was gonna meet up with the herd somewhere n-north of town."

"Headin' north, huh?" Seaforth said, releasing Edgar's shirt so that the man's feet hit the floor. Then he looked at Edgar again. "Did you say bought?"

Edgar reached for the money in the till to hand it over . . .

O NE MAN HAD been riding with Seaforth since the Civil War. His name was Teddy Garfield, but everybody called him Gar.

As Seaforth came out of the store Gar asked, "What was all the yellin'?"

"A couple of cowpokes came in and bought some supplies," Seaforth said.

"Did they pay?" Gar asked.

"They did, but that don't matter," Seaforth said. "These supplies are ours."

"So whadaya wanna do? Get 'em back?"

"Yeah, I do," Seaforth said, "but I think there's somethin' else we can get from 'em, too."

"Like what?"

"Like a herd of cattle."

Seaforth told Gar what Edgar had told him, and Gar reacted the same way.

"There ain't no more trail drives."

"Well, it looks like there is," Seaforth said, "and they can't be movin' that fast. Makes it easy for us to catch up with 'em."

"So now we're gonna be rustlers?" Gar asked. At fifty years old he had never rustled cattle in his life. Worked them, yes; rustled, no.

"It ain't rustlin'," Seaforth said. "It's payback for what they took."

Gar shrugged.

"You're the boss."

He had been saying that to Seaforth for over twenty years, so why stop now over a bunch of cows?

Seaforth looked at the horses tied to the hitching rail, and some others over in front of the saloon.

"The boys quenchin' their thirst?" he asked.

"You said they could, once we reached town," Gar reminded him.

"Okay, well," Seaforth said, "a herd can't move fast, so let's get a beer and plan."

"I'll get a beer," Gar said, "but you plan, because you're—"

"—yeah," Seaforth said, "I know, the boss."

JAKE AND DUNDEE caught up to the herd by midday. They could see the dust in the distance. As they approached, the cows seemed to be moving well and then as they rode past they waved at Desi, who was eating the drag dust.

"Any trouble?" Jake called.

"Everything is fine, jefe," he called back.

When they got to the front of the herd Jake saw Chance riding there, sitting straight in the saddle. Once again he hoped his friend had gotten past whatever crisis he had been facing the night before.

"Looks like everythin's movin' along just fine," Jake said, coming up alongside his friend.

"You didn't have to rush back," Chance said.

"We didn't," Jake said. "In fact, we had a little problem."

"Trouble?"

"Not trouble, just a slight problem with a store clerk.
I'll tell you about it later. We're gonna take these supplies up to Carlito."

"Go ahead," Chance said. "We're fine here."

AFTER THEY OFF-LOADED their supplies Jake and
Dundee rode back to the herd, freeing Curly to
return to the *remuda*. The rest of the afternoon went
by uneventfully, and by the time they camped and unsaddled their mounts, they were all pretty satisfied
with the way the day had gone.

Carlito got supper going on the fire, and everybody
had coffee while they waited. Jake told the story of the
reluctant store clerk, which the others found odd.

"What else is a clerk in a mercantile store supposed
to do but sell supplies?" Curly asked.

"Apparently," Dundee said, "they were all already
sold, if you believed what he was sayin'."

"How does a whole store full of supplies sell?"
Curly asked.

"And, accordin' to him, to the same buyer," Dundee
added.

"Sounds like somebody puttin' their claim in on a
town," Chance commented.

"That's what I was thinkin'," Jake said.

"So no trouble gettin' out of town with the supplies?" Chance asked.

"There wasn't nobody on the street," Dundee said.
"Seems like all the folks were stayin' inside."

"Yep," Chance said, "that sounds like a town under
the thumb of a buncha gunslicks."

"Well," Dundee said, "they weren't there when we
was, so I guess we got lucky."

"Let's just hope we stay lucky," Chance said.

"Whadaya mean?" Dundee asked.

"Did you tell the clerk who you were, or what we're doin'?" Chance asked.

"Well . . . I didn't," Dundee said.

"Jake?" Chance said, looking at his friend.

"I, uh, mighta told him my name," Jake admitted, "but I didn't tell 'im what we're doin'."

"I hope not," Chance said. "We don't need some cheap gunnies gettin' in our way."

"To be on the safe side," Jake said, "we'll post an extra watch."

"Why don't we make that you and me?" Chance suggested. "While Desi and Taco go out to watch the herd, I'll stay awake here in camp. Then when Dundee and Curly go out to relieve them, I'll wake you up."

"Deal," Jake agreed. "Then tomorrow we'll be on the lookout, too, just till we put some distance between us and Three Rivers."

CHAPTER FOURTEEN

W HILE JAKE WAS on watch that night he went over the time he and Dundee had spent in Three Rivers. He knew he had lost his temper and told the clerk his name, but he also knew he had not told him about the drive. But the man might have overheard something that was said between him and Dundee. If that was the case, then whoever was running Three Rivers might come looking for them. On the other hand, why? To get back a few cans of peaches and beans, and some bacon?

But there was no harm being on the alert.

W E WANT WHOEVER'S ridin' drag to keep an eye behind us," Jake said at breakfast. "Carlito and Curly, keep alert for anyone comin' at us from ahead. Whoever's ridin' flank, same thing."

"You really think somebody's gonna come lookin' for those supplies you and Dundee bought?" Curly asked.

"I don't know," Jake said, "but there's no harm in bein' ready."

"What about Indians?" Dundee asked, "We ain't talked about that. Do we have to worry about them, this trip?"

"We shouldn't," Jake said. "There might be some who don't want to stay on the reservations, but we won't have to worry about that until we get to Indian Territory."

"What about rustlers?" Taco asked. "We used to worry about them all the time."

"With trail drives dryin' up, rustlers have had to look for other ways to make their money," Chance said. "They're still rustlin' horses, but not so much cattle anymore."

"Let's just concentrate on gettin' through Texas," Jake said. "It's still gonna take weeks. When we cross into Indian Territory, we can worry about other things. Right now we just need everybody to have the same goal."

They all agreed they did, and began to break camp.

SEAFORTH BAILEY HAD decided to let his men relax for a day and get a good night's sleep before they went looking for this Big Jake Motley and his herd.

Teddy Garfield still wasn't sure about this rustling business, but he had sworn his allegiance to Seaforth Bailey years ago, and he was a loyal man.

Over breakfast in a small café that was serving only him and his men—no other customers were allowed in at the time—two of the men were sitting with Garfield. They were Dennis Finch and Al Keenan, the two most recent recruits to Seaforth's Raiders.

"What's the Major got in store for us now, Mr. Garfield?" they asked.

Though Garfield was the Major's second in command, he craved no rank, hence the men simply called him Mr.

"That'll be up to the Major to say, boys," he replied. "Don't ask me. You know how he likes to tell us himself."

"Yeah, but you know everythin' he knows, don't ya, sir?" Keenan asked.

"That may be," Garfield said, "but nevertheless, I'm not saying. So just eat your flapjacks and be patient."

"Yes, sir."

Garfield rarely spoke of the things he knew. He kept them to himself. For one thing, the Major didn't like being outdone. That was the reason Garfield had not told Seaforth what he knew of Big Jake Motley.

He had heard of Motley and the Big M, both of which had some years of success before falling on lean times. Garfield had also heard rumors of the sale of the Big M. If Big Jake Motley was taking a herd north to sell, it was probably his last.

A man faced with that would not give up his herd easily. He only hoped that Major Seaforth Bailey would take that into account. He could tell him and see, but the Major might not appreciate being advised in such a way.

The alternative would be to wait until he was asked for his opinion—which was the way he usually went.

The front door of the café slammed open and Major Seaforth Bailey entered. Garfield knew he had spent the night in the local whorehouse and would have eaten breakfast there.

"Have you men had enough rest?"

"Yessir!" they all shouted.

"And your fill of breakfast?"

"Yessir."

They all shouted but for Garfield, who simply sat and watched.

"Then get out there and saddle your horses," Seaforth ordered. "We pull out in one hour."

Ten men leaped to their feet and ran from the café to follow orders.

Garfield speared the last of his steak on his fork and ate it.

Seaforth walked over and sat across from him.

"Coffee?" Garfield asked.

"Why not?" Seaforth said. "We've got an hour."

Garfield poured coffee into a white mug for Major Seaforth.

"Have you gotten over your dislike of the thought of rustlin'?" Seaforth asked.

"Like you said, Major," Garfield answered. "It's not rustling."

"Yes, I know what I said," Seaforth replied. "What do you say?"

"Frankly?"

"Don't I always want you to talk frankly, Gar?"

"No," Garfield said, "sometimes you'd like to kill me when I speak frankly."

"Well, this time I have a feeling you're not telling me everything," Seaforth said. "So let's both be very frank . . . this time."

Garfield put his fork down.

"I think it's a long way to go for some licorice."

Seaforth took a piece from his pocket, popped it into his mouth, and said, "It's my licorice."

"Okay," Garfield said, "let me tell you what I think I know . . ."

SEAFORTH SURPRISED GARFIELD by listening to him in silence, and never interrupting. That wasn't like him.

"So it's this Motley's final trail drive, then," Seaforth said.

"That's the way it seems."

"And you think that'll make him fight harder."

"Seems to make sense."

Seaforth nodded, digesting the information while chewing yet another piece of licorice.

"That doesn't matter," he finally said. "The only thing that does is how many men he has."

"Yes," Garfield said, "I thought you'd say something like that."

"We said we were being frank," Seaforth pointed out. "I'm taking that herd, Gar. Will you be with me?"

"Aren't I always with you, Sea?" Garfield asked.

"Yes," Seaforth said, "yes, you are." He stood. "We better get mounted."

"Right."

They left the café together.

WHEN THE LAST of the men rode up to them in front of the café, they were at their full force of twelve.

"Okay, we're ridin' north," Seaforth announced. "When we reach this herd we'll scout it, see how many men they have, and then I'll form a plan. Until then, nobody fires a shot without a word from me. Got it?"

Some of the men said, "Yes, sir," and others just nodded.

Seaforth looked at Garfield, who said, "Got it."

AS SEAFORTH'S RAIDERS rode out of Three Rivers, the townspeople drifted out of their homes and stores and into the street. As always, they exchanged fervent hopes that this time the raiders would meet their match and not return. In the past, citizens would pack their things and leave while the raiders were gone, but this lot had stayed, and continued to hope against hope that they would get their town back, someday.

Maybe one day soon.

W ITH ALL SEVEN of them keeping alert, their eyes flicking in all directions, by the second night outside of Three Rivers they had not spotted any riders. Once they had seen a buckboard with a man and a woman on it, but the couple had simply waved at them in passing.

On that second night they sat around the fire, consuming another Carlito meal with relish after a hard day driving the herd up a hill, across a deep gully, and retrieving fifteen head that seemed to have suddenly decided they wanted to go east.

Jake sent Curley and Desi after those fifteen, since they were still the men—along with Carlito—he knew the least about. Both men had performed very admirably and driven those cows back into the herd with relative ease.

Taco had seemingly regained his youthful vigor; Desi proved he was a good *vaquero*; Curly showed that he had been truthful, at least once in his past, about working cows and horses; and Dundee was a quick learner.

But it was Chance who brought Jake the most pleasure. His friend seemed to be winning his battle against the lust for whiskey, had lost some of the belly that had flopped over his belt weeks ago, and had finally—after much complaining—managed to regain his seat.

As for Jake Motley himself, he felt good being back in the saddle and at the helm of a trail drive. But he knew they still had many days and miles ahead, during which his age and condition could betray him.

He just hoped they weren't going to have to deal with some petty gunslicks along the way.

"We still keepin' watch tonight?" Curly asked.

"Yeah," Jake said, "Chance and me, we'll take turns stayin' awake. The rest of you can pick your shifts to watch the herd."

Since the four of them had been getting along so well, they decided that Dundee would take the first watch with Desi, followed by Curly and Taco.

Carlito cleaned his equipment, left a pot of coffee on the fire, and turned in.

"These boys are doin' okay," Chance commented to Jake.

"These two old men are doin' okay, too," Jake countered.

Chance grinned and patted his stomach.

"At least I lost some of this flab."

"And I can breathe," Jake said. "First week or so I never thought I'd be able to take a deep breath again."

"You hid it well," Chance said. "I thought I was the only one suffocatin' on account of my age."

"Now we just gotta get through the next five weeks or so without givin' in to the years."

"Well," Chance said, "at least I don't feel like one of us is gonna die in the saddle anymore."

"No," Jake said, "I think we'll make it. I just don't know what condition we'll be in when we get there."

"Why don't we put some money on it?" Chance suggested. "That might keep us goin'."

"You mean, like the old days?"

"A friendly wager," Chance said. "I say before we get to Dodge City, you'll fall out of the saddle before I do."

"A bottle of whiskey?" Jake said.

"Done!"

The two men shook hands across the fire.

S EAFORTH BAILEY HAD one man in his pack whom he valued almost as much as Teddy Garfield. His name was Sequoia, a half-breed. The breed was his tracker, and while a herd was not hard to track, it was Sequoia's abilities that convinced Seaforth he was making the right call.

They found one of the trail drive's cold camps, and Sequoia needed only moments to walk it, study the ground, and make his pronouncement.

"Six men," he said, "maybe seven."

"That's all?" Seaforth asked.

"They do not need more," Sequoia said. "They cannot have more than five or six hundred head in the herd."

Later, when they made their own camp, the men sat around the fire and questioned Sequoia.

"You can tell that from lookin' at the ground?" Dennis Finch said.

"It is very clear," Sequoia said.

Al Keenan asked, "The number of men, or cows, is clear?"

Sequoia looked at him with his cold, flint-gray eyes and said, "All."

Finch and Keenan looked at Garfield across the fire.

"He's been at this a long time," Gar said. "He should know."

All the men looked at Sequoia, whose age was a mystery to them. The breed outrode them all, never seemed to get tired, and could have been forty or sixty.

"Everybody turn in early," Seaforth commanded. "Tomorrow's gonna be a big day."

CHAPTER FIFTEEN

WHEN SEAFORTH BAILEY spotted the herd it was easy to see that Sequoia had been right on all counts. It looked to be five or six hundred head, and including the man on the chuckwagon, there was a crew of seven.

Sequoia had spotted the herd first, riding ahead of the rest of the raiders. When he rode back to fetch Seaforth they both rode on ahead, leaving the other ten men behind so the dozen raiders wouldn't attract attention.

Sequoia didn't bother pointing, since the herd was spread out ahead of them as they topped a rise and reined in.

"What do you think, Sequoia?" Seaforth asked.

"The herd is fit," the breed said. "They have probably come from South Texas, and have not had time to lose weight on the drive."

"And the men?"

"They seem to know what they do," the breed commented. "I see two men who are very experienced, perhaps much older than the others."

"Well," Seaforth said, "if Gar is right, one of these fellas is called Big Jake Motley, and he'd be in his fifties or sixties."

"Fifties, I think," Sequoia said.

"Okay," the Major said, "let's go with that. Two of them in their fifties?"

"Yes."

"The odds are in our favor, then," Seaforth said. "Twelve to seven, and two of them are old codgers."

Sequoia turned and stared at his boss.

"What?" Seaforth asked.

"The old codgers are the experienced men," the breed said. "Do not underestimate them."

"I don't underestimate anyone," Seaforth said. "You got anything else you want to tell me?"

"Yes."

"What is it?" Seaforth asked impatiently.

Sequoia turned his attention back down to the men and the herd.

"They have seen us."

TACO RODE FROM drag all the way up front to where Jake was leading and fell in alongside him.

"On the ridge behind us, jefe," he said.

"I see 'em," Jake said. "Just two?"

"Sí, jefe," Taco said, "but they might just be scouts. There will be more if they are from Three Rivers."

At that moment Chance came riding up.

"See 'em?" he asked.

"Yeah," Jake said, "we were just sayin' there's gotta be more than two."

"Whadaya wanna do, Jake?" Chance asked.

"Let's break out the pistols," Jake said.

"Right," Chance said.

"But tell the boys not to shoot unless you or I do," Jake told Chance.

"That's what I was thinkin'," Chance said.

He rode on ahead to the chuckwagon, where they had all stored their pistols. He also gave the word to Carlito and Curly.

"Tell the others," Jake said to Taco.

"Sí, señor." He rode back to inform Dundee and his cousin, Desi, of the order.

S EAFORTH AND SEQUOIA rode back to the rest of the men, fell into stride with them.

"What'd you see?" Garfield asked.

"Just what the breed said there would be," Seaforth said. "Five, six hundred head, and seven men."

"So what's the plan?" Gar asked.

"Right now, we'll just ride along behind them for a while."

"Why?"

"They spotted us," Seaforth said. "Now I want to give them time to think."

"We might be giving them time to plan," Garfield said.

"They can plan all they want," Seaforth said. "They're a cook and six cowpunchers, two of which are well past their prime."

"But they've got guns, right?"

"So?"

"Anybody with a gun is dangerous," Garfield said.

"We are twelve men who know how to use our guns," Seaforth said. "I think we've got the upper hand, don't you, Gar?"

"Whatever you say, Major," Garfield said.

"That's what I like to hear," Seaforth said. "Now

we'll give them a few hours to think it over before we ride down and give them the opportunity to simply hand the cattle over with no bloodshed."

"And do you think they'll go for that?"

Seaforth grinned and said, "I certainly hope not."

W HERE ARE THEY?" Chance asked, coming up alongside Jake again.

"They're givin' us time to think," Jake said.

"Why would they wanna do that?"

"Because they think they're gonna scare us."

"Well," Chance said, "I'm concerned, but I can't say that I'm scared."

"Me neither," Jake said. "But a few hours might help us rather than hurt us."

"In what way?" Chance asked.

Jake looked at Chance and said, "I don't know. I'm thinkin' about it."

S EQUOIA RODE UP ahead again, and came back.

"They are still moving," he said.

"Any change in their formation?" Seaforth asked.

"No," Sequoia said, "the usual. Two on each flank, and one drag."

"And the chuckwagon and *remuda* ahead?"

"Ahead," Sequoia said, "but not so far ahead."

"They're stayin' bunched, then," Seaforth said. "Good. We can take 'em all at once."

Garfield looked at his leader, and thought how much easier it would have been if they could have taken the chuckwagon and *remuda* first.

"You got somethin' to say?" Seaforth asked him.

"Not a thing, Major," Garfield said. "Not a thing."

* * *

BY MIDDAY JAKE was wondering what the holdup was. Then Chance came riding up alongside him again. He and his friend both had pistols in their belts now, and wore them with equal discomfort.

"What are they waitin' for?" Chance asked.

"For our nerves to get the best of us," Jake said.

"Well, they're gettin' their way," Chance said. "I don't know about you, but my nerves are startin' to get the better of me."

"I know what you mean," Jake said.

"Think they'll wait until we make camp?"

"No, then they'd have to come in the dark. They'd be just as much at a disadvantage as we would."

"Good thinkin'," Chance said, "unless they figure that's what we'd think."

"Look, we're gonna keep watch," Jake said, "but I think they'll wait at least until mornin', maybe hit us before we start up for the day."

"Or maybe they won't hit us at all," Chance said. "Maybe there was just the two of them."

"Maybe, maybe," Jake said, "but I doubt it."

SEAFORTH HAD HIS raiders fall back about a mile and then camp.

"Let's set a watch," he said to Garfield, "just in case they send somebody back to take a look at us."

"Right," Garfield said.

"And I want them to be sharp."

"I'll start with Sequoia," Garfield said.

"Good. And tell them I'll shoot anybody who falls asleep on watch."

Garfield knew that, after himself and Sequoia, they

did have a few good men among the others. Major Seaforth Bailey, however, never acted that way. It was as if he always expected the men to fall down on the job. Garfield knew he could put together a crew of at least six from this band that could accomplish anything.

If he had to.

He went to find Sequoia and start the watch.

CHAPTER SIXTEEN

CARLITO HANDED JAKE a plate of bacon and eggs, with biscuits and a cup of coffee.

"Where did you get the eggs?"

"I was saving them, jefe."

"So why make 'em today?"

Carlito shrugged.

"Just in case."

Chance came walking over and Carlito handed him a plate.

"Where'd he get the eggs?" Chance asked, sitting across from Jake.

"He said he was savin' them."

"Then why make 'em now?"

"Accordin' to him," Jake said, "just in case."

Chance looked at Jake, then checked around them.

"So far, so good," he said, and started eating.

WHEN GARFIELD STOOD up from his bedroll he saw the men gathered around the fire. As he walked over he noticed that they were all eating. He also saw that the cook, this morning, was Seaforth.

"What's going on?" he asked.

"What's it look like?" Seaforth said. "Breakfast."

"We're taking the time to have breakfast?"

"Why not?" Seaforth asked. "That herd isn't going anywhere."

Garfield wondered what had convinced the Major to make such a decision, but the food smelled good and he was hungry.

"Fine, then," he said. "Hand me a plate."

Seaforth loaded up a plate with beans and a hunk of bread and passed it over to Garfield.

"I want you all to eat well," the Major told them. "We might be killing some men today, and I want you all to do it on a full stomach."

The men took their plates and moved away from the fire to sit in groups.

Garfield stayed at the fire with Seaforth.

"What's the plan?" Garfield asked. "I know you don't care if they kill on an empty stomach or a full one."

Seaforth laughed.

"You know me too well, Gar," the Major said. "I just want them all to be calm when the showdown comes."

"Showdown?"

"Yes," Seaforth said, "I've decided we're simply going to ride up and tell them we want the herd."

"And you think they'll just hand it over?"

"Definitely not," Seaforth said.

"So what happens when they say no?"

"Well, then we take it." Seaforth pointed to Gar's plate. "How're your beans?"

CARLITO PASSED PLATES of bacon and eggs to all the other men, and then took one himself.

"This is a treat," Dundee said. "Thanks, Carlito."

Jake knew Carlito was thinking the condemned men deserved a hearty meal. He was just making sure if they all died this day, they died well fed.

Jake and Chance ate their food while keeping a sharp lookout. They weren't taking any chances of being surprised while everybody had a plate in their hands.

"Dundee, Curly," Jake shouted, "eat up and then get out to the herd. We don't want no surprises this mornin'."

"Got it, boss," Dundee said.

The two young men wolfed down their food, then saddled up and rode out to the herd.

JAKE FINISHED HIS breakfast, gave the empty plate to Carlito, then picked up his pistol and stuck it in his belt.

"Can you hit anythin' with that?" Chance asked, also sticking his in his belt. Both were rather aged Peacemakers.

"Can you?" Jake asked.

"Jake, I could always hit what I aimed at with a handgun," Chance said. "You couldn't. I'm askin' you if you've gotten any better."

"I don't think I've fired it since the last time I saw you," Jake said.

"Seriously?" Chance looked down at Jake's gun. "Have you even cleaned it? Will it even fire? What if those jaspers come after us today—"

"I cleaned it," Jake said, cutting him off. "It'll fire."

"I hope everyone else's will," Chance said.

Taco and Desi finished eating and went to saddle their horses. They each had a revolver shoved into their belt.

Jake and Chance were saddling their horses when Curly came riding up to them.

"Company, boss," he said. "Lots of it."

"Where?" Jake asked.

Curly pointed behind them, to the ridge where they had seen the two men. Now they saw a dozen riding toward them.

"Okay," Jake said. "Get everybody over here."

"Right," Curly said.

"What if they go straight for the herd?" Chance asked.

"Look at 'em," Jake said. "They're circling around to come right into camp."

"What the hell for?"

"They're gonna talk first," Jake surmised.

While they waited, Dundee, Curly, Desi, and Taco came riding up behind them. Even Carlito came over from his wagon, carrying a rifle.

"Carlito, stay out of sight in your wagon, with your rifle ready," Chance ordered.

"Sí, *patrón*!"

"Good idea," Jake said.

The dozen riders came right into camp with their horses. The man in front was wearing a Confederate coat and the insignia of a major. He was also wearing a Confederate pistol holster on his right hip, the kind with the flap that folded over the gun.

As the riders arrived they spread out behind their leader, which suited Jake. That made them all accessible targets. If they had been grouped behind him some of them would have been shielded.

"Good morning, gentlemen," the man in the gray jacket said. "My name is Major Seaforth Bailey. These men behind me are Seaforth's Raiders. No doubt you've heard of us."

"Never," Jake said, and he could see that annoyed the man.

"I'm Jake Motley. What can we do for you and your men?"

"Is that Big Jake Motley?" Seaforth asked.

"That's what some people call me," Jake admitted.

Seaforth looked at the six men in front of him. He could see their pistols in their belts, and rifles in their hands.

"Your men are all armed," he said.

"Well," Jake said, "you can never be too careful."

"Perhaps I should get to the point, then," Seaforth said.

"We'd appreciate it," Chance said. "We've got some work to do."

"Mr. Motley, you were in Three Rivers a couple of days ago, and you took some supplies from the mercantile," Seaforth said.

"I bought some supplies," Jake said.

"Yes, well, those supplies were spoken for—by me."

"The whole store?" Jake asked.

"Indeed," Seaforth said, "right down to the licorice."

"Licorice?" Jake looked at Dundee, who just shrugged. He hadn't seen the young man take any candy.

"Yes," Seaforth said, "*my* licorice."

"I think you're bein' a little ridiculous, Major," Jake said. "There was plenty of supplies in that store. Enough for everyone."

"I beg to differ," Seaforth said. "There was just enough there for me and my men. I'm afraid I'm going to have to demand you return them. All of them."

"I don't think we can do that," Jake said. "We've already eaten some of the bacon and"—he looked at Dundee again—"I'm sure, some of the licorice."

"That's too bad," Seaforth said. "I'm going to demand some sort of recompense."

"Some what?" Chance asked.

"Payment," Seaforth said.

"We paid," Jake reminded him.

"But you didn't pay me," Seaforth said. "I'm afraid you owe me."

"Now you're mistaken," Jake said. "We don't owe you a thing."

"I'm sorry you feel that way," Seaforth said. "The only way I can figure to settle this is for my men and me to take your herd." The man shrugged. "It's only fair."

"Who are you kiddin'?" Chance asked.

"Sorry?" Seaforth asked. Then he looked at Jake. "Who's this man?"

"My partner," Jake said, "and my friend."

"I didn't know you had a partner."

"Well, you know now," Chance said. "And you're not takin' our herd."

"Are you going to stop us?" Seaforth asked.

"We are."

"In case you can't add," Seaforth said to Chance, "you're outnumbered two-to-one."

"There's a rifle pointed right at you, Major," Jake said. "If you and your men try anythin', you'll be the first to die."

"You could be bluffin'," Seaforth said, after a moment of consideration.

"I could be," Jake said, "but I ain't."

"Well," the Major said, "that's all right. This was only meant to be a conversation."

"And the conversation is over," Jake said. "You're not takin' our herd, and we're not returnin' any supplies."

"You're being very unreasonable."

"Isn't that jacket kind of old?" Chance asked. "The war's been over for more than twenty years."

Seaforth ignored the insult to his jacket.

"Looks like I do agree on one thing," Seaforth said. "This conversation is over . . . for now."

Major Seaforth Bailey waved his arm and his men all turned their mounts and headed back the way they had come, with him leading the way.

CHAPTER SEVENTEEN

WELL," CHANCE SAID to Jake, "whadaya think of that?"

"I think they'll be back," Jake said. "That man is too arrogant not to come back with his 'raiders.'"

He turned as the other men gathered around.

"So what do we do now, jefe?" Taco asked as Carlito got down from his wagon and joined them.

"We get under way," Jake said, "and we stay ready, because they're gonna come back."

"You do not think they will go away?" Carlito asked hopefully.

"No," Jake said, shaking his head definitively. "That kind of man doesn't give up."

"What kind of man?" Curly asked.

"Arrogant," Jake said, again. "An arrogant man has to get his way, and won't give up until he does. Or until somebody stops him."

"So who's gonna stop 'im?" Dundee asked.

"We are," Jake said. "Or I am. This is my herd. If

any of you want to turn back, or just ride away from this, do it now. I'll understand."

"I won't!" Chance said. "We're sure as hell not gonna let Jake face twelve men alone . . . are we?"

"I am not," Taco said. "I am with you, amigo."

"As am I, jefe," Desi said.

Chance looked at Dundee and Curly.

"Well," Dundee said, "sure, why not? We've come this far."

"Yeah, I'm in," Curly said. "Where else would I go, anyway?"

They all looked at Carlito.

"I still have a lot of cooking to do," he said.

"Okay, then," Jake said, "let's get this herd movin'. Dundee, you take drag—"

"I'll take drag," Chance said. "If they decide to shoot somebody in the back, I don't want it to be one of these fine young men."

"Okay," Jake said. "Desi and Taco, right flank, Curly and Dundee left. Tie the *remuda* to the back of Carlito's wagon." He turned to Carlito. "Don't ride too far up ahead of us. I want to keep you close, and safe."

"Sí, *patrón*."

"Right," Curly said.

They all mounted up and started the herd moving.

THE TWELVE RIDERS rode back up and over the ridge, out of sight of the drovers down below. Then Seaforth and Garfield separated themselves.

"What'd you think of him?" Seaforth asked.

"Stubborn old buzzard," Garfield said.

"Do you think he was bluffing about the rifle?"

"No," Garfield said, "I think he was dead serious."

"As do I."

"So," Garfield asked, "when do we hit them?"

"I haven't decided," Seaforth said. "I might want to make the old buzzard stew a bit. Did you form any opinions about the other men?"

"Yes," Gar said. "The partner is also a stubborn old buzzard. The two young white hands were nervous. The Mexicans weren't."

"That's good," Seaforth said. "It'll work to our advantage if two of them are scared."

"I didn't say they were scared," Garfield said. "I said they were nervous. There's a difference."

"Yes, yes, of course," Seaforth said.

He turned in his saddle to look at his own men.

"What about our boys?" he asked.

"What do you mean?"

"Are they scared? Nervous?"

"Some of them are scared, some nervous," Garfield said.

"Are they reliable?"

"Most of them are."

"And the ones who aren't?"

"They'll be the first to get killed," Garfield told him.

"As long as we take that herd," Seaforth said, popping a piece of licorice into his mouth. "What about you?"

"I'm not nervous," Gar said, "or scared."

"That's good," Seaforth said. "Neither am I. I guess if we'd felt this way during the war we would've made names for ourselves."

"We were kids," Gar said.

"We were smart then, and we're smart now," Seaforth said.

Garfield didn't know how smart it was to go after this herd, not when Big Jake Motley had so much invested in it. A man was never so dangerous as when he was on his last legs. But there was no way he could tell Seaforth that.

"Yeah, well . . ." was all Gar said.

"Just make sure nobody overreacts," Seaforth said. "Make sure they key on you and me. I don't want anybody shooting until we do."

"Whatever you say, boss."

As Gar turned his horse to ride over to the others Seaforth yelled, "And don't call me boss!"

J AKE HAD HIS men concentrate on the herd while he kept an eye out in front, and Chance stayed alert behind them. On occasion a few cows would wander off, and one man would go after them, so Jake rode back to tell them to make sure they did everything in twos, just in case. He didn't want any of them going off alone and being bushwhacked.

Jake was wondering if Major Seaforth would decide to hit them before they reached San Antonio, or after they passed the town. That would probably depend on whether or not Major Seaforth wanted to take a chance on having to deal with the law there.

Having considered that, Jake decided to ride back to where Chance was and see if he agreed.

"Between here and San Antonio?" Chance repeated. "That makes sense. If he's got Three Rivers under his thumb, like you say, he's not gonna want to go anywhere near San Antonio."

"All right, then," Jake said. "That means he'll move somewhere between now and tomorrow afternoon. I'll tell the men."

Chance nodded and waved.

W E WANT TO hit them before San Antonio," Seaforth said to Garfield.

"Obviously," Gar said. "There's too much law there.

They've got a new modern police department, and they still have a sheriff."

"Twenty miles," Seaforth said. "Let's take them twenty miles before San Antonio. That'll be tomorrow afternoon. Then we'll drive the herd back toward Three Rivers."

"Then what do we do with them?" Garfield asked.

"We sell them," Seaforth said.

"To who? He's probably taking them to Kansas, which makes sense. What the hell are we going to do with them in Texas?"

"Look," Seaforth said as they sat around a small fire. "We'll deal with that when the time comes. First I want to take them."

Garfield dumped the remnants of his coffee into the fire.

"Then we better move," he said, "we're letting them get too far ahead."

"They're moving slow," Seaforth pointed out.

"Then I suggest if you want to hit them before San Antonio, we get ahead of them."

"Between them and San Antone," Seaforth said, standing. "Good idea. Get the men ready. We'll circle around them so they don't see us. Let them keep wondering."

Garfield said, "Yeah, good idea," glad that he'd gotten Seaforth to go along while thinking it was his idea.

JAKE HAD TO circle the entire herd in order to tell Taco and Desi, then Dundee and Curly, what he and Chance had decided. That done, he rode up to Carlito to inform the cook, who had his rifle next to him on his seat.

"Sí, jefe," Carlito said, "I will be alert."

"Good man," Jake said.

"Jefe, there will be killing, no?"

"There will be killin', yes," Jake said, "if anybody tries to take my herd."

"Señor," Carlito said, "I have never killed a man before."

"Then you're gonna have to make a decision, Carlito," Jake said. "Fire that rifle, or hide in your wagon."

"Sí, señor."

"Just remember," Jake said, "if they take the herd, and they find you in the wagon, they'll probably kill you . . . or . . ."

"Or, señor?"

Jake shrugged.

"They might just make you cook for them."

CHAPTER EIGHTEEN

WHEN THEY STOPPED the herd and camped for the night, Jake became dead sure the raiders would hit them the next day.

"I could ride to San Antonio for help," Dundee said, over the campfire. "It would only take me a few hours."

"A few hours to get there, and a few to get back," Chance said. "We'll need your gun here."

"Two-to-one ain't great odds," Curly said.

"Curly, if you wanna ride out, just say so," Jake replied. "No hard feelin's. This is my herd, not yours. Lord knows I ain't payin' you enough."

"That ain't what I'm sayin'," Curly said. "If I cut and run now, that don't say much about me as a man, and I'd have to live a long time with it."

"I agree," Dundee said. "We gotta stay."

Jake looked at Desi. He already knew Taco would be staying.

"Sí, jefe," Desi said, "I am staying."

"Okay, then," Jake said, "here's what I want us to do when they come . . ."

A FTER HE FINISHED outlining his plan for the attack, they all had more coffee and considered their roles.

"Carlito," Jake said, "get the bottle."

"Sí, jefe."

"Bottle?" Chance said.

"I had Carlito put a bottle of tequila in the wagon," Jake said. "I thought we'd have a drink in Dodge City, but if we're gonna be in a firefight tomorrow, why wait?"

Carlito returned with the bottle and a big smile. The men all held their cups out—except for Chance.

"Of course," Jake said, "I'm just talkin' about sweetenin' our coffee."

That drew a few groans, but they kept their cups out anyway, and Chance reluctantly did the same.

"Guess if I'm gonna take a bullet tomorrow, like you said, why not?"

Carlito put a few drops into everyone's coffee, and then they all sat back, sipping.

"We'll stand watch tonight, though, just in case they decide to come in the dark," Jake added. "You boys split the herd watch, and Chance and I will stand watch here in camp."

As usual, Curly and Dundee took one watch while Taco and Desi took the other.

"Carlito," Jake said, "you get some sleep. I want you to make a good breakfast bright and early tomorrow."

"Sí, jefe."

As Carlito stood up to turn in Jake said, "And take the bottle with you."

Carlito grinned and said, "Oh, sí, jefe."

* * *

WHEN CURLY AND Dundee were out with the herd and all the Mexicans had turned in, Jake and Chance sat at the fire and talked.

"How you holdin' up, old-timer?" Chance asked.

"I'm a whole year older than you, you bastard," Jake said. "I'm fine—a little sore, but so far, so good. What about you?"

"The same," Chance said. "I'm breathin' better these days than I was that first week. A coupla times I thought I'd just choke to death."

"Well, thank God you didn't," Jake said. "Now you'll be around tomorrow to get shot to death."

"Not a chance," Chance said. "If I die on this drive it'll be in the saddle while drivin' this herd—probably ridin' drag."

"Did you see that fella sittin' just off that Major's left shoulder?"

"I did," Chance said. "Real steady eyes. I'm peggin' him as his *segundo*."

"Yeah, I'd keep my eye on him when they come back," Jake said. "And they've probably got a few other good boys."

"Taco's gonna be okay," Chance said, "and probably Desi. I don't know about those two kids."

"They got good attitudes," Jake said. "They'll be fine, especially if they can do what I told them to do."

"We'll have to wait and see," Chance said. "There may not be time."

"I don't see how those twelve men could hit us without warnin'," Jake said. "We're gonna have to see them comin'."

"Unless there's a bottleneck somewhere," Chance said.

"I don't think so," Jake said. "Not between here and San Antonio, anyway."

"You been this way more than I have," Chance said. "I'll take your word for it."

Chance looked into his cup, licked his lips, then drained the last of his sweetened coffee from it.

"I'll take the first watch," Jake said. "You turn in. Tomorrow's gonna be a hard day."

"The hardest," Chance said. "We're cowpunchers, not gunnies, and tomorrow we're gonna hafta kill or be killed."

CHANCE TURNED IN and Jake sat and thought about what his friend had said.

Jake would certainly be sorry if any of his men were killed, but when you took the job driving a herd you accepted the responsibility of doing whatever you had to do to get the cows to market. And they had all made their choice to stay when he gave them the opportunity to leave. So guilt could no longer figure into the situation. Now it just remained to stick to the plan and defend the herd. He was also convinced that Carlito would do what he had to do, despite the fact that he had never killed before.

In the West, men were faced with that choice every day—kill to eat, or starve; kill to defend yourself, your home, what was yours, or die doing it.

He poured himself another cup of coffee, wished he had kept the bottle of tequila instead of having Carlito take it to his wagon. He wondered if he would be able to find the bottle without waking the cook, but decided against it. He had made the rules about drinking on the trail. They had all had a taste, and that was that. The rest of the bottle would be saved for Dodge City.

He only hoped they would all be alive to drink it.

* * *

GARFIELD WALKED UP to the top of the ridge and looked out. In the distance he could see the cattle milling around in the moonlight, and the flicker of their campfire in the cattle drive camp. It would be so easy to just walk in there in the dark and kill them all. But that wouldn't have been in keeping with the image Seaforth Bailey had for Seaforth's Raiders. No, they were going to have to ride in and take the herd in a blaze of glory—all the glory Seaforth still thought he had missed during the Civil War.

Garfield didn't know who had come out of that war more damaged: Seaforth, for what he wanted, or Garfield himself, for trying to help him get it?

When Garfield felt the presence next to him he knew it was Sequoia, the half-breed. That was because he hadn't heard him approaching. The breed was even more of an oddity than most, because Garfield knew he was half-white, but nobody seemed to know what the other half was.

"You and me," the breed said, "we could go down there and finish it before it start."

"I know we could."

"Then why do we not?"

Garfield looked at the breed.

"Because that's not what he wants."

"And why is what he want more important than what we want?" the breed asked.

"You know," Garfield said, "I ask myself that all the time."

He turned and walked back to camp.

CHANCE MCCANDLESS SPELLED Jake four hours later, at the same time Taco and Desi went out to relieve

Curly and Dundee. The two white hands came into camp as he was pouring coffee.

"Enough for two more?" Dundee asked.

"One," Curly said. "I'm goin' to sleep."

"Sure," Chance said. "Have a seat."

Dundee sat across from Chance, who handed him a cup of coffee.

"Quiet," Dundee said, accepting the cup. "Too quiet out there. Do you think they're watchin' us?"

"They've probably got someone watchin'," Chance said.

"I don't understand Jake's reasonin' for why they won't attack us at night," Dundee said.

"Arrogance?"

"Yeah, that. How does a man get like that?"

"Well," Chance said, "it has to do with the way they're educated, I guess . . . or not educated . . . or the kind of upbringin' . . . " He stopped, then tried again. "Uh, okay, I don't really know. I mean, I've known a lot of arrogant men in my time, but not well enough to understand why they're arrogant."

"Well, with this man," Dundee said. "it seems to come from the war. I mean, he's still wearing a Confederate jacket and insignia."

"Yeah, he is," Chance said, "but the way the jacket looked, it's like he put the insignia there himself. I get the feelin' he wasn't a major durin' the war."

"Ah," Dundee said, as if he was getting it, "so out of this arrogance he, sort of, promoted himself."

"Yeah, right."

Dundee thought a moment, then said, "I still don't get it."

"That's good, really," Chance said.

"Why good?"

"Because it means you'll never become arrogant yourself," Chance explained.

"I wouldn't want to," Dundee said. He finished his coffee and put the cup down. "Thanks for the coffee. I'm gonna turn in."

"We'll be gettin' an early start, after breakfast," Chance told him.

"Right," Dundee said. "We'll be ready."

Dundee turned in, and Chance prepared another pot of coffee.

CHAPTER NINETEEN

CHANCE WOKE JAKE, Curly, and Dundee the next morning as Taco and Desi came riding into camp.

"Breakfast," he announced.

They all staggered to the fire, each in his own form of rest or unrest. Chance felt surprisingly alert for having been on watch the past four hours.

Carlito handed out plates of his chuckwagon chicken, pecos strawberries, and sourdough bullets—bacon, beans, and biscuits—to everyone, then sat down with his own plate.

"Okay, after we eat I want everyone to stick their heads in a barrel of water and wake up," Jake said. "Today's gonna be the day."

"Are you predictin'," Dundee asked, "or hopin'?"

"I guess I'm predictin'," Jake said. "But it feels like a pretty damn sure thing, to me."

"Me too," Chance said. "We're far enough away from any law for it to make sense."

"So we make our own law?" Curly asked.

"We do," Jake said.

"The law of the gun?" Dundee asked, touching the pistol in his belt.

"No," Jake said, "the law of the trail."

"Jake's law," Chance said. Jake looked at him. "Nobody takes what's ours," he continued.

"Understand?" Jake asked.

They all said they did.

"Then eat up, wash up, and wake up!"

W HEN THEY WERE all fairly refreshed and mounted they started the herd moving north. Once again, Chance rode drag. It just seemed to make sense to have the most experienced man there. The best way to take a herd was to stampede it over the men who were guarding and guiding it. You started the body of a herd stampeding by lighting a fire under the ass end. It was, therefore, Chance's job to make sure that didn't happen.

Of course, if the men trying to steal the herd didn't know that . . .

W E'RE GONNA STEAL the herd from the front?"

The speaker was a man named Gus Walker. In his forties, he was possibly the only member of Seaforth's Raiders who had experience working cattle. The others had experience using their gun, taking what they wanted, and killing.

"Yeah, that's the plan," Garfield said as they rode, giving the herd a wide berth. "Why?"

"Well, everybody knows the way to steal a herd is to stampede it," Walker said. "You can't very well do that from the front."

"Tell that to the Major."

Gus Walker looked over at Garfield like he was out of his mind.

"You tell 'im," he said. "If I tell Major Bailey he's wrong he'll shoot me."

"If he hears you call him Major Bailey he'll shoot you," Garfield said. "It's Major Seaforth."

"Right," Walker said, "Seaforth. I still ain't tellin' him he's wrong."

"We'll do it his way, then."

"Fine. Where and when?"

"As soon as we find a likely place up ahead to ambush them," Garfield answered.

"Bushwhack?" Walker said. "The boss don't like to ambush people. He likes to go head-on."

"I know," Garfield said. "It's just . . . an option."

"A what?"

"Another way to do something," Garfield explained.

"The men like the way the Major does things now," Walker said.

"I know," Garfield said.

Before they could go on, Sequoia rode back to fall into place and join them.

"The Major wants you," the breed said to Garfield.

"We'll talk later," Garfield said to Walker, and rode on ahead.

"What's goin' on?" Walker asked.

"Only they know," the breed said, and then before Walker could speak again, "I must ride on ahead."

That left Walker riding on his own, which he didn't like, so he fell back and joined the rest of the men.

"What were you and Garfield talkin' about?" a man named Gardner asked him.

"Options," Walker said.

"What are options?"

"Other ways of doin' things."

"What's wrong with the way we do them now?" Gardner asked.

"I don't know," Walker said.

N O AMBUSH," SEAFORTH said. "That's not the way we do things."

"Then why is Sequoia scouting up ahead?" Garfield asked.

"He's looking for a likely place for us to hit the herd," Seaforth said. "When we do it, it will be head-on."

"Major—"

"Who have you been talking to?"

"What? Nobody. I just—"

"The men will follow my lead," Seaforth said, "will you?"

"You know I will," Garfield said. "I always do, don't I?"

"You make me think you always do."

"What's that mean?"

"You think I don't see when you're trying to get into my head?" Seaforth asked. "Give me an idea and then try to convince me it's mine."

Garfield looked at Seaforth with renewed respect.

"You know about that?"

"I do," the Major said, "and I let you think it works."

Garfield studied Seaforth for a few moments, saw something in the man's eyes he used to see back in the day.

"Yes," Seaforth said. "I'm not as arrogant and stupid as you think I'm getting."

"Sea—"

"Never mind, Gar," Seaforth said, "just be at my side and everything will be all right."

"Yes, sir," Garfield said, happy to apparently have

the old Seaforth back, at least for a while. He wasn't even chewing the damn licorice!

T HE DAY BEGAN badly, and went downhill from there. Crossing a deep gully, several of the cows managed to snap a leg, which meant they had to be put down. The carcasses could not simply be left where they were, so they had to be butchered and the meat stored on the chuckwagon. This meant they were going to eat well for many nights to come—if they survived that long.

They also encountered a pack of Texas red wolves that got pretty brave and came close enough to the herd to claim some stragglers, or calves. In the end, the only way Jake could figure to get rid of them was to let them have their kill, which would keep them feeding for some time while he and his men moved the herd farther away. Dundee and Curly wanted to shoot the wolves, but after wounding a few they realized there were just too many and stopping to hunt wolves would end up slowing down their progress.

Another problem was a spring rain that appeared, and suddenly dried-up gullies were gushing with flowing water. Many of the cows didn't want to cross, and some of the horses resisted as well. As they had done a couple of weeks before, the men had to swim across, coaxing their horses along behind them, while the flow of the main body of cattle pushed the reluctant cows across. It took time . . .

When they were all on the other side—as if to rub their noses in the trouble—the rain stopped.

"If we had waited . . ." Dundee said, looking back across the flowing gully. Already the water had begun to slow down.

"It would have just cost us more time," Jake said. "Let's check on the condition of the horses, and each other."

"Not to mention the chuckwagon," Chance said.

They checked the horses first, and found all but one had gotten across safely. One of the *remuda* had broken its leg and was put down.

The chuckwagon had virtually floated across successfully, and the mule team had survived. Carlito had injured his arm, but not badly. He assured Jake that he would still be able to cook with his arm in a sling for a short while.

"And I will fire my rifle, if I must," the cook added.

"Good," Jake said.

They carefully checked the wheels of the chuckwagon. All seemed intact.

Lastly, they checked each other. Curly had a gash on his head that he had not even felt when it occurred. They cleaned it thoroughly. Dundee had injured his left hand, but he was right-handed, so he would be able to fire his pistol.

Chance had some bruised ribs, as something in the water had jabbed into him, possibly a tree trunk. But he was able to move, so they didn't seem to be fractured.

Jake, Desi, Taco, and Dundee had arrived on the other side in one piece.

The sky cleared, and that seemed to be the end of the storm, which it seemed had appeared only to torment them.

"I suppose the only way it could've got worse," Jake said, "was if Seaforth and his raiders had been waitin' here for us."

"They're not here, and I don't think they're behind us," Chance said.

"What're you sayin'?" Dundee asked.

"That I think they circled around us and are waitin' someplace up ahead."

"Can we change direction and avoid them?" Curly asked.

"Not a chance," Jake said. "We're just gonna have to keep goin', and hope for the best."

"Then let's move 'em out," Chance said.

"Should we change mounts?" Curly asked. "I can bring the *remuda*—"

"No," Jake said, "all our horses have gone through the same ordeal, and I don't want to take the time. Let's just move!"

CHAPTER TWENTY

"WHAT'S HOLDING THEM up?" Seaforth wondered aloud. "They should have been here by now."

"There was a storm," Garfield said. "Sequoia told us it was pretty bad. It would have slowed them down. Or might have damaged their chuckwagon."

Seaforth was sitting on some rocks with Garfield, Gus Walker, and four others. Across from them—far enough away so that the herd could get between them—was Sequoia with five men. When Seaforth gave the signal, they were going to attack the trail drive. Sequoia's group would handle the flanking riders on their side, and whoever was riding drag. Seaforth's group would handle their flanking riders, and Jake Motley, who the Major assumed would always be at the front. Their responsibility would also be the cook driving the chuckwagon.

"Let's just stay calm and wait, Major," Garfield said. "They'll be here."

"Those boys across the way better keep calm," Seaforth said. "I hope they're not getting impatient."

"With Sequoia leading them?" Garfield said. "He keeps his head better than any three of us. Relax, Sea. You have a good plan, here."

"I'd like to do this without stampeding the herd," Seaforth observed. "It'll be hell to round them all up again."

"You won't have to round them up again," Walker said.

Seaforth looked at him, then at Garfield.

"Walker," Garfield said.

"What do you mean, Walker?" Seaforth asked.

"I've worked cattle, Major," Walker said, moving closer. "Even if they stampede, most of them will stay together."

"Is that a fact?"

"Yessir!"

"Walker," Seaforth said, "when we get this herd I think you're going to be a trail boss. What do you think of that?"

"That suits me just fine, Major," Walker said, with a smile.

Garfield hoped that being the trail boss didn't make Walker think he was in for a bigger cut.

THEY GOT THE wet herd moving again, as well as themselves. Rather than changing into dry duds, they just decided to let the wet clothing dry on them.

And finally, with the sun out and doing its job to get them dry, suddenly there was a crack and the chuckwagon leaned to one side, almost throwing Carlito off. He stopped his team and then stepped down. By the time Jake rode up to him, he had found the problem.

"The rear right wheel, jefe," he said. "It broke all the way through."

"We checked the wheels when we got out of the water," Jake pointed out.

"We did," Carlito said, "but we did not see the crack."

"Okay," Jake said, "Do you have another wheel?"

"Sí, jefe. In the back of the wagon."

"I'll get Taco and Desi over here to change the wheel," Jake said. "You sit somewhere and relax."

"Sí, jefe."

As Jake headed back to the herd Chance was riding toward him.

"What's the holdup?" he asked.

"There's a broken wheel on the chuckwagon."

"But we checked."

"I know. We didn't see a crack, and now it's all the way through. I'm gonna get Desi and Taco to change it."

"Okay," Chance said, "I'll make sure Curly and Dundee stick with the herd, don't let them stray."

"Right. Let's go."

CARLITO HAD A wheel in the back of the wagon, up against the canvas side, where it didn't take up much room. Taco and Desi slid it out the back and got to work replacing the cracked one.

With Chance, Curly, and Dundee looking after the herd, Jake stood watch over the wagon repair, and kept an eye out for raiders.

It was getting late in the day and Jake was considering just making camp right there once the repairs were done. If Chance was right and Seaforth and his men were ahead of them, waiting, then maybe this would make them nervous, instead of the other way around.

Jake rode slowly around the area, saw that it was not well traveled ahead of them. When he rode back to the wagon Taco and Desi were just setting the wagon back down on the ground.

"How's it look?" Jake called.

"It is solid, jefe," Desi said.

"I was just going to have Carlito climb aboard to make sure," Taco said.

"He's got that bad arm," Jake said. "Why don't you do it?"

"Of course," Taco said. "As you say, jefe, I will do it."

Jake watched as Taco climbed onto the wagon seat, bounced up and down on it a few times, then picked up the team's reins and urged them forward several yards before stopping.

"It looks good," Desi said.

Taco dropped back down to the ground, walked to the wheel, examined it, touched it, then turned to Jake.

"It is fixed, jefe," he announced.

"Good," Jake said.

"We should exchange mounts now—" Taco started, but Jake cut him off.

"No. I've decided we're gonna camp here. I'll go and tell the others. One of you make a fire for Carlito."

"I will do it," Desi said. "And I will help him prepare the meal."

"I will unsaddle the mounts and picket the horses," Taco said.

"Good. And keep an eye out."

"We will."

Jake rode back to the herd, told Chance, Curly, and Dundee they were making camp.

"Dundee, you and Curly stay with the herd. I'll have someone come out and get you when the meal's ready."

"I should stay out here, too," Chance said. "Just till we know the herd is bedded down. They've been through a lot today, and I can feel the tension."

"Okay," Jake said, "but if I spot Seaforth and his men, I'll fire a shot. That means come a-runnin'."

"Got it," Chance said.

Jake rode back to camp.

* * *

WITH DESI'S HELP, Carlito was able to prepare a warm meal for them. By this time all their clothing had dried but there was still some dampness inside everyone's boots. And they didn't dare take them off to sit with their feet by the fire, for fear that Seaforth and his men would choose just that moment to attack. That would leave them all defending the herd barefoot.

"I tell you what," Jake said while they ate. "Let's get our boots off two at a time, try to dry them out, and put on some dry socks. Two at a time should be safe."

Jake went last, waiting until everyone else had dry feet beneath them. He sat and stared straight ahead. Even if Seaforth's Raiders didn't come in a group, they might send someone back to scout them.

"Your turn, Jake," Chance said. "I'll keep watch."

"I'm figuring they'll wanna know what the holdup was, so they'll send a scout back."

"I'll keep an eye out," Chance said, seating himself with his rifle across his knees.

Jake went to the fire, dried out his boots as well as he could, donned dry socks, and then pulled the boots back on. Desi and Taco were out with the herd by this time. They had camped early because of their ordeal, so it was not yet dark, and too early to turn in for the night. Another thing they all had to do was clean their guns, to make sure that they would fire after having been drenched by the rain and the running water in the gully.

Dundee and Curly were in the midst of doing that, moving quickly just in case. When they were done Jake cleaned his rifle and pistol. He assumed the others had already done the same.

He walked back over to where Chance was and sat next to him, handing him a cup of coffee.

"Thanks."

They sat and drank together.

"Anythin'?" Jake asked.

"No," Chance said, "nothin's movin', and I don't like it."

"What are you thinkin'?" Jake asked.

Chance pointed.

"I think somebody's out there watchin' us, and he's so good we can't see him."

"One of Seaforth's men?"

Chance nodded.

"I saw a breed with them," he said. "I'm thinkin' it's him."

"That would make sense," Jake said. "If he don't wanna be seen, we ain't gonna see 'im."

"Well, let him go back to his major and tell him where we are," Chance said. "It's a good bet they'll just wait for us tomorrow, and by then we'll be recovered from the ordeal we had today."

"I hope so," Jake said. "I don't know how many more days like this I can take."

SEQOUIA SAT AND watched the camp, secure in the knowledge that they could not see him. He watched as they repaired the wheel on the chuckwagon and then made camp. He knew that three men were watching the herd. He also knew he didn't have the time to ride back to Seaforth and bring him and all his men here. By then all the activity in camp would be done, and they would be on the alert.

Once he saw the two old cowpokes sit together with coffee and stare out toward him, he smiled. They knew someone was close by, watching.

He backed off, mounted his horse, and headed back to Seaforth's Raiders. Tomorrow would definitely be the day.

CHAPTER TWENTY-ONE

CARLITO WOKE THE next morning, stiff and in pain, but insisted on preparing breakfast. This time both his cousins helped him.

"Chance and I are thinkin'," Jake said as they ate, "that if we can make the next ten miles without incident, Seaforth and his raiders will hit us."

"Is the plan still the same?" Curly asked.

"Pretty much." Jake looked at Carlito. "Can you shoot, señor?"

"Sí, jefe," Carlito said, "I will shoot."

"Curly, how's the hand?" Jake asked.

Curly held it up, flexed it, winced, and said, "Good."

"And you?" Jake asked, turning to face Chance. "How're the ribs this mornin'?"

"Kept me awake for a while," Chance admitted, "didn't make gettin' to my feet very easy this mornin', but I'll be damned if they'll keep me from ridin' and shootin'."

"I got a suggestion," Dundee said.

"What's that?" Jake asked.

"Why don't you let a couple of us ride on ahead and pick some of them off?"

"A couple of you?"

"Yeah," Dundee said, "whoever's the best shot with a rifle."

"And who would that be?" Chance asked.

"Me," Dundee said, with a smile.

"And me," Taco said.

"And how many would you get?" Jake asked. "Two, three? Then the other nine or ten would ride ya down and kill you."

"Ah, they'd never catch us," Dundee said, "would they, Taco?"

"No, señor," Taco said, "they would not. They would not even see us."

"No?" Jake said. "They'd see the sun shinin' off all those silver button conchas you're wearin' a mile away, Taco. After all, you keep 'em nice an' shiny."

"Not a good idea, boys," Chance said.

"Let's stick to the plan," Jake said. "If we show them we're not gonna give up easy, we might discourage 'em."

"You really believe that?" Dundee asked.

"No," Jake said. "What we're all gonna try to do is kill the leader, that Major Seaforth. When they come, concentrate your rifle on him. If we get him, the rest will probably just give up."

"What makes you think that?" Curly asked.

"Because," Jake said, "he's the only one complainin' about his damned licorice."

SEAFORTH'S RAIDERS CAMPED for the night, and while they were gathered around the fire Seaforth addressed his men.

"According to Sequoia, the trail drive is still on its

way here. They had some problems to deal with, including a broken wagon wheel on their chuckwagon. But our plan is still in place. So eat your fill and get your rest. Tomorrow's the day payment comes due."

As usual, while the men sat around one fire, Seaforth and Garfield sat at a second. No one but Sequoia ever dared to approach them. But while the breed was able to sit at either fire, it was Garfield who was the linchpin between Seaforth and his men.

"Just make damn sure nobody's drinking," Seaforth told Garfield.

"There's no whiskey in camp," Garfield assured him.

"There better not be."

Seaforth popped a piece of licorice into his mouth, and Garfield wondered how much of the damn stuff the man had left. The smell of it was starting to gag him.

But Garfield's respect for the Major had been renewed, candy or no candy. Seaforth wanted what he thought he was entitled to, and whether Garfield agreed or not he would—as always—back Seaforth's play. What Teddy Garfield did not know about himself was that since he had no goals, no ideals, and no morals of his own, he was perfectly willing to support all of those things that existed inside Major Seaforth Bailey.

He drifted over to the other fire while Sequoia joined Seaforth.

"I want you up and out there early tomorrow morning," Seaforth told him. "Make sure they're progressing, and then come back and inform me."

"Yes, sir."

"And, Sequoia . . ."

"Yes, sir?"

". . . this time let them see you."

"Is that wise, Major?" the breed asked.

"Maybe not," Seaforth said, "but right now that's the way I want to play it."

"You are the boss," Sequoia said.

"Yes, indeed," Major Seaforth Bailey said, "that's what I am."

THE SKY WAS clear, the ground was dry, all the animals were fresh, and they seemed to be moving toward trouble with no impediments.

Jake looked back at the herd, figuring they had maybe lost only a dozen head or so on the trip. He wondered what he would have done if Major Seaforth had asked for, say, a dozen head in return for the supplies. Would he have given them to him? Probably not. Jake knew he was a stubborn ol' cuss, and there was just no way he owed Seaforth a nickel.

They were keeping the herd nice and tight, with Curly and Dundee on the right flank, Desi and Taco on the left, riding closer to the front than usual. If and when Seaforth and his men appeared, they were going to have to move fast.

Chance, however, riding drag, was still stuck at the back of the herd, and if the raiders came from ahead, it would take him a moment or two to realize, and then a few seconds to get into the fight.

If the raiders decided to come at them from either side, that suited Jake just fine. That would make for two smaller forces, rather than one large one.

But Seaforth was possibly a former military man, unless the Confederate jacket he was wearing had been bought or stolen. If he was military, there was going to be some strategy involved. Jake and Chance had both served during the Civil War, but neither of them had been an officer.

Chance was of the opinion that the Major's insignia on the jacket had not been earned. So it was unknown what level of strategy, if any, would be implemented.

Jake's strategy was simple. Try to do as much damage as quickly as possible, if not to defeat them, then to discourage them. Of course, he knew there was a chance the raiders could strike hard and fast and defeat them. If that happened at least he would have gone down protecting what was his.

S EQUOIA RODE BACK to a point from where he could see the drovers, but they could not see him. They were moving at a good speed. It wouldn't be long before they were in range.

He turned to ride back to Seaforth and his men, but remembered that the Major had told him to let the drovers see him. He didn't understand the reason, but he rode up to a high point from where he would be able to see them, and they would be able to see him.

J AKE RODE UP alongside the chuckwagon, which had stopped.

"Jefe," Carlito said, pointing.

"I see 'im," Jake said.

He saw the man sitting on a horse at the top of a ridge ahead of them. There was no way he could tell whether the man was alone. He might have just been a scout. Or, the other eleven men might have been waiting on the other side of that ridge.

Chance came riding up alongside Jake.

"A scout?" he said.

"Looks like it," Jake said.

"Why's he sittin' there where we can see him, all of a sudden?"

Jake looked at Chance.

"Orders?" Jake asked.

"So Seaforth wants us to know he's watchin'."

"That's what I think."

"You think Seaforth and his men are just on the other side of that ridge?"

"If they are, they'll come ridin' down at us as we get alongside it," Jake said.

"And if not," Chance said, "his scout will ride back and tell him to expect us."

"Either way," Jake said, "we're close."

"What do you wanna do?" Chance asked.

"Get the men in here," Jake said. "Let's make a slight change in the plan."

S EQUOIA FELT HE had given the drovers enough time to see him. He turned and rode off the ridge, heading back to where he had left Seaforth's Raiders. It would take him an hour to get there, the drovers and the herd longer than that.

That would give Seaforth plenty of time to ready his raiders.

E VERYTHIN' READY?" JAKE asked.
 Curly and Dundee came to the back of the chuckwagon and looked out.

"We're ready, boss," Curly said.

"What about the herd?" Dundee asked. "Once the shootin' starts, aren't they gonna stampede?"

Jake looked at Chance, who was sitting his horse right next to him.

"They might," Chance said. "We'll have to leave it to Taco and Desi to try and see that they don't."

"That's askin' a lot of them, ain't it?" Dundee asked. "Control the herd while shootin' at the raiders?"

"Let's hope the three of you can do a lot of damage from the wagon," Chance said.

"And on the other hand, they might not stampede," Jake said. "If the raiders come for us and the chuckwagon, we should be far enough away from the herd for them not to be spooked."

"Hopefully," Chance said.

"Well," Jake said, "after what they've already been through . . ."

"Gunshots are gunshots," Chance said. "We just better be ready."

"What if we are?" Jake asked.

"Are what?" Chance asked.

"Ready," Jake said. "What if we're ready . . . but they're not?"

CHAPTER TWENTY-TWO

H ERE THEY COME!" Jake shouted.
Up ahead of them there were suddenly twelve
riders, coming straight at them.

Chance, Desi, and Taco rode back to the herd and
drew their guns.

Curly and Dundee were inside the chuckwagon, the
sides of which had been shored up with supplies—sacks,
barrels, anything that could be used for cover.

It was Carlito's job to get the wagon turned sideways, and also out of the path of the herd.

There was always the chance that a stampeding
herd would actually run in the wrong direction. It was
Chance, Desi, and Taco's job to make sure they stampeded in the right direction.

Seaforth chose to come straight at them, which
worked into Jake's plan. At least they would have the
herd going in the most advantageous direction.

* * *

MAJOR SEAFORTH CHOSE a place where he and his raiders would be hidden from view by a slight rise in the terrain. Only Sequoia sat at the top, watching and waiting. And when he saw the dust being kicked up by the herd, he rode back down to where the raiders were waiting.

"They are here," he said.

"Get ready!" Seaforth shouted. "We're riding up this hill. When we get to the top you'll see the herd, and the drovers. I don't want a bunch of dead cows. Fire at the chuckwagon driver and anyone ahead of the herd first. Then we'll take the rest of them."

They drew their guns and waited. The sound of the herd approaching was the signal to ride up the hill and, as they rode over the crest and saw the herd and the drovers, to start firing.

JAKE WATCHED AS the chuckwagon broke left and, at the same time, he broke right. Behind them Chance, Desi, and Taco started firing into the air, spooking the herd into a stampede—right at the raiders.

Jake had gone from not wanting a stampede, to making use of one.

The stampeding cattle headed right for the approaching raiders.

GARFIELD LED THE charge of Seaforth's Raiders at the approaching trail drive. Seaforth—as if he were a real major—hung back to observe as he sent his men into battle. As he watched he saw the chuckwagon turn, the *remuda* behind it, and the lead rider—presumably Big Jake Motley—go the other way.

And then he saw the herd coming at his men, in full stride and, immediately, he knew he had been outmaneuvered.

There was no way to recall his men.

Dammit!

THE HERD STAMPEDED by Jake and headed straight for the oncoming riders. From the other side Jake could hear Dundee, Curly, and Carlito firing from the cover of the wagon.

From behind him came Chance, Desi, and Taco, their job having been done.

Up ahead, Jake saw the raiders realize what was happening and, as he had hoped, some of them broke left, and some broke right. A couple of horses panicked as the herd approached, reared and dropped their riders, and then ran off, riderless.

"Let's go!" he shouted at the men.

They rode alongside the stampeding herd part of the way, then broke off to face Seaforth's men. They were outnumbered five-to-four, but the horses beneath those five raiders were skittish. As Jake, Chance, Desi, and Taco approached they began to fire, which further incited the raiders' horses. They tried to return fire, but it was difficult as they also tried to control their mounts. One by one they were dropped from their saddles by the lead flying from Jake's and his men's rifles.

ON THE OTHER side of the herd four of Seaforth's men had veered and were fighting their mounts. The dust from the stampeding herd filled the air like an incoming fog. Carlito, Curly, and Dundee fired into it, despite the problem with visibility. These were their orders, to lay down a rapid-fire volley, whether they could see or not.

Inside the clouds of dust Seaforth's men realized they were being shot at. They tried to see where the firing was coming from, but by the time they spotted the chuckwagon, it turned sideways, the canvas rolled up, and rifles jutted out. Then it was virtually too late.

Two of them tried to ride at the chuckwagon, firing, while the other two turned their horses to run. But it didn't matter. Either way they went down in the face of the rain of flying lead.

J AKE, CHANCE, DESI, and Taco were firing with deadly intentions. Perhaps their shots were not particularly well aimed, but there were enough of them. They saw two men fall, and the other three men turned and rode off.

"Should we follow?" Taco asked.

"No," Jake said, "let's try to stop the herd before they run themselves down." He certainly didn't need any of those cattle losing weight on this drive.

The four of them put up their rifles and rode after the herd.

O N THE OTHER side Curly and Dundee saw Jake's plan had worked. The raiders were dead, but the cattle were still stampeding. The men ran to their already saddled horses, mounted up, and rode after them.

Carlito remained in the wagon and stayed alert, rifle ready, in case any of the men stood up.

S EAFORTH WATCHED AS his men scattered in front of the oncoming herd, watched them fall, victims of a hail of lead from goddamned cowpokes.

He saw that some of his men got away, and thought he recognized them. When they came riding back up the hill toward him he saw that he was right. Garfield, Sequoia, and Gus Walker had survived.

"Jesus," Garfield said, "what happened?"

"They stampeded the herd themselves," Walker said, before Seaforth could answer.

"And they secured that chuckwagon so it was like a little fortress," Seaforth added. "Those damned waddies outsmarted us."

Us? Garfield thought.

"How many of us made it back?" he asked Seaforth.

"Just you three."

"So now we're the ones who are outnumbered," Garfield observed.

"It doesn't matter," Seaforth said, "because I have another plan."

"Another plan?" Garfield asked. "I hope it involves getting more men."

"We don't have time for that," Seaforth said.

"Then what do you have in mind?"

"An ambush."

"What?" Garfield asked. "We don't ambush people."

"We do now."

T HEY MANAGED TO track down the herd after they had run about ten miles, slowing down when they were exhausted. For the most part, the cattle had stayed together. Some had wandered off, and the men had to take time to track them down and bring them back. The animals were too winded to resist.

By the time they thought they had the herd back together—having lost maybe another dozen head— Carlito caught up to them in the chuckwagon.

"Is everyone all right?" he asked, dropping down from the seat.

"Yeah, we're good," Jake said. "They're out gatherin' the herd back in."

"The herd is all right?"

"Tuckered out," Jake said. "We lost a few head. Some were shot, some ran off."

"And no one is hurt? My cousins?"

"They're fine."

"And Señor Big Ears?"

"Yeah, he's fine, too."

"And you, jefe?"

"Yeah," Jake said, "we got through it without anybody gettin' shot, except for a few cattle."

"And the other men?"

"Most of them are dead," Jake said. "A few got away, and Seaforth stayed out of it. He sent his men in to do his dirty work, like a real major."

"Not even a scratch?" Carlito asked.

Jake grinned.

"Not even a scratch."

Y OU SURE YOU want to do this, Sea?" Garfield asked.

They managed to find the herd again, and had taken cover behind an outcropping of rocks.

"Yes, I want to do it," Seaforth said. "And I'd do it myself, but you're a better shot."

"He won't forget this, you know."

"He'll still have to take his herd to market," Seaforth said. "We don't have enough men to take them now. But we can do this."

"Why not do it to him, then?" Garfield asked.

"No," Seaforth said, "the other old-timer. I want him to feel it."

"Sequoia can get closer—"

"No," Seaforth said, "you're my right hand, Gar. If you do it, it's like me doin' it."

"They are camping," Sequoia said.

"Good," Seaforth said. "We'll have to get this done before dark."

Garfield leaned on a rock and sighted down the barrel of his rifle.

"Don't rush," Seaforth said. "Take the shot when you know you have it."

"Right."

Garfield took a deep breath and waited.

J AKE DECIDED THEY might as well camp right there. He would rather have kept moving for another hour or two, but the herd was too winded for that. They'd have to keep a sharp eye out for survivors of the raiders.

He didn't like that they now found themselves near outcroppings of rocks on either side. He wondered, if Seaforth had seen them, if he and his remaining raiders would have waited here to ambush them. But the raiders probably hadn't ridden this far, and didn't know it was a much likelier place for an attack later.

Or an attack now.

Carlito had started a fire, but Jake was thinking this might be a mistake. They should probably move on a little farther, toward a more flat area, with no rocks for anyone to hide behind.

At that moment Chance came riding in, with Desi and Taco.

"Dundee and Curly are stayin' with the herd," he said.

"Chance, I'm thinkin' maybe we should keep movin'—"

"The cattle are worn out," Chance argued.

"I don't think Seaforth is gonna give up," Jake said, "and this place is too accessible—"

Desi and Taco walked to the fire and started talking with their cousin while he started cooking.

"Well," Jake said, "at least dismount—"

Jake saw the blood blossom on his friend's chest even before the sound of the shot came to him from a distance.

Chance McCandless fell from the saddle, dead before he hit the ground.

CHAPTER TWENTY-THREE

JAKE RUSHED TO his fallen friend while the others scanned the horizon in every direction for a shooter.

"Chance, dammit!" Jake said.

He turned and looked at his men.

"Anybody see where that shot came from?"

"Could've been those rocks," Dundee said.

"Or those," Curly said, pointing.

"We did not see, jefe," Desi said.

"Is Señor Chance . . . ?" Taco asked.

"Yes, Taco," Jake said. "He's dead."

Then they heard the sound of horses, but they quickly began to fade away.

"Seaforth," Jake said. "It couldn't have been anyone else."

Jake stared out into the distance as the pounding of hooves receded.

"Should we go after them?" Dundee asked.

Jake turned and looked down at Chance.

"No," he said, "we have to bury Chance and then move on."

"But, boss—" Dundee said.

"Chance would want us to deliver this herd," Jake said. "Once we do that, I'll be back here to find Seaforth."

"We will all come back, señor," Taco said.

"No, Taco," Jake said, "this was my doin'. I convinced Chance to come on this drive, I went into Three Rivers to that store, and I refused to give anythin' back to Seaforth. I'm sure he wanted one last shot before he and his remainin' men left. And who knows, they might hit us again before we leave Texas."

Jake walked to where Chance was lying, stared down at his friend.

"I guess I should've left you sleepin' in the back room of that cantina, amigo."

"Oh no, señor," Taco said, "Mr. Chance, he was very happy to be out here on a drive again, with you. He told me so."

"Did he?" Jake asked. "Thanks for tellin' me that, Taco. Now let's get him buried good and proper. I'll say a few words, and then we'll be on our way to Dodge City tomorrow."

"Sí, señor," Taco said.

"I have two shovels in my wagon, jefe," Carlito said.

"Good, Carlito," Jake said, and then to Taco, "Let's get them, Taco. You and me, we'll dig."

"Sí, señor."

As it turned out, Jake got winded and needed somebody to take over, so the others all took turns. When they had a hole about six feet deep they wrapped Chance in a blanket and lowered him down.

"Do you think it was Seaforth himself who took the shot?" Dundee asked Jake while Desi and Curly filled in the grave.

"It was probably his *segundo*, or that breed scout,

but it don't matter. I'll have them all for this, no matter how long it takes me to track them down."

Jake said a few awkward words over his friend's grave, broke a couple of planks of wood off the chuckwagon—with Carlito's permission—to form a cross that he could actually scratch Chance's name into.

They sat around the fire that night in glum silence, until Carlito and Desi turned in. Curly and Dundee rode out to sit on the herd.

That left the two men who had actually known Chance a long time, sitting together.

"It was deliberate," Jake said.

"Señor?" Taco said.

"They deliberately waited until they had a clear shot at Chance," Jake continued.

"Why did the Major not just kill you, señor?" Taco asked.

"Seaforth wanted to punish me by killin' Chance," Jake said. "Killin' me woulda made it too quick."

"And will he stop there?"

"I doubt he'll follow us all the way to Kansas," Jake said. "And he probably won't even trail us into the territories. So if he doesn't hit us again in Texas, I don't think we'll have to worry about him."

"Would you like to take a watch, then, Señor Jake?" Taco asked.

"Yeah, Taco, I would. I'll turn in and you wake me in four hours."

"Sí, jefe," Taco said.

Jake walked, shoulders slumped, to his bedroll, lay awake for a long time playing back memories of Chance in his mind, until exhaustion finally overcame him.

S O YOU'RE GOING to let them go?" Garfield asked.

"We'll let them go for now," Seaforth said, "but

Big Jake Motley is going to come after me, once he delivers his herd."

"Because we killed that one man?" Garfield asked.

"They were two of a kind," Seaforth said. "Those old-timers had been riding together a long time. He's not just going to forget that we killed him."

"He's a cowpoke," Garfield said, "and probably a sodbuster. Why worry about him coming after you?"

"I'm not worried about it, Gar," Seaforth said, "I'm counting on it."

"So what do we do in the meantime?" Garfield said. "We're down to four men."

They looked over to where Gus Walker was sitting at the second fire with Sequoia.

"We rebuild," Seaforth said. "We have months before Big Jake comes after us. By then we'll be at full force again."

"Do you think he's going to come alone?" Garfield asked.

"I don't think even that old fool would be that stupid," Seaforth said.

"So will he bring the law?"

"Oh, no," Seaforth said, "he won't be looking for justice, he'll be looking for vengeance."

"You're giving this old cowboy a lot of credit," Garfield observed.

"You saw the way he faced us," Seaforth said. "And you don't get a name like Big Jake for no reason. At one time he was an influential man. Now he's at the end of his life, and he doesn't give up easily. No, he'll be coming, I'm sure of that."

THEY MADE IT through Texas without seeing any sign of Seaforth, his men, or his scout, the breed. Once they crossed the border into the Indian Territory, they were more on the lookout for Indians off the reservations, or comancheros, who were like human buzzards.

They did encounter one band of Indians, who looked as if the group was made up of braves from the Apache, Comanche, Quapaw, Kiowa, and Osage tribes. They weren't looking to steal anything, they just wanted a few cows for some meals, and Jake decided to give in, without even asking for anything in trade.

They encountered some rain, had to cross running streams, but nothing as bad as they had faced in Texas. They finally crossed the border into Kansas at a town called Liberal. Jake figured by that time they had lost maybe fifty head.

He and Carlito rode into the town, which was sleepy and small, but had a general store. They picked up some supplies without encountering any resistance, and found out from the clerk that they were about seventy miles from Dodge.

When they got back to camp they told the others they had about s week left to get to their destination.

Carlito's supper that night was his SOB stew, which was prepared from calf parts. The death of Chance still hung over them heavily, like ever-present storm clouds, especially for Jake, whose attitude on the trip since the shooting could only be described as morose.

The other men talked at the fire, but Jake usually just sat eating and didn't partake in any of the conversations. For one thing, he was now the sole old-timer in the group, didn't really fit in with the other, younger men. And he didn't let on to anyone, but his muscles were aching even more than they had been the first week of the drive. He was just hoping he had the strength to make it through the last week.

They kept two men on the herd each night, but didn't keep any other kind of watch. They no longer feared an attack from Seaforth's Raiders, Texas wolves, Indians, or comancheros. With a week left they were feeling home free. But the two men babysitting the herd made sure they kept a sharp eye out for anything untoward that might come along.

Jake was getting a full night's sleep now, but it didn't seem to help. Each morning he rolled out with a groan, tried to keep the others from realizing he was wearing down. Without Chance to buck him up with a sharp word or a sly look, he was dragging.

The closest to his age was Taco, who was in his forties, but the Mexican seemed to be holding up quite well. Unbeknownst to Jake, all the men were feeling the strain of the drive, and of Chance's death.

When they left their camp outside of Liberal, everyone was looking forward to the end of the trail.

CHAPTER TWENTY-FOUR

BARBED WIRE.

One of the biggest reasons the trail drives from Texas to Kansas were dying out was barbed wire. Ranchers decided to fence off their property, which kept herds from being driven across their land during a trail drive. Having to push a herd around these fenced areas made the trail drives just too time-consuming and difficult. In addition, it cut down on places where the herds could graze. If the cattle couldn't eat during a drive, they arrived at their destination emaciated.

Jake had expected to encounter some fenced-off areas, and was surprised that they had not—until they reached Kansas. The ranchers in Kansas not only wanted to protect their grazing grounds, but also wanted to keep their own cattle from any diseases the Texas cattle might be carrying.

The first time they encountered a barbed-wire fence and had to redirect the herd, Jake realized they were not going to make Dodge City in a week.

"We can cut the wire," Dundee said, "drive the herd through, and then put the wire back up."

"And start a war," Jake said. "No, we'll go around."

Apparently, word had gotten out about a herd being driven through Kansas, for the next time they encountered the wire, they also had to deal with armed ranch hands. Jake tried to explain his cattle weren't diseased, but the rancher they were dealing with was having none of it.

"Go around," he ordered Jake.

It took two weeks to make the one-week trip to Dodge from Liberal, but they finally drove the herd into the Dodge City stockyards. It was only after the cattle were closely examined that they were accepted, and driven into the stock corrals.

Jake had no doubt that barbed wire was going to further divide the range, and would even cut down on the need for large crews of cowhands to keep the cows from overgrazing certain areas. He was actually glad he was never going to have to try to drive a herd through Texas again. Avoiding barbed wire in the near future would be next to impossible.

"You boys are free to eat or drink all you want," Jake told his men. "Put your horses up at a livery, and get yourselves situated in hotel rooms, and after I've sold the cattle, we'll settle up. And don't get into trouble."

"Sí, jefe," Taco said, "we will be waiting."

Taco and the others turned their horses and rode away from the stockyards.

J AKE HAD HOPED to get eight to ten dollars a head for his cattle. He was therefore very disappointed when the best offer he got was five. Unfortunately, there was only one man making the offer and setting the price, which left Jake with no choice but to accept.

The count on the herd when it arrived in Dodge City showed that Jake had accurately surmised that he'd lost about fifty head on the trip. He collected his better than two thousand seven hundred dollars and went looking for his men to settle up with them.

BECAUSE HE HAD promised Chance a percentage and his dead friend had no family to give it to, he decided to divide that money up among the rest of the men. So they all got paid more than they had been expecting. By the time they were all sharing end-of-the-trail drinks in the Long Branch Saloon, Jake had half of his money left.

He had one drink with the men and then went to the Dodge House to get himself a room. Once he was behind the locked door, he collapsed onto the bed and gave in to the pain he felt in his old joints and bones.

JAKE WOKE HOURS later, with hunger and depression fighting for supremacy. Pain was bringing up a poor third. The pain would fade away eventually. The hunger could be taken care of by a meal. But only one thing was going to ease the depression, and that was tracking down and killing Seaforth Bailey and however many raiders he had left.

At that moment, the hunger was the easiest thing to handle. He left the hotel in search of a meal, found himself standing in front of Delmonico's steak house, and went in.

Dodge City was once the queen of the cow towns, a wild and woolly place where men like Wyatt Earp and Bat Masterson made their bones. It was no longer as popular, or as open, as it once was, but the steak house was still a busy place at suppertime.

Jake managed to get a table in the middle of the crowded dining room, drew some looks from diners who made a habit of eating there and so were able to recognize a stranger in their midst.

He ignored everyone and ordered a chicken dinner, because after two months of driving cattle, he was tired of looking at beef. He washed it down with a big mug of ice-cold beer, then chased it all with a piece of rhubarb pie and a cup of coffee.

When he stepped outside it was dark, and quiet. He thought he could hear the ghosts of Dodge City around him—or maybe it was Chance's ghost, asking him when he was going to avenge his death.

Tomorrow, old friend. I start tomorrow.

IN THE MORNING he had a hearty breakfast, then began to put together the gear he would need to hunt Seaforth Bailey.

Jake had never been a gunman, never worn a badge, but as a young man, he had joined on several posses when asked. So he had an idea of what he would need.

First, a good horse.

He went to the largest livery in town—the one where he had put up his horse and his animals from the drive—and told the hostler exactly what he wanted.

"I need a reliable animal, lots of stamina, five or six years old . . . and, oh, a gelding."

"Jesus, you know exactly what ya want, don't ya?" the old hostler said.

"Have you got somethin' like that, or do I have to go somewhere else?"

"No, no," the man said, "I got just the thing for you. Come on out back."

They went out the back door of the livery to a corral that had about a dozen horses in it.

"Which one?" Jake asked.

"The red sorrel," the man said. "Just recently gelded. Go on in and take a look."

Jake entered the corral, put his hand on a couple of the horses to get them to move aside. When he reached the sorrel he admired the strength of it, the flaxen mane and tail, no sway to its back, good teeth, strong neck and flanks.

He walked back to the hostler and said, "I'll take him."

"I ain't toldja the price."

"Whatever you say."

"You don't wanna dicker?" the man asked, surprised.

"I don't have the time."

Jake had all the money from his sale of the cattle on him. If he had to, he was going to spend it all to avenge Chance McCandless. The hostler quoted his price, and Jake paid it. He also told the hostler he could have the other animals—the entire *remuda*.

"If yer gonna throw them in, I'll lower the price," the man offered.

"Don't bother." He took the money out and handed it to the hostler.

"I got a better saddle than the one you rode in on," the hostler said. "I'll throw that in."

"Good, thanks. I'll take it. I'll pick everythin' up tomorrow mornin', first thing."

"I'll have him saddled. You wanna know his name?"

"I ain't givin' him a name," Jake said.

"He's already got one," the man said. "I'm callin' him Red."

"Good enough."

Jake left the livery, went to the mercantile, bought some new clothes, and ammunition for his pistol and rifle, both of which he considered reliable. He also had

Chance's guns. He'd get rid of the extra rifle, but he was going to keep Chance's Peacemaker as a backup to his own. His rifle was a Winchester '76, which fired heavier ammunition than the popular '73 model. It would kill a bear as easily as a man.

The rifle he'd carried during the war had been an 1860 Henry, but the Henry became the basis for the Winchester, which was among the first repeaters manufactured. He had a '73 when they first came out, but when the '76 appeared he quickly switched his allegiance.

He bought enough supplies to keep himself going for a week or so—coffee, beans, beef jerky, and some cans of peaches. Eating this way would make sure that by the time he got back to Texas he would have lost some weight. He had lost very little on the drive, thanks to Carlito's cooking.

If he was going to hunt men, he needed to be in better condition. Rather than shape him up, the trail drive had shown him just what terrible condition his body was in. He had given in to age a long time ago; now it was time to try to fend off the effects of it—at least until he did what he had to do.

The last thing he bought was a holster. He had never worn one before, outside of a kind with the flap that folded over the gun, during the war. This one had no flap, was simply a leather pouch designed to attach to his belt and hold a pistol. He simply needed the gun to be easily accessible for his hunt.

He left with his supplies in a gunnysack, which he brought back to his room. In the morning he would tie it to his saddle horn, put his extra clothes and Chance's gun in his saddlebags. He put on the newly purchased holster, shoved his gun into it so he would get used to wearing it.

He left the hotel again as it started to get dark, and headed for the Long Branch.

HE THOUGHT HE would find some of the boys at the saloon. As it turned out, only the Mexican cousins were there—Taco, Desiderio, and Carlito, seated at a table with a whiskey bottle in the center.

The bar was crowded, and all the tables were filled. Nobody paid the least bit of attention to Jake as he crossed the room.

"'Evenin', boys," he said. "Mind if I join you?"

"Jefe!" Taco said, glad to see his friend. "Please, *sientate*. Sit."

Jake sat in the empty fourth chair at the table, and a saloon girl came right over.

"Beer," he told her. "Anythin' more for you fellas?"

"No, jefe," Desi said, raising his shot glass of whiskey, "we are doin' well."

Jake waited for the girl to bring him his beer, lifted it, and wet his whistle.

"Where are Curly and Dundee?" he asked.

"They have been at the whorehouse since last night," Taco said. "They are young men!"

"I am a young man!" Desi complained. "Why am I not at the whorehouse?"

Taco slapped his cousin on the back and said, "I have been wondering the same thing myself, *cabrón*."

That was a word Jake had heard before—dumbass! The cousins laughed.

"When are you leaving town, señor?" Taco asked.

"Tomorrow mornin'," Jake said. "I've got a new horse and saddle, some new duds, and I'm on my way."

"And supplies, jefe?" Desi asked. "For your hunt?"

"Yeah," he said, "supplies for my hunt."

"I still wish you would allow me to accompany you, Señor Jake," Taco said. "I would also like to avenge the death of Señor Chance."

"No, Taco," Jake said. "This is my fight. I started it, and I've got to finish it. I just thought I'd find you boys here and have one last drink."

"Gracias, jefe," Carlito said. "We are happy you wanted to share your time with us."

At that moment the batwing doors swung inward and several men entered, dressed in trail clothes, with guns tucked into their belts.

"*Ay, mierda,*" Desi cursed.

CHAPTER TWENTY-FIVE

JAKE LEANED OVER to Taco.

"What did he say?"

"Shit!" Taco whispered.

Jake turned in his seat, saw the four men who had entered. They looked around the saloon, then walked to the bar. They used their elbows to make room, and nobody complained. He noticed the pistols they all had in their belts.

"What's that about?" Jake asked Desi.

"Those four men, señor," Desi said, "they do not like Mexicans."

"So you've had trouble with them before?" Jake asked the three cousins.

"Sí, señor," Desi said, "on the street."

"They shouted their feelings so that everyone could hear them," Taco said, "especially us."

"And what did you do?" Jake asked.

"We stayed out of trouble, señor," Carlito said, with a broad smile. "But I do not like the look of these hombres. *Muy malo.*"

And then, as if on cue, a loud voice shouted, "Well, lookee here, boys, what we got in the Long Branch."

The speaker walked over to the table Jake was sharing with his boys, and the other men followed him. They were of a type, young—none older than thirty—and had obviously been drinking elsewhere.

"It's them damn Mess-i-cans we saw on the street today," the speaker said. "What are you Mess-i-cans doin' in a white man's saloon?" He leaned in close. "Didn't we tell you to leave town?"

The loud voice had drawn everyone's attention to them, and the room went quiet. Jake knew they were seconds away from a bloodbath, because he could see the angry looks on the faces of Taco and Desi and the worried look on Carlito's. He also knew that none of the Mexicans were carrying a gun. He had to act fast, before one of these men pulled a pistol from his belt and did something stupid.

Jake stood up quickly, drawing his gun from his new holster, and brought the butt down on the man's head. The speaker dropped to the floor in a limp heap.

His three friends stared down at him in shock, and then back at Jake, who was still holding his gun.

"You shouldn'ta done that to Eddie, mister," one of them said.

"Take your friend out, and all of you sober up," Jake told them. "If I see you startin' trouble again I'll turn you over to the law. Got it?"

None of them answered, but all three reached down to help their friend to his feet and, supporting him between them, they walked out.

A sudden raucous round of applause went up from the crowd, and Jake quickly stuck his Peacemaker back into his holster and sat down.

"Gracias, jefe," Carlito said. "I thought a very bad thing was going to happen here."

"So did I," Jake said.

The same saloon girl came over and put a fresh beer in front of Jake with a big smile.

"That's from Andy, the bartender," she said, "as thanks for keepin' trouble from happenin'."

Jake picked up the ice-cold glass, turned to the bartender, and raised it in thanks. The big-bellied man nodded and waved back.

"And thanks from me, too," the girl added. "You kept Big Andy from havin' to use that damned shotgun he keeps under the bar."

The applause died down and everyone went back to doing what they were doing before the excitement.

Jake finished his beer and stood up.

"Well, boys, I'll be off in the mornin'. I wanna thank you all for everythin' ya done."

"You paid us, señor," Taco pointed out.

"And very well, señor," Desi added.

"Nevertheless," Jake said, "I couldn't have done it without you. Thanks."

He shook all their hands and left the Long Branch.

THE EXHAUSTION WAS creeping into Jake's bones again as he walked back to the Dodge House Hotel. But as he stepped up onto the boardwalk to approach the front door it became obvious he wasn't going to be allowed to just turn in.

"Hey, old man!"

He turned, saw the four men from the saloon fanned out in the street in front of the hotel. They were barely illuminated by the streetlamps. On the other hand, he was brightly lit, so there was small chance they could miss him. Now he was sorry he was wearing the holster. He could have gotten the gun out of his belt much quicker.

But it was fairly obvious that he wasn't going to get to ride back to Texas and avenge Chance McCandless. Not if these young fellows had their way.

He couldn't tell them apart, so he didn't know which one he had hit until he spoke.

"You think you're pretty slick, hittin' me on the head with that gun butt," Eddie said.

"I was just tryin' to keep anyone from gettin' killed, son," he said.

"I ain't your son," the young man said, "and I don't need no reason to kill a Mess-i-can."

"Well, those Mexicans happen to be friends of mine, so I couldn't let you do it."

"Then instead of killin' them," Eddie said, "we're gonna kill you."

"And *then* we'll go back and kill them," one of the other men said.

"Is this really necessary?" Jake asked. "I've still got some things I wanna live to do."

"You shoulda thought of that before you butted in," Eddie told him.

"But it was you who butted in," Jake said, figuring the longer he could keep talking, the longer he could live. "I just reacted."

"Well, react to this!" the spokesman said, but before he could draw they all heard the voice from the dark behind them.

"Oh, señor," Taco said, "I would not do that."

The four men froze.

"Is that you, Mex?" one of them asked.

"It is all of us, señores," Desi replied. "We suspected you would not allow our amigo to go peacefully to his hotel to sleep."

"So if you kill him," Carlito chimed in, "we will kill you."

Jake could see the men were conflicted.

"Looks like a Mexican standoff to me, fellas," he said. "Which is kinda ironic, don't you think? Seein' as how you don't like Mexicans."

"All right, señores," Taco announced. "You have three guns pointed at your backs. Now carefully drop yours to the ground, *por favor.*"

"You wouldn't shoot us in the back," Eddie said, without much conviction.

"I wouldn't count on that," Jake said. "After all, they're Mexicans."

The four men looked at each other, and then, one by one, removed their guns from their belts and dropped them to the ground.

"Where are your horses?" Jake asked.

"Down the street."

"Get on them and leave town," Jake said.

"In the dark?" Eddie asked.

"Right now," Jake said, "or I can't be responsible for what my crazy Mexican friends might do."

The men looked at each other again, then started walking away.

"And in case you're plannin' on grabbin' your rifles," Jake said, "my friends will go with you and keep you covered until you leave."

"What about our guns?" Eddie asked.

"I'll be givin' them to the sheriff," Jake said. "If you ever come back, check with him."

As the four men walked off down the street, Desi and Carlito followed with their guns out. Taco came across the street to Jake.

"Taco," Jake said, "thanks for this."

"You need us, jefe," Taco said, "for your hunt."

"I appreciate the offer, I really do," Jake said, "and what you did tonight, but I still have to go it alone tomorrow."

"As you wish, señor."

"Good night, Taco," Jake said, "and if I don't see you tomorrow . . . *adiós.*"

"*Vaya con dios,* Señor Jake."

JAKE WOKE THE next morning, ready to go. He'd had a dream about Chance McCandless, during which he promised his friend he would find his killers and exact vengeance on them.

"You're no bounty hunter, Jake," Chance had told him.

"I'll get the job done, Chance," Jake said, "I promise you."

"Just don't get yourself killed doin' it, old man," Chance said, and faded away.

When Jake woke he felt as if Chance had really appeared to him, to warn him.

He washed up, put on his new clothes and his holster, picked up his rifle, saddlebags, bedroll, and gunnysack of supplies, and left the room. In the lobby he checked out and settled his bill. When he left by the front door he was pleased not to find anybody with a gun waiting for him.

He walked to the livery, where the hostler, as promised, had the sorrel gelding saddled and ready to go. The saddle he had put on the horse was a plain one, but good leather and in perfect condition.

"Nothin' fancy," the man said, "but it's fine quality."

"It'll do fine," Jake assured him. "Thanks."

"Good luck with whatever you're gearin' up for, friend."

"Thanks."

Jake walked the horse outside, then tied his bedroll in place, hung the sack from the saddle horn, tossed his saddlebags over the horse's back, slid his rifle into the scabbard, and mounted up.

He was ready for his manhunt.

CHAPTER TWENTY-SIX

THE FIRST DAY was Jake and the sorrel gelding called Red getting to know one another. He walked him, cantered him, galloped him. He moved him side to side, backed him up. The horse responded to his touch very well. He thought the animal would have been very handy during a roundup—only he wasn't going to be doing any more roundups, was he?

Since he wasn't pushing a herd anymore, he made it to Liberal in half the time it had taken him to get to Dodge from there.

He camped outside of Liberal that first night, having no reason to ride in. He built a small fire, just enough to make a pot of coffee, and ate the beef jerky with it. Then he sat and thought about his past with Chance McCandless. They had been in the war together, cowhands together, and then when Big Jake Motley bought the Big M, he made Chance his foreman. When he married Abby, Chance was his best man.

But then things began to go sour on the ranch, and Abby died. That was when Chance left. Jake knew

Chance loved Abby, and he sometimes thought his friend had left the Big M because of it. And if he had, Jake could certainly understand why. She was a wonderful woman.

Jake didn't feel the need to keep watch that night. He doubted the four men from Dodge would follow him out here. They had already been humiliated twice. And there was practically no chance Seaforth Bailey would come this far for revenge—not when the man probably knew that Jake would be coming for him.

He had seen many men like Seaforth Bailey during the war, men who thought they should be officers but never were. And he had met many men over the years who claimed more in the way of achievements during the war than they ever truly accomplished. But he felt that this man—though arrogant as hell—probably had some degree of intelligence. And if he didn't, his *segundo* probably did. Either way, they would have to figure that Jake would come for his own revenge. After all, that had to be why they had chosen to shoot Chance in the first place. They knew it would hurt Jake, and they knew he would have to come for them once the herd was delivered.

He had no other choice. There was no way he could look ahead to his remaining days until he got this done.

HE CROSSED INTO Indian Territory the next morning, and hoped he would have the same luck they'd had when they encountered Indians with the herd. Of course, this time he had very little to give them.

He decided not to travel through as much Indian Territory as they had done with the herd. Instead he headed for the Texas Panhandle, which meant he didn't have to ride through much of the territories. So by heading for Shamrock, Texas, he gave himself about fifty or sixty miles of Indian Territory to travel, which would probably take him two days if he didn't push the sorrel.

He didn't want to push the horse, because there was no point in wearing him out. They'd get where they were going eventually. There was no great rush. He wanted them both to be in decent shape when they arrived near Three Rivers.

He camped his second night in the territories, knowing that he would be crossing into Texas the next morning. What he hadn't expected was to wake up and find that he had company . . .

HE DID A breakfast of coffee and beans, and while he was eating it he heard the approaching horses. From the sound, he could tell they were not shod. That meant Indian ponies.

He pulled his rifle closer, touched the pistol in his holster, and then continued eating as they approached.

There were three of them and, once again, they were a mix of tribes. As they approached his camp he could see that two were Quapaw and one Osage. He certainly felt better having to deal with them than with Apaches or Comanches.

He did his best to seem relaxed as he looked up at them.

"We are hungry," one of them said.

"Step down, then," Jake said. "I'll put on some more beans."

The three braves slid off their ponies and walked to the fire.

"No meat?" one asked as Jake emptied another can of beans into the pan.

"Sure," he said, "I can add some beef."

He took out some beef jerky and added it to the pan. "Coffee?" he asked.

"Uh," the Indian grunted, which Jake took to mean yes.

"I only have two cups," he said. "You'll have to share."

He dumped his own cup out, filled it and his second cup, then handed them across the fire to the braves. The two Quapaws shared one and the Osage drank his own. All three braves had rifles, which they laid down on the ground next to them.

Once the beans and jerky were ready, he handed two plates across to the three braves, who once again shared. They picked the beef out with their fingers, then tipped the plates and shoveled the beans into their mouths with their hands.

"More coffee," one of the Quapaws said.

"Sure."

Jake filled both cups again.

While they drank, the Osage looked at Jake and said. "You trade?"

"I don't have anythin' to trade," he said. "Sorry. I'm only able to feed you."

The Osage looked at the sorrel.

"Good horse," he said. "You trade for pony."

"I can't do that," Jake said. "I need that horse to get where I'm goin'."

The three braves looked at each other. They handed their empty plates back to Jake.

"Gun," one of the Quapaw said. "You trade gun."

"Again," Jake said, "I'm gonna need it where I'm goin'."

"You got more meat?" the Osage asked.

"Sure," Jake said, and handed over the rest of his beef jerky. He could pick up more at the first decent-sized town he came to, if not just waiting to get to Shamrock.

One of the Quapaw walked to his horse and came back with a blanket.

"This for food," he said, holding the blanket out to Jake, who didn't dare reject the offer.

"Thank you," he said, accepting the blanket.

The three braves went back to their horses, mounted up, and rode away.

A worn blanket for some beans and beef jerky. It didn't sit right with Jake. He figured he'd have to be on the lookout these last few miles, before he crossed into Texas.

He broke camp quickly, wanting to get on the move before the braves changed their minds and came back. After stomping out the fire, he saddled the sorrel and urged the animal into a gallop.

H E HAD ONLY gone a few miles when he realized he was being followed. It had to be the three Indian braves he had shared breakfast with. He wondered why they would trail him, rather than try to rob him while they were in his camp. Maybe they hadn't decided to rob him until after they had traded with him.

He only had about another mile to go to get to Texas when he heard the galloping ponies behind him. Then there was a shot, which made the intentions of the three braves clear.

Rather than stand and fight, he decided to outrun them with the sorrel. He dug his heels in and the horse leaped forward. It was nerve-wracking to have three Indians chasing him, screaming at the top of their lungs and firing wildly with rifles they didn't know how to use. It was also invigorating, the way this sorrel was eating up the ground.

He felt fairly sure if he beat the Indians to Texas, they wouldn't follow him. It was one thing to rob white men riding through Indian Territory, but another to do it in Texas or Kansas. That would bring the army in, for sure.

Hopefully, these three weren't hotheads who would stay after him. If that was the case, he'd have to stop and fight them. He wasn't afraid, he just didn't want to take a chance on getting killed before he could kill Seaforth Bailey. After that, he would fight any would-be young gunnies or braves who wanted it.

He continued to let the sorrel have his head. They put enough distance between themselves and the Indians that he couldn't hear them screaming, and they had stopped shooting because he was out of range.

And then he was in Texas . . .

H E SLOWED THE sorrel, but didn't stop riding until they had reached Shamrock.

It was a small town, not much going on as he rode in. The sorrel had cooled down some from his run, but Jake wanted to get him cooled down a bit more. Then he wanted to get himself fed before they continued on. He doubted that two Quapaw Indians and one Osage would follow him into town.

He was dismounting in front of a café on the main street when a man approached him. The badge on his chest was tarnished, with no shine to it. The man wearing it was much the same.

"Howdy," the man said.

"Afternoon, Sheriff."

"Looks like you just rode in."

"I did."

"From where?"

"Indian Territory," Jake said. "I had a few braves on my trail, and had to outrun them or outfight them."

"If you don't mind me askin'," the middle-aged lawman said, "which did you do?"

"I outran them."

"That's a good-lookin' sorrel," the sheriff said. "My name's Sheriff Bart Jefferies."

Jake frowned, but the sheriff spoke again before he could say anything.

"Don't even try," Jefferies said, "you never heard of me. No reason you should. Nothin' much ever happens here in Shamrock, but we do get some trouble ridin' in from the territories every once in a while."

"Not from me," Jake said. "I doubt those braves actually followed me into Texas."

"That's good to hear," the lawman said. "And there's nobody else on your trail?"

"I'm not wanted, if that's what you mean. I just spent two months drivin' a herd from Brownsville to Dodge City, and now I'm headed back." It wasn't exactly true. He wasn't going all the way back to Brownsville, just as far as Three Rivers, but there was no reason for the lawman to know that.

"A herd?" Jefferies said. "I thought all the drives from Texas dried up."

"They have," Jake said. "I'm sure mine was the last one. At least, it was my last."

"And you paid off your men in Dodge?"

"All of 'em," Jake said. "So you see, there's nobody on my trail at all."

"I hope you don't mind me askin'," Sheriff Jefferies said. "I usually check with strangers when they ride into town. Any idea how long you'll be stayin'?"

"Long enough for my horse to have a blow, and for me to have a steak and pick up a few supplies. Then we'll be on our way."

"I ain't runnin' you out, you know," Jefferies said.

"That's okay, Sheriff," Jake said. "I never had any intention of stayin' in a hotel. I'll probably be sleepin' under the stars all the way."

"Well, they do a good steak right in there," the lawman said, with a nod. "It's called Sarah's Café. And down the street is a general store. Should have whatever you're lookin' for."

"Good to know," Jake said. "I was hopin' I wouldn't have to look around."

The lawman touched the brim of his hat and said, "You enjoy your meal now."

"I will."

He left the sheriff standing there and went inside.

OVER A STEAK, he had to admit it felt good to be back in Texas. He'd had no idea what he was going to do, where he was going to go after he and Chance delivered the herd. Now he knew Texas was in his blood, even if he no longer had a home there.

By the time he finished his meal he figured his horse had enough time to rest.

As he stepped outside the café, he knew he'd have more conversations like the one he'd had with the sheriff if he continued to stop in towns. Thankfully he had only one stop to make in Shamrock and that was to replace the food he'd lost by feeding the Indians. From then on out he figured to stay on the trail for days at a time.

CHAPTER TWENTY-SEVEN

From shamrock to Abilene, west of Fort Worth, was a week of campsites and sparse meals of beef jerky and beans, washed down with strong trail coffee. Rather than ride into Fort Worth, he avoided the hustle and bustle of the larger town and opted to stop in Abilene to restock.

Abilene was small but busy, probably due to some spillover from the nearby larger town. It was the first town he had stopped in since Shamrock, but his goal was the same. A short respite for the sorrel and a good, hot meal for himself. He felt that the condition of his broken-down old bones was improving, but he still needed a decent meal every so often.

There were more choices than there had been in his previous stop. He was determined to stay away from saloons, as they were often places where trouble simmered and eventually boiled over. He also ignored some of the larger eateries on the town's main street, and eventually found one that appealed to him. It was small, but as he dismounted, the smells coming from it were mouthwatering.

He tied the sorrel off and went inside. Apparently, the place was not a popular location for lunch, as there were plenty of tables available. After a week of beef jerky, Jake went for a chicken lunch, and enjoyed it. When he paid his bill and stepped outside, he found two men standing by his horse. One was older, in his forties, built thick in the middle. The other one might have been his son.

"This yours?" one asked.

"That's right."

"Nice animal."

"Thanks."

"New in town?" the other asked.

"Just passin' through," Jake said. "Figured to have a meal, pick up some supplies, and move on. You the law?"

"Us? Naw, we're just appreciative of good horse-flesh," the first man said. "I got a ranch outside of town, and raise horses." He touched the sorrel's neck. "This one sure is nice."

"Again," Jake said, "thanks."

"You wouldn't be interested in sellin' him, wouldja?" the man asked.

"Afraid not," Jake said. "Just bought him myself a couple of weeks ago."

"You don't look like the type to drift," the man said.

"Had a ranch for a long time down around Browns-ville," Jake said.

"That a fact? I pretty much know who most of the big ranchers are in Texas. My name's Dan Paxton, this is my son, Joe."

"Glad to meetja," Jake said. "Jake Motley."

"I knew it!" Paxton said, snapping his fingers. "Big Jake Motley, right? The Big M?"

"Used to be the Big M," Jake said. "I don't know

what the new owner is callin' it, these days." That wasn't quite true, but the truth didn't much matter, at this point.

"You just have a meal in there?" Paxton asked.

"I did. It was okay."

"Like I said, you don't look like you're driftin'."

"I'm not," Jake said. "Drove my last herd to Dodge, and now I've got some business back around Three Rivers way."

"I tell you what," Paxton said. "Why don't you let me show you some hospitality? A good meal, a comfortable bed, and you can get started again in the mornin'."

"Why would you do that?" Jake asked.

"I like men who know horses," Paxton said. "And you have a reputation for knowing horses and cattle."

"Didn't know I had any reputation left," Jake said.

"I don't know what's goin' on in your life," Paxton said, "but the Big M used to be known in Texas, and so did Big Jake Motley, but everybody falls on hard times somewhere along the line. Lemme just show you some appreciation."

Paxton's son, Joe, hadn't said a word yet, but now he commented, "Give this fine animal a night off."

Jake took a deep breath. He could use a night in a real bed.

"Okay, Mr. Paxton," he said, "I accept your invitation."

"The name's Dan," Paxton said, extending his hand.

THE PAXTONS WERE in town to pick up some supplies, so Jake walked over to the general store with them.

"We're buildin' another corral," Paxton told Jake. "And my wife gave me a list. She's a helluva cook."

"Glad to hear it," Jake said. "I've gotta pick up a few things myself."

"Save your money," Paxton said. "We'll outfit ya tomorrow before you leave."

So Jake stood by while the Paxtons made their purchases, helped them load their buckboard, and then followed them from town to the Paxton Ranch.

When they reached the ranch it reminded Jake a lot of the earlier days of the Big M, when it was still growing. There was a two-story house he was sure Paxton had built himself, a large, new-looking barn with a corral in front, and a few hands working some horses.

"Do you have any cattle?" Jake asked.

"No," Joe Paxton said, "what Pa does is raise horses, pure and simple. That's our business."

The Paxtons drove their buckboard right into the barn, and a few of the men came trotting over.

"Get this stuff unloaded," Dan ordered, stepping down from the seat. "This is Mr. Jake Motley. Take care of his horse, and treat him well."

Jake could tell that Dan Paxton was a good man with horses, because he referred to the sorrel as "him" and not "it." Only dedicated horsemen did that.

"Come on, Jake," Paxton said. "We'll go up to the house and I'll introduce you to my missus. Joe, get one of the men to bring Ma her supplies."

"Right, Pa."

Jake collected his saddlebags from his horse and followed Paxton.

"Any other kids, Dan?" Jake asked as they walked.

"No, just Joe. But he's a good one. You?"

"We never had any," Jake said.

"And your wife? Is she waitin' in Brownsville for you?"

"She died some years back," Jake said. "Things went downhill from there."

"I'm sorry," Paxton said. "I didn't know."

When they reached the house a handsome, middle-aged woman came out onto the porch to greet them. She wore a simple blue dress that reminded Jake of the kind Abby used to make for herself. Suddenly he wasn't so sure this was such a good idea.

"Jenny, this is Big Jake Motley, from South Texas," Paxton said. "Used to own and run the Big M down there. He was passin' through and I invited him to eat with us and spend the night."

"You must be ridin' a fine horse, Mr. Motley," she said. "My husband enjoys people who know horses. Welcome. Please come in."

"Thank you, ma'am."

"Where's Joe?" she asked as they entered the house.

"He's seein' to your supplies," Paxton said. "Probably puttin' them in the kitchen as we speak."

The house had obviously been furnished to the lady of the house's taste—frilly and clean—and, thankfully, did not remind Jake of Abby's preferences. Jenny Paxton's taste was more girlish than Abby's had ever been. Jake had input into what went into the house, probably more so than Dan Paxton did.

"How about a drink?" Paxton asked.

"Daniel," Jenny Paxton said, "why not let Mr. Motley wash up and see his room before you ply him with liquor?"

"She's right, as usual," Paxton said. "Let's get that done and then I'll pour you some good brandy."

J AKE GOT WASHED up and put on a clean shirt to have supper with the Paxtons. When he came downstairs Paxton handed him the promised brandy.

"You strike me as a beer man," the rancher said, "but try this."

Jake sipped and said, "It's very good."

"Let's sit," Paxton said.

He had a desk in the front room, by the window, which reminded Jake of his own, but other than that the furniture was different. The chairs and sofa in his own house had been more rustic and handmade. This furniture looked like it was bought from a catalog. It was also cushiony, which was meant to be comfortable, but he didn't like the way he was sinking into it.

"What was it like?" Paxton asked. "I mean, your last trail drive."

"It was sad," Jake said, "and hard, but also very satisfying. I hadn't been on a drive in a while, leavin' that to my younger hands. Took my bones a while to get comfortable in the saddle again."

"With that sorrel?"

"No," Jake said, "I bought that one when I left Dodge. I decided to spend some of my herd money on a good animal."

"Well, that's a good one, all right."

Joe Paxton entered at that point, looking freshly scrubbed, which made him appear eighteen rather than in his twenties, which was what Jake had first figured.

"Can I have some of that, Pa?" he asked.

"One glass, son," Paxton said.

Joe poured it and sipped it appreciatively. He took his drink to a chair and sat.

"We were just talkin' about Jake's herd," Paxton told his son.

"How many head did you drive, Mr. Motley?" Joe asked.

"I only had six hundred for this final drive," Jake said. "Far cry from the days when we drove two or three thousand."

"Wow," Joe said, "that musta been somethin'. I've taken horses to market in Fort Worth, but I've never been on a cattle drive."

"It's very different," Jake said.

They went on to talk more about the differences between driving a herd of cattle and a herd of horses, until Jenny Paxton came in and announced supper was ready.

The conversation continued over supper as Joe Paxton asked question after question.

"I just wish the cattle drives weren't gone," he said eventually. "I'd sign up for one in a minute."

"No, you wouldn't," Jenny said. "Your father needs you right here."

"It's backbreakin' work, Joe," Jake told him. "You're not missin' anythin'."

After supper Joe excused himself to go and do some chores.

"Maybe we can talk some later?" Joe said to Jake.

"Sure thing," Jake said.

After Joe left and Jenny was in the kitchen, Paxton and Jake sat at the table and drank coffee.

"Sorry about all the questions," Paxton said. "The boy's startin' to think he's missin' out on somethin'."

"That's okay," Jake said. "If I can discourage him, I will."

"I appreciate that," the rancher said. "I really don't need him goin' off on his own right now. Maybe in a few years, when he's older."

"How old is he?"

"Nineteen," Paxton said.

"He's still just a boy," Jenny said, coming in from the kitchen.

"He's a young man, Jenny," Paxton said, "but I still don't want him to leave."

"I've been on my own since I was fifteen," Jake said. "Might be why I'm so tired, these days."

"You seem to have done all right for yourself," Jenny said. "The Big M and all."

"It was goin' well for a time," Jake admitted. "But then my wife died, my best friend left . . . everything fell apart. I can tell Joe all that, if you like."

"I'm sorry," Jenny said. "I know that's all very personal, but if hearin' it will keep him home—"

"We'll keep 'im home, Jen," Paxton said. "There's no point in makin' Jake talk about his troubles."

Jenny sat across from Jake and asked, "So what are you up to now?"

"I'm huntin' a man."

"Taken up bounty huntin', then?" Paxton asked.

"No," Jake said. "During the drive, down around Three Rivers, he tried to take my herd, and killed my best friend."

"What will you do when you find him?" Jenny asked.

"Kill 'im," Jake said.

She stood up, said, "Please don't tell Joe that story," and went back to the kitchen.

CHAPTER TWENTY-EIGHT

PAXTON OFFERED JAKE a cigar out on the front porch. He accepted, and they sat there together, smoking.

"You know," Paxton said, "if you do want to tell Joe that story—"

"If it comes up, I will," Jake said. "But if he wants to go, can you really stop him?"

"I don't know," Paxton said. "He's never really tried to go, so I haven't had to find out."

"Well, then, I hope you never do," Jake said.

They smoked a while longer before Paxton spoke again.

"Who's the man you're huntin'?" he asked. "The one who killed your friend."

"My friend, my partner . . . almost my brother," Jake said. "The man's name is Seaforth Bailey."

"Seaforth's Raiders?" Paxton asked.

"You've heard of them?"

"Well, sure," Paxton said. "I was down that way once, deliverin' some horses. I heard stories. Are they really an old Civil War band, like Quantrill?"

"No," Jake said, "but they wanna be."

He explained about the general store in Three Rivers, the licorice, the meeting with Seaforth, the gun battle, and the final shooting.

"You don't think you can take care of them yourself, do you?" Paxton asked. "I mean, there were four left the last time you saw them, but there'll be more now."

"I'll find out when I get there," Jake said.

"You're not worried about gettin' killed, are you?" Paxton asked.

"As long as I kill Seaforth," Jake said, "no."

"Jake," Paxton said, "you're only a few years older than I am. You've got a lot of life ahead of you."

"Abby's dead, now Chance is dead," Jake said, "and the Big M is gone. What life?" He stood up. "This is all I've got left. I'm gonna turn in. Tell Joe if he wants to talk, we can do it in the mornin', before I leave."

"I'll tell 'im."

Jake tossed the remnants of the cigar off the porch and went into the house. He was on his way up the stairs when Jenny appeared at the bottom.

"Jake?"

He turned and came back down. When he reached the bottom she put both hands on his chest.

"Please don't tell Joe anythin' that will make him think leavin' home is an adventure."

"If you want," he said, "I'll leave in the mornin' without talkin' to him again."

"No, no," she said, removing her hands, "don't do that. It'll just make him wonder all the more. Daniel needs Joe here, Jake, to run the ranch."

"Seems to me you just have to make Joe understand that," Jake said. "I'll see what I can do, Jenny."

"Thank you, Jake."

"Thanks for the meal," he said, "and the hospitality."

"See you in the morning," she said. "I'll have a big

breakfast ready. It'll take you through the day, if need be."

"Good night," he said.

He went up to his room and turned in. The bed was comfortable, and he fell into a dreamless sleep.

IN THE MORNING he woke to the smell of coffee and bacon, feeling refreshed—unbelievably so. He didn't know if it was the meal, the bed, or the company. Maybe his old bones just needed a good night's sleep in a real bed.

Or maybe he needed to stop thinking in terms of old bones.

AT BREAKFAST JENNY was very quiet as she loaded the table with eggs, spuds, bacon, flapjacks, and biscuits. Joe, on the other hand, was very talkative, still full of questions for Big Jake Motley. Dan Paxton added to the conversation every so often, but for the most part it was Jake either answering or fending off Joe's questions.

Jenny was right about breakfast. There was enough food there to carry Jake for a week, so he stocked up, eating his fill and more. When he was done Jenny kissed his cheek and wished him luck. Dan and Joe Paxton walked him outside.

"I'll get your horse for you, Big Jake," Joe said, and ran over to the barn to saddle the sorrel.

"You did your best with those questions," Dan said to Jake. "I appreciate it."

"I tried not to let any part of my life sound like an adventure," Jake said, "even though most of it was."

"And the adventure's not over, is it?"

"I guess not."

"You know," Paxton said, "after you're done, if you want to come back here, you're more than welcome."

"I appreciate that, Dan," Jake said, shaking the man's hand. "I'm gonna walk to the barn and have a few last words with Joe."

"That's real kind of you."

Jake stepped down from the porch and walked to the barn. As he entered he saw Joe finishing up with the sorrel.

"I was gonna bring 'im over to you, Big Jake," Joe said.

"I know," Jake said, "I just wanted to talk to you alone before I left."

"You know," Joe said, handing him the reins, "I'm thinkin' about comin' with you."

"I had a few friends who wanted to come along, and I told them no," Jake said. "I'll tell you the same. This is somethin' I have to do alone."

"I get it," Joe said, looking glum.

"But I'll tell you somethin' your father can't do alone, Joe," Jake said, "and that's run this ranch. I wish I'd had a son to help me. Maybe I'd still have the Big M."

"You really think so?"

"Both your parents need you here," Jake said. "Don't be in a hurry to ride off, Joe. You've got a lot of years ahead of you."

"I guess you're right, Big Jake." They walked out together, shook hands, and Jake mounted up.

As he rode out he looked back, saw that Joe had joined his father on the porch, and the two men waved. Jake waved back, then urged the sorrel into a canter. He hoped the Paxtons would have better luck with their ranch than he'd had with the Big M.

CHAPTER TWENTY-NINE

MAJOR SEAFORTH BAILEY watched as Teddy Garfield lined up all the new recruits in Seaforth's Raiders on the main street of Three Rivers. Standing off to the side were Sequoia and Gus Walker, who were watching with interest.

As Garfield got the ten men in a straight line, Major Seaforth stepped down from the boardwalk and approached. The citizens of Three Rivers were all inside, some watching from their windows or doorways.

In the months since Big Jake Motley had fought the raiders off and moved on with his herd, Seaforth had come to terms with the defeat. Motley had outdone him, strategy-wise, but Seaforth also believed he just didn't have enough men back then. Now, with these ten, he'd have a force of fourteen. He still felt sure that Jake Motley would be coming back for him, alone, or with some of his hands. Either way, Seaforth's Raiders would be ready for him.

"The men are ready, Major," Garfield told him.

Seaforth popped a piece of licorice into his mouth and said, "Thank you, Gar."

He had told Garfield he didn't want any of the men to be too young or too old. He wanted experienced fighting men. What he was looking at were ten men in their thirties and forties, many of them scarred in some way from past battles. And, more importantly, none of them lived in or had any ties to the town of Three Rivers.

"You men are all prepared to do what is necessary to be one of Seaforth's Raiders?"

"Yessir!" they all shouted.

"Do you see these three men?" he asked, indicating Garfield, Sequoia, and Walker.

"Yessir!"

"They have been with me a long time," Seaforth said. "They are your superiors, understand?"

"Yessir!"

"And this man," Seaforth went on, indicating Garfield, "is my second in command. You obey him as you would me."

"Yessir!"

"Now, when I dismiss you, you will be ready at a moment's notice," Seaforth said. "You can go to a saloon or a café, but none of you may go to a whorehouse. Is that understood?"

This time the "Yessir!" was not as enthusiastic.

"I said, is that understood?"

"Yessir!"

"Then . . . dismissed!"

The men scattered as Garfield walked up to Seaforth.

"These were the best you could do?" Seaforth asked.

"You didn't want young men, so yeah, this was it," Garfield said. "They've all fought before."

"And from the looks of them," Seaforth said, "they lost."

He walked away and entered a saloon, which he used as a base of operations. None of the new men dared go into that place, so they went to the only other saloon in town, across the street.

Sequoia and Walker came over to Garfield.

"What a group," Walker said.

"They'll be fine when the fighting starts," the breed said.

"And when's that gonna be?" Walker asked. "Does the Major still think Motley's comin' back for him?"

"Definitely," Garfield said. "And so do I. He's going to have to get his revenge for me shooting that other old-timer right off his horse."

"It was a good shot," Walker admitted.

"It was a cinch," Garfield said. "I'm going into the saloon with the Major. I want you two to keep an eye on those new men. Nobody goes to a whorehouse. Got it?"

"Got it," Walker said.

"And that includes both of you."

"We understand," Sequoia said.

Walker and the breed went across the street while Garfield followed the Major into the saloon.

Inside, he stopped at the bar and got himself a beer, then joined the Major at his table.

The only thing he didn't like about sitting with Seaforth was the constant smell of licorice coming off the man.

"Why don't you chew tobacco, like a normal man?" Garfield asked.

"I like licorice," Seaforth said. "Why don't you chew tobacco?"

"I don't like it," Garfield said. "I'd rather just smoke a cigarette."

Garfield sipped his beer while Seaforth poured himself another whiskey from the bottle on the table.

"Are we going to do anything else besides wait for Big Jake Motley?" Garfield asked.

"We'll have plenty to do after we've finished with him," Seaforth said.

"I've been thinking about a few things," Garfield said. "We could even do them while we're waiting. There's a payroll coming in on a stage—"

"We can do all of that after," Seaforth said, cutting him off.

Garfield put his head down and drank his beer.

G US WALKER AND Sequoia entered the other, smaller saloon where the new men were gathered. This one was called the Red Cherry, while the other, larger saloon was called the Sunrise. They were just places to drink. No gambling, no girls, no music.

Some of the men were at the bar, others were seated at tables in twos and threes. The breed and Walker each got a beer and walked to an empty table.

"How long have you been with the Major?" Walker asked.

"Long time," Sequoia answered.

"Then you know," Walker said, "if he's ever wanted one man as much as he wants this Big Jake Motley."

For a moment Walker thought the breed wasn't going to answer, but then Sequoia said, "No, there's been no other. This is the only one."

"Well," Walker said, "I hope he gets 'im soon. I'm gettin' tired of waitin' for some action."

Sequoia sipped his beer before responding.

"You must show these others how to wait," he said. "Do not show them impatience."

"I'll do my best," Walker said.

The breed was the only one Walker could talk to. He didn't dare speak to the Major without first being spoken to, and Garfield didn't want to hear anything he had to say. The ten new men weren't worth speaking to—at least, not yet. Maybe once he got to know them one or two might be interesting. But until then, it was only Sequoia, who actually did more listening than he did talking.

"Yes," the breed said, "that would be wise."

Seaforth had known Garfield a long time, long enough to recognize that the man was becoming impatient with him. But that was okay, because Seaforth Bailey was becoming impatient as well. He had expected Jake Motley to be back by now—no, he actually had expected to have killed him by now. The wait was becoming interminable, but he couldn't let that show, not to the men, and not to Garfield.

A payroll sounded tasty to him, and maybe it was just the thing he needed to distract him while he waited for Motley a bit longer.

"Gar."

"Yes?"

"Go get two beers," he said, "and then tell me about this payroll."

CHAPTER THIRTY

A PPROACHING SAN ANTONIO eight days later, Jake was wondering if Seaforth was expecting him. How far would he go? Would he send a scout to watch for him? His intention had been to ride to Three Rivers to find the man, but what if the man found him before that?

He decided to skirt San Antonio, stop in a smaller town to refill his burlap sack with supplies. He found a small town called Wayfair that had a trading post. He was able to get what he needed, and a drink while waiting for the owner to tally his bill.

"There ya go," the man said, handing him his gunnysack. "That's a smart way to carry your supplies, instead of packin' your saddlebags."

"I thought so," Jake said. "Thanks."

"Sure thing."

He started out, but decided to try to find out some information. After all, he was only about seventy miles from Three Rivers.

"Maybe you can help me with somethin'," Jake started.

"What's that?" the white-haired clerk asked.

"Three Rivers."

"What about it?" the man asked.

"I was thinking of stopping there for supplies, until I saw your store."

"Well, you're lucky you did."

"Why's that?"

"Three Rivers is a closed town."

"How'd that happen?"

"There's a group called Seaforth's Raiders got it sewed up," the clerk said. "Nobody's allowed to even buy supplies there. This Major Seaforth's laid claims to the entire stock in the general store."

"Is that still goin' on?" Jake asked. "I thought I heard those raiders had come to a bad end."

"Not that I know of," the clerk said. "In fact, from what I hear, they got more men than ever in that group. Or I should call 'em a gang, because that's what they are."

"Is that right?"

"They got delusions that they're like Quantrill's Raiders, but they ain't even close. I'm just glad they don't hardly come this far north."

"Stay to themselves, do they?"

"Not hardly," the man said. "They just hit a payroll wagon 'bout a week ago."

"What about the law?"

"Ain't no law around Three Rivers," the clerk said, "and don't nobody else want to claim jurisdiction. Say, why you askin' so many questions? You got some business with that gang?"

"I might."

"I'd advise against it," the clerk said. "They say that Major's a madman, and you look like you're alone."

"I appreciate the advice."

He left the trading post, tied the sack to the sorrel's pommel, and mounted up. It sounded like madman

Major Seaforth wasn't twiddling his thumbs, waiting for Jake Motley to come and find him. Neither was he hiding out. And if he had more men than he had before, Jake was going to have to figure out a way to get to him. He didn't like the thought of killing him the way they had killed Chance, from a distance. He wanted to put a bullet in the man's gut from close up, which meant he was at least going to have to deal with his *segundo* as well as the breed scout.

He turned his horse and rode out of Wayfair, deep in thought and alert.

H E IMMEDIATELY RECOGNIZED the place where the raiders had attacked, and Chance died. He stopped at the gravesite. The cross had been knocked over, probably due to weather or predators. There had been some digging but the body of his friend seemed to have gone undisturbed.

He dismounted and did his best to prop up the cross. Then he stood there and stared at it.

"Sorry, old-timer," he said. "You should have had dozens of years left, if I hadn't dragged you on this drive. But it wasn't really my fault, it was that Seaforth fella, and I'm gonna take care of him for ya."

Jake didn't know if it was Seaforth who took the shot, his *segundo*, or the breed, so he just figured he'd be killing all three of them.

But one at a time, if he could.

He mounted up and headed south. Three Rivers was less than a couple of hours away.

H E CAMPED OUTSIDE of Three Rivers, making a cold camp, not wanting to attract any attention. It was spring into summer, so having no fire was not a problem. He supped on beef jerky and washed it down with water from his canteen. Tomorrow he wanted to take a look at Three Rivers from a distance, see if Seaforth's Raiders were there. That would tell him what his options were. If they weren't in town, he could ride in and wait. If they were then he might have to do something to draw them out.

He turned in for the night, but kept his gun close.

H E WOKE WHEN he heard somebody step on a dry twig. It snapped, and he came rolling out of his bedroll, gun in hand.

"Wow," someone said, "that's a good move for an old codger like you."

"What?" He squinted into the dark. The voice was familiar. "Who is that?"

"Do not worry, señor," Taco said. "It is only us."

They came into view, then, as his eyes got used to being awake in the dark. He saw Taco, Dundee, and Curly.

"Where's Desi?" he asked.

"He had to go back to Mexico," Taco said. "And he took Carlito with him. But we thought you would need our help."

"I told you if we snapped a twig he'd hear it." Curly laughed. "They said you'd sleep right through it."

"Well," Jake said, holstering his gun, "since the three of you are here we might as well build a fire and put on some coffee."

"Got anythin' to eat?" Dundee asked.

"Yeah, we can make some beans."

"I'll get some wood," Dundee said.

When he came back with the wood he and Taco got the fire going. Jake put the coffee and beans on the fire, and then they sat around and waited.

"Why no fire before now, Jake?" Dundee asked.

"I didn't know who'd be around," Jake said. "How'd you three find me?"

"Taco's a pretty good tracker," Curly said. "And he figured you'd be runnin' a cold camp."

"I know you, señor," Taco said.

"Yeah, you do."

"We saw Chance's grave," Dundee said. "Figured you were there. That cross looked like it was freshly dug back in."

"Yeah, it got knocked over," Jake said. "I been thinkin' about diggin' him up, but then I don't know where to bury him. South Texas? Old Mexico?"

"He called Mexico his last home," Taco said. "Perhaps there."

"Yeah, maybe," Jake said. "If I'm still alive after this, maybe I'll do that."

"You hear anythin' about Seaforth and his raiders?" Dundee asked.

"Yeah," Jake said, "heard he's got more men than ever."

"So he restocked," Curly said. "That don't matter. We took 'em once, we can take 'em again."

"There's four of us this time," Jake said, "and more than a dozen of them."

"Yeah," Curly said, "but you've got a plan, right?"

"I was gonna take a look at Three Rivers tomorrow and, if they're not there, ride in and wait."

"Wait for a dozen men?" Dundee asked.

"More," Curly reminded him.

"And if they are in town?" Dundee asked.

"Figure out a way to draw them out."

"I don't like this plan," Taco said.

"What about joinin' up?" Dundee asked. "I'm sure they never had a good look at me or Curly. We could ride in and join up, and then be on the inside."

"Too dangerous," Jake said. I don't want you guys gettin' killed—at least, not without me."

"Then what do you suggest?" Dundee asked.

"Let's just wait till mornin'," Jake said, "and see what comes up."

"We settin' a watch?" Curly asked.

"Well," Jake said, "now that we've got a fire, I think we have to."

CHAPTER THIRTY-ONE

THE NEXT MORNING they woke, doused the fire, saddled up, and moved out.

"Taco," Jake said, "ride up ahead and see what you can see. You're scouting for their scout."

"Sí, señor."

As he started to ride ahead Jake called, "Taco!"

"Sí, señor?" Taco said, turning in the saddle.

"If you see him, just ride back here and tell us."

"Sí, señor."

As Taco rode ahead Dundee asked, "Are we gonna take a look at Three Rivers today?"

"Yeah," Jake said, "but from a distance. I don't want them seein' us until we're ready."

"That sounds okay to me," Curly said.

"Three Rivers is about two hours ahead," Jake said. "Let's be real alert."

"Agreed," Dundee said.

* * *

AFTER ABOUT AN hour and a half they heard a horse coming their way. Curly raised his rifle.

"Easy," Jake said. "It's one rider, probably Taco."

As the sound came closer the rider appeared, and it was, indeed, Taco.

Curly put his rifle up and they waited for the Mexican to reach them.

"I saw him," Taco said.

"The scout?"

"Sí, the breed," Taco said.

"And did he see you?" Jake asked.

"I do not think so," Taco said.

"How far are we from town?" Dundee asked.

"It is just over that far rise," Taco said. "We can observe it from there."

"Then let's go," Curly said.

"But if we can see the town," Taco added, "they can see us."

"We'll keep low," Jake said.

"Sí," Taco said. "We can leave the horses and approach on foot."

"All right," Jake said. "Curly, you stay with the horses."

"Why me?" Curly demanded.

"You're still the wrangler," Jake said.

"Yeah, yeah . . ."

They left their horses in Curly's care and made their way up the rise. As they reached the top they got down on their stomachs and crawled the rest of the way. From their vantage point they were able to look down at Three Rivers.

"Nothin'," Dundee said. "They ain't there."

"Yeah, they are," Jake said.

"How can you tell?" Dundee asked. "There's nobody on the streets."

"It's because there's nobody on the streets that I know they're there," Jake said. "The people are staying inside."

"Their horses must be in a stable," Taco observed.

"I agree," Jake said. "And they must be in a saloon, a café, or a whorehouse."

"Except for the breed," Dundee said. "He's out here, somewhere."

"Right," Jake said, looking around. "Let's back out of here."

They backed down the rise, then got to their feet and ran back to Curly and the horses.

"Well?" Curly asked.

"They're down there," Jake said.

"We can't go down and get them, can we?" Curly asked hopefully.

"Definitely not," Jake said. "Especially now that we heard there's more of them than ever."

"Then what do we do?" Dundee asked. "Can you take a shot from up here, Jake?"

"No," Jake said. "Chance was the marksman with a rifle, not me. What about you boys?"

"Dundee might be able to make the shot," Curly said. "Not me."

"Not me," Taco said.

"And I don't want Dundee to kill Seaforth," Jake said. "I wanna do that myself."

"Well," Curly said, "I'm stumped. I'm glad the play is yours to call, Jake."

"Let's mount up and ride," Jake said. "I want to put some distance between us and Three Rivers. I don't wanna be spotted while I'm tryin' to decide what to do."

They all mounted up and rode back the way they had come.

* * *

THEY FOUND A place to camp, inside a circle of rocks Jake had spotted earlier in the day. They wouldn't be able to be spotted from a distance.

"Are we buildin' a fire?" Dundee asked.

"Not till it's dark," Jake said. "The rocks will hide the flame, and the dark will hide any smoke."

"What about the smell?" Curly asked.

"The breeze is blowing toward us from town," Jake said. "They won't smell our coffee from there."

"And the breed?" Taco asked.

"I don't think he'll be out here in the dark," Jake said.

They collected what they needed to make a fire and, as darkness fell, built it, and put the coffee on. Following that, Jake filled the pan with beans, enough for the four of them. They decided against bacon because that smell would be too strong.

As they sat around the fire and ate they decided Taco would take the first watch, and then they would each take a two-hour turn. That way they would all get enough shut-eye.

"What are you thinkin'?" Dundee asked Jake, after he had sat in silence for a while, not taking part in the young men's conversation.

Curly spoke before Jake could answer.

"Do you think you could ride down there and get Seaforth to face you man-to-man, without his raiders?"

"I doubt it," Jake said. "I don't think the man has the nerve. But also, I ain't no gunman. In a shoot-out like that, I don't know if I'd survive."

"And I do not think his men would stay out of it," Taco added. "Riding into town would be the death of you, señor."

"I agree."

"How far are we from San Antonio, d'ya think?" Dundee asked.

"About seventy-five miles," Jake answered. "Why? Do you wanna ride back there?"

"There's somethin' that I can handle better than a gun," Dundee said.

"What's that?"

Curly snapped his fingers.

"Dynamite!"

"Right!" Dundee said.

"Dynamite might even up the odds," Jake admitted. "But you wouldn't be able to ride back here as fast as you ride there. Not with dynamite. So we're talking six or seven days."

"Pleasanton," Taco said.

"Taco's right," Jake said. "Pleasanton is a decent-sized town. It should have a mercantile, which, hopefully, would have some dynamite."

"How far is it?" Dundee asked.

"Half the distance," Jake said. "And I think we'll all go. There's no point in any of us just sittin' and waitin'."

"Suits me," Dundee said. "I could use a beer."

"No beer for you," Jake said.

"And why not?" the young man asked.

"Because you're the one who's gonna be handlin' the dynamite," Jake reminded him.

THEY KILLED THE fire before daylight so that the smoke would not be seen. That meant a very early breakfast of coffee and beef jerky.

By the time the sun was up they were on their horses and riding north again, to Pleasanton.

Taco kept an eye behind them, in case the breed scout happened to be following them. But once they put some distance between themselves and Three Rivers, it was no longer a factor.

They reached Pleasanton around ten a.m., found the main street busy with foot traffic, horses, and wagons.

"Busier than I remember," Jake said. "The mercantile must be bigger than it used to be, too."

They rode directly to the store and reined in their horses in front of it. Four men riding in was bound to attract attention, so it was no surprise when they felt themselves being watched.

"They're suspicious of strangers," Jake said. "I can feel it."

"They have a bank," Dundee pointed out. "Maybe we look like a gang of bank robbers."

"I do not look like a bank robber," Taco said. "I am a lover, not a robber."

"Maybe they're worried about their women with you," Curly said.

"That I would believe," Taco said.

"No point in all of us goin' inside," Jake said. "Taco, you and Curly stay out here with the horses."

"This is the last time I'm bein' the wrangler," Curly announced.

"Agreed," Jake said, and went into the store with Dundee.

The clerk behind the counter was laughing and talking to his customers, calling them by name, and as each customer turned to leave with their purchases they gave Jake and Dundee curious glances.

"Can I help you gents?" the clerk asked when his regular customers had left.

"Yes," Jake said, "my friend wants to buy some dynamite."

"Dynamite," the middle-aged clerk said. "You're a pretty young fella to want to handle dynamite."

"I've had plenty of experience," Dundee told him.

"What'll you be usin' it for?" the clerk asked.

Dundee looked at Jake.

"Boulders," Jake said. "We've got to move some big boulders."

"How many sticks do you want?" the man asked.

"A couple of dozen," Dundee said. "If you've got 'em."

"I've got 'em," the clerk said, "but I don't sell explosives to just anybody."

"Why's that?" Jake asked.

"The last time I sold somebody explosives," the man said, "they used it on our bank vault."

"Well," Jake said, "we'll be takin' the dynamite and leavin' town right away."

"Not so fast," a voice behind them said.

They turned and first saw Taco and Curly, then noticed that neither of them had their guns. Behind them stood several men, one of whom was wearing a sheriff's badge.

"I'm gonna need your guns, gents," the sheriff said.

"Why?" Jake asked.

"You're buyin' dynamite," the lawman said, "I want to talk to you about that, at the jail. So first . . . I'll need your guns."

CHAPTER THIRTY-TWO

PEOPLE GATHERED TO watch as the sheriff and his unofficial deputies walked the four strangers from the mercantile to the jail.

When they entered what appeared to be a customary Old West jail, the lawman tossed their guns on top of his desk. The other men formed a semicircle around the four men, guns in hand.

"Gents, my name's Sheriff Roy Gates. I'll need your names."

Jake, Dundee, Curly, and Taco said their names.

"Mr. Motley," Gates asked, "is that Big Jake Motley, from down Brownsville way?"

"That's right," Jake said. "I'm surprised you've heard of me."

"I've heard enough to know that you're not a bank robber," Gates said. "At least, up to now."

"What makes you think we're here to rob your bank?" Jake asked. "All we did was stop in your mercantile."

"To buy dynamite," Gates said.

"Yeah, your clerk said somethin' about your bank vault gettin' dynamited," Jake said. "That still doesn't explain why you'd suspect us."

"I don't suspect you," Gates said. "I just want to talk to you. I've been the sheriff here longer than most men hold this job. Mr. Motley, you're my age, you know men like us have to be careful."

"Sheriff," Jake said, "you're keepin' us from doin' somethin' very important. Please, go ahead and ask your questions so we can buy our dynamite and leave."

"You still intend to buy dynamite?"

"Yes."

"What for?"

Jake had lied to the clerk about the reason, but he thought the truth would probably work better with somebody like Sheriff Gates.

"We're not going to use the dynamite to rob a bank, Sheriff," Jake said. "We're gonna use it to kill a man."

Gates looked surprised.

"You're admittin' to me that you intend to murder a man?" he asked.

"It ain't murder," Jake said, "it's revenge."

"Against who?"

"A man who killed my best friend."

"I think you better explain."

"Can we sit?" Jake asked.

"Get these men some chairs," Gates said.

One of the men actually had to leave the office and come back with two chairs so all four of them could sit.

"I sold my ranch and drove my last herd to Dodge City," Jake said.

"A trail drive? When?"

"We started out almost three months ago," Jake said. "Along the way we went up against a man named Seaforth Bailey who had appointed himself a major."

"Seaforth's Raiders?"

"He tried to take our herd, and we fought him off," Jake said. "But after, from a distance, he killed my best friend, a man I rode with for over forty years. Like you said, we're the same age, Sheriff. You know what that kind of friendship means."

"I do."

"Well, now I've come back for my revenge, only Seaforth has even more raiders than he had when we fought him off before."

"So you're figurin' to even up the odds with dynamite?"

"That's it."

Gates looked at his unofficial deputies and said, "Put your guns up, boys, and go back to your jobs."

"You sure, Sheriff?" one of them asked.

"I'm sure," Gates said. "These men aren't here to rob the bank."

The men lowered their guns and filed out of the office.

"Maybe you want your men to wait outside for a short time," the sheriff said to Jake.

"It's okay," Jake told the others. "It looks like I'll be right out."

Taco, Dundee, and Curly all stood and followed the deputies out of the office.

"Okay, so you're not gonna rob our bank," the lawman said, "but you're tellin' me that you're gonna kill a man."

"Out of your jurisdiction," Jake pointed out.

"That may be, but you're still admittin' that you're gonna break the law," Gates said. "I might have to notify the sheriff in Three Rivers."

"Well, that would be tough, since there is no sheriff in Three Rivers."

"I see. Then I might have to contact the sheriff wherever you do it."

"I don't know where I'm gonna do it," Jake said.

"Look, Sheriff, I'm not gonna ambush him, or shoot him in the back. He'll see it comin' and he'll have just as good a chance of killin' me."

"So, a fair fight, then?"

"Well, not a dime novel shoot-out in the street," Jake said, "but pretty fair, yeah. I'm only gonna use the dynamite to keep his raiders at bay, if we can."

"So you're not plannin' on blowin' up Three Rivers."

"The citizens there haven't done nothin' to me," Jake said. "Why would I wanna blow up their town?"

Gates stood up.

"I'll walk back to the mercantile with you so you can get your dynamite."

T HEY ALL WALKED back to the mercantile with the lawman while townspeople watched curiously. Jake and Dundee went inside with the sheriff, who told the clerk, "Sell 'em what they want."

"If you say so, Sheriff."

Gates looked at Jake.

"I don't know if you were plannin' on stoppin' in one of our saloons, but I'd prefer you didn't."

"That's fine," Jake said. "Since we'll be transportin' dynamite I don't want any of us to be drinkin'."

"I don't blame you."

When they had the dynamite, Dundee carried it outside, put it in his two saddlebags, then gave the blasting caps to Curly and the fuses to Jake.

"We keep all that apart and we won't have any trouble," he said.

"Then let's get movin'," Jake said. He turned to the lawman. "Thanks for the hospitality."

"You're bein' sarcastic," Gates said, "but I coulda tossed you all in jail for a while."

Jake could have argued about that, but decided to

just get himself and the boys out of Pleasanton without any more trouble.

As he mounted up Sheriff Gates said, "I'm gonna wish you luck, Big Jake. I hope it all works out for you."

"Thanks for that, Sheriff."

The other three had already started to ride out, so Jake urged his sorrel to follow.

B ECAUSE THEY HAD been delayed in Pleasanton, they camped that night some distance away from Three Rivers. It was just as well, since Jake still had to sit and ponder how he wanted to use the dynamite.

Their camp was not as hidden from view as it had been days earlier, but they still built a small fire after dark, just large enough to make coffee and some beans.

"Dynamite always makes me nervous," Curly commented, looking over to where the saddlebags had been set down on the ground, away from the fire.

"Like I said," Dundee relied, "if we just keep the dynamite away from the blasting caps and fuses, there shouldn't be any problems."

"I'm just stayin' away from everythin'," Curly said. "I've seen you use too much dynamite."

"That was a onetime thing!" Dundee said.

"What happened?" Taco asked.

"Never mind," Dundee said. "It ain't even worth talkin' about."

"I don't think we want any huge explosions," Jake commented.

"Jake, we can use the sticks one at a time. One stick'll take care of several men."

"Do we have to bury the sticks, or can you throw them?" Jake asked.

"Either way," Dundee said, "but if we bury them somebody would still have to light the fuses."

"So what do you suggest?"

"I think we have to get Seaforth and his raiders to charge us, and then we start tossing the dynamite in among them. By the time they realize what's goin' on, most of them will be on the ground."

"And who's gonna be throwin' dynamite?" Curly asked.

Dundee looked at his friend.

"Two of us," Dundee said. "You and me."

"Whoa," Curly said, "not me."

"I will do it," Taco said.

"Okay," Dundee said, "you and me, Taco. I'll show you how to do it."

The two men stood up, walked away from the fire to the saddlebags.

"Are we far enough away from them?" Curly asked. "In case somethin' goes off?"

"Dundee's your partner," Jake said. "Don't you think he knows what he's doin'?"

"Usually."

"Except for that one time?" Jake asked.

"We had a job blastin' some boulders from a field," Curly said. "But one of them was close to the house. Dundee just used too much dynamite and . . . boom, no more house."

"Okay, well," Jake said, "that was a while ago, right? And only one time?"

"Yeah, it was a while ago," Curly said, "but it only takes one time, don't it?"

CHAPTER THIRTY-THREE

THEY SET TWO-HOUR watches again, the last one having the job of stomping out the fire before the sun came up, but not before having a cup of hot coffee waiting for everyone.

"Thanks," Jake said as Curly handed him a cup.

Breakfast was just a piece of beef jerky for each. They could have a huge meal after, if they were still alive. Jake, for one, didn't mind having an empty stomach if he was going to end up dead.

But ending up dead was a good possibility, and Jake wanted all the younger men to realize that.

"Before we get started I just wanna make sure you all know—" he started, but they cut him off.

"Yeah, yeah, we know, Jake," Dundee said.

"We could all end up dead."

"Señor Chance was our friend, too, señor," Taco pointed out. "Not so good, like you, but still our amigo."

"Yeah, like Taco says," Curly added, "we comprende the risks."

"That's all I want, then," Jake said. "Let's get mounted.

IN THREE RIVERS, Major Seaforth was eating his breakfast alone, as he usually did, in the saloon he had chosen to use as his headquarters. The other men could eat anywhere they wanted, but not in his place. And since no customers were allowed inside while he was there, he simply had the bartender cook his meals.

He looked up when Garfield came through the bat-wing doors. His *segundo* was the only one permitted to approach him while he was eating.

"Sit down and have some coffee," Seaforth told him.

Garfield sat and the bartender hurried over with the coffeepot and another cup.

"Tell me," Seaforth said.

"Sequoia came back in last night," Garfield said. "Nothing to report."

"Either he's losing his eyesight, or Big Jake's not here yet."

"There's another possibility," Garfield pointed out.

"What's that?"

"Motley's being real careful, making sure Sequoia doesn't see him."

"You think he's that good?" Seaforth asked.

"I didn't think he was good enough to fight us off when we went for his herd," Garfield said. "So now I don't know what to believe."

"Have Walker go out with the breed tomorrow," Seaforth said. "I want two scouts. If Big Jake is that good, I don't want him sneaking up on us."

"Walker's no scout."

"He can learn," Seaforth said. "What about the other men?"

"They all did their jobs when we took that payroll," Garfield said.

"They were sloppy," Seaforth said. "I was almost sorry I let you talk me into doing that job."

"We got the money," Garfield said.

"I want you to work with those men and get them sharp," Seaforth said. "If we're thinking that Jake Motley might be more than an old drover, we better be ready. Understand?"

"Yes, sir."

"Don't 'yessir' me, Gar," Seaforth said. "Just get it done."

"Right."

Garfield drank down his coffee and stood up.

"And get Walker and the breed out there."

"Right."

Garfield turned and left the saloon, leaving the bat-wings swinging behind him.

Seaforth continued to eat his ham and eggs, but was having second thoughts about the way he was handling this Jake Motley thing. Maybe he should just take all his men out there and hunt the man down rather than waiting for the man to hunt him down. But what if he was wrong? What if Motley was too much of a coward to come after him? Then he would be wasting a good portion of his time that could be spent more profitably.

TACO HANDED JAKE his spyglass.

They were once again on their bellies, looking down at the quiet streets of Three Rivers.

"Where'd you get this?"

"I always carry it, señor," Taco said.

"And keepin' it to yourself!"

"And now you have it," Taco said, with a big smile.

Jake aimed the glass at the town and peered through it. At that moment a man came out of a building and started across the street. He was recognizable as the man who had been sitting his horse right next to Major Seaforth, probably his second in command. At the time, he had looked like a confident man.

But if he was in town, were they all there?

"That's one of 'em," he said, handing the glass back to Taco.

Dundee and Curly were waiting at the base of the rise, with the horses, keeping the animals quiet.

"Sí, señor," Taco said, "I recognize him."

"But just because he's there doesn't mean they all are," Jake reasoned.

"I could go down, Señor Jake," Taco offered. "Have a look around. Perhaps their horses are in the livery."

"You'd be takin' a big risk, Taco," Jake said. "If they catch you they won't kill you. They'll try to make you tell 'em where I am."

"They will not catch me, jefe," Taco said. "I promise you."

"Let's get off this hill before somebody spots us," Jake said, and they backed down.

"So?" Dundee asked.

"We saw one of them down there."

"Where there's one there's more, I'll bet," Dundee said.

"Taco wants to go down and have a look."

Dundee and Curly looked at the Mexican.

"If you do that," Curly said, "you better not let that breed get wind of you."

"I realize that, señor," Taco said.

"Curly," Jake said, "why don't you take Taco's spy-glass and keep an eye on the town. Let us know if any-thin' happens."

"Right."

Curly grabbed the glass from Taco's hand and scurried up the hill.

"Jake, why don't we just drop some dynamite on that town and see who comes scurryin' out?" Dundee suggested.

"There are innocent people in that town, Dundee," Jake reminded him.

"How innocent can they be if they let somebody like Seaforth operate from there?"

"They're afraid of him and his men," Jake said. "I think you might be too young to understand that kind of fear."

"You might be right," Dundee said.

"Señor?" Taco said.

Jake looked at the man he now considered to be his oldest friend.

"All right," he said, "but be careful. I'm not lookin' to lose another friend."

"I will be careful, amigo," Taco said. "But I do not think they would even recognize me if they did catch me. I do not think they saw me that clearly the last time we met."

"You might be right," Jake said. "But be careful anyway."

Taco smiled broadly.

"Always, amigo!"

THERE WAS ONLY one other saloon in Three Rivers. It was the smallest one, but it was the one the raiders used for their headquarters. The owner/bartender there actually didn't mind much, because there were a dozen of them, and at least they paid for drinks.

Garfield entered the saloon, looked around, and

saw Sequoia sitting in a corner, alone. Walker was sitting with three of the new men he seemed to have managed to bond with. Garfield left him there, got two
beers, and went to talk to Sequoia.

He sat across from the breed and pushed the fresh
beer across to him.

Sequoia nodded to him and accepted the beer.

"The Major needs you to go out again and scout,
and take Walker with you."

"Why take Walker?"

"You want to take someone else?"

"I did not mean that," the breed said. "Why do I
need to take anyone?"

"Seaforth wants two sets of eyes out there."

Sequoia shrugged.

"He is in command."

"Yes, he is," Garfield said.

"When does he wish us to go out?"

"Finish your beer first."

Sequoia nodded.

Garfield finished his beer, stood up, and left.

SOMETHIN'S HAPPENIN'," CURLY called down to them,
before Taco could leave.

Jake hurried up the hill, took the spyglass away
from Curly.

"One man went into a building. He came out, then
two more came out and went to the stable."

Jake nodded, trained the spyglass on the stable. Before long, two men came riding out, and headed out of
town. One of them was the breed.

"Okay," he said, giving the glass back to Curly.
"Keep watchin'."

He went back down the hill.

"Taco, the breed just left town with another man,"

Jake said. "That should make it easier for you to get in and out. Just take a quick look around, get a head count, and then get back up here. We'll wait."

"As you wish, amigo," Taco said, mounting up. "I will see you soon."

CHAPTER THIRTY-FOUR

Taco rode as close to town as he dared, then dismounted, tied his horse to a stand of bushes, and went the rest of the way on foot.

He made his way to the rear of the general store, without going through town. Instead, he carefully snuck behind the buildings.

When he reached the livery he moved to a single rear door and pressed his back to it. There was a corral behind the stable, but it was empty. If the raiders were there, all their mounts were inside.

He tried the door, found it unlocked, and slipped inside. By the light from the two open front doors, he could see all the horses in their stalls. He doubted Seaforth was permitting any of the locals to keep their animals there. When he counted a dozen plus the breed scout and the man who had ridden out with him, Seaforth's Raiders was now made up of fourteen men.

As he started to back out the rear door, he felt something poke him between his shoulder blades.

* * *

GARFIELD WATCHED AS Sequoia and Walker rode out of town, and then—for some reason—he decided to walk around town, which was as quiet as ever. He just had a feeling he should stay on the street. In the past, gut feelings like that had proven helpful to him, so there was no point in going against it now.

He walked down the street on one side, then crossed over and headed up the street, toward the livery stable.

SHIT!" CURLY SAID, because from his vantage point, he could see both men. Taco was heading for the back of the livery stable while the other man was heading for the front.

"Jake!" he called down the hill. "You better get up here."

Both Jake and Dundee scampered up the hill because of the tone of Curly's voice.

As Jake reached the top he took the spyglass from Curly.

"See 'em?" Curly asked.

"Yeah, I see 'em," Jake said. "Damn, I told Taco to be careful."

"Looks to me like he's bein' careful," Curly said. "He left his horse behind, and he stayed behind the buildings until he reached the livery. I don't know what the hell that other feller's doin'."

Jake trained the spyglass on the other man, and recognized him.

"That's Seaforth's right-hand man," he said.

"Yeah, but what's he doin' on the street?" Dundee asked.

"Bein' careful," Jake said.

As they watched, Taco opened the back door of the

livery and went in. All they could do was wait and see
what happened.

G ARFIELD WAS APPROACHING the livery when something flashed in the corner of his eye. Quickly, he
walked to the front of the livery and peered in. He
didn't see anyone, but he did see the back door open
and close.

He left the front, circled around to the back door,
and waited there.

T ACO IMMEDIATELY KNEW it was a gun barrel. He
raised his hands.

"Tómalo con calma, señor, por favor," Taco said.

"I'll take it easy when you ease your gun out of your
belt and hand it back to me . . . señor."

"Of course, señor." Taco did as he was told and
handed his pistol back. He thought he knew which
man was behind him. He knew, during the gun battle
over the herd, that he had gotten a good look at Seaforth's *segundo*. What he didn't know was whether or
not the man had gotten a good look at him.

The gun barrel disappeared from his back as the
man stepped away.

"Okay, turn around, but keep your hands raised."

Taco turned, saw the man he was expecting, holding
a gun on him. His own gun was in the man's belt.

"Are you here with Big Jake?" the man asked.

"Señor?" Taco frowned. "Who is this Big Jake? I
am here alone."

"To do what?"

Taco shrugged and said, "You will forgive me, señor, but I am afraid I was looking to steal."

"You admit that?"

"Señor," Taco said, "you are holding my life in your hands. What good would lying do?"

"I don't know," the other man said, "but I'm going to take you to talk to someone and we'll find out."

WHAT DO WE do?" Dundee asked as they watched the man march Taco through the street at gunpoint.

"Relax," Jake said, even though he was anything but, "he's takin' him to see Seaforth."

"They'll kill 'im for sure," Dundee said. "We gotta get down there."

"It'd take too long," Jake said. "We've gotta hope they don't recognize him."

"We gotta do somethin'!" Dundee insisted.

Jake looked at him.

"Can you throw a stick of dynamite that far from here?" he asked.

"Wha—hell, no!"

"Then calm down," Jake said. "Like I said, all we can do is wait."

Jake put the spyglass to his eye again, watched as Seaforth's second in command walked Taco into a building, probably a saloon.

SEAFORTH LOOKED UP from his table as the batwing doors swung open and Garfield entered with a Mexican at gunpoint.

"What do we have here?" Seaforth asked.

"I caught this Mex sneaking into the livery stable, Sea," Garfield said.

"Did he say what he was doing there?"

"Yep," Garfield said, "he says he was looking for something to steal."

"Is that right?" Seaforth looked at Taco. "Are you here with Big Jake Motley?"

"Señor," Taco said, "I do not know this man. I am here alone. I was hungry, and I was looking for something I could steal and trade for some food. *Por favor*, I am sorry. Please do not kill me for being hungry."

Seaforth looked at Garfield.

"You recognize him?" he asked.

"No."

Seaforth then looked at Taco.

"Sit down, Mex."

Taco sat across from Seaforth.

"What do you want to do with him, Sea?" Garfield asked.

"There's only two other men who were with us when we hit the herd," Seaforth said. "You and I don't recognize this man. Maybe Walker or Sequoia will."

"So you want to hold him until they come back?"

"Right."

"Where?"

"Let him sit right there," Seaforth said. "I'll have the bartender give him something to eat while we wait."

"Why are you going to feed him?" Garfield asked.

Seaforth looked Taco right in the eye and said, "I'd hate to have a man die on an empty stomach."

JAKE, CURLY, AND Dundee waited with bated breath to hear a shot from down below.

"Maybe we can't hear it from here," Curly said.

"I think we're close enough to hear a shot," Jake said.

"Then what's goin' on?" Dundee wondered.

"Obviously," Jake said, "neither of them recognizes Taco as bein' with us."

"Somebody else might," Curly said.

"The breed might," Jake said, "but he's not in town right now."

"So they're gonna hold Taco until the breed comes back?" Curly said.

"That gives us time to get him out," Dundee said.

"There could be a dozen or more men down there," Jake reminded them.

"Taco went to find out just how many men there were," Dundee pointed out, "and he got caught."

"Jake," Curly said, "we gotta get 'im out."

"The town's quiet," Jake said, "there's nobody on the street, and now that they've got Taco, their attention is on him."

"Yeah?" Dundee said. "And all that means . . . what?"

Jake looked at Dundee and Curly.

"All that means, let's go get 'im outta there."

CHAPTER THIRTY-FIVE

J AKE, DUNDEE, AND Curly slid back down the hill and put their heads together.

"I don't think we can help it," Dundee said. "The town's gotta take some damage."

"We don't know where all the men are," Jake said.

"Gotta be in a saloon," Curly said. "That's where I'd be sittin' if I was waitin' for my boss to make a decision."

"Well," Jake said, "from the short time we were there I only remember two saloons."

"So which one are they in?" Dundee asked.

"I'm gonna guess Seaforth's man took Taco into that saloon to see the Major."

"And what about the other men?" Curly asked.

"I'm gonna say that Seaforth is too arrogant to drink in the same saloon as his men," Jake said. "So whichever one he's in, they'll be in the other one."

"We can't be sure of that," Dundee said.

"Well," Jake said, "that's what we're gonna find out first."

* * *

Taco ate the food the bartender supplied for him, washed it down with a mug of beer.

"You were pretty hungry," Seaforth said.

"I told you, señor," Taco said. "I have not eaten in some time. Gracias for this." Taco pushed the empty plate away.

"Now that you've been fed," Seaforth said, "do you want to change your story?"

"My story, señor?"

Seaforth looked over at the bar, where Garfield was standing and watching, working on a beer.

"Yes," Seaforth said, "about coming here to steal."

"But, señor," Taco said, "that is why I came here. I saw the town was so quiet, I thought I could come in and get out quickly."

"Where's your horse?" Seaforth asked.

"Just outside of town," Taco said. "A few hundred yards from the livery."

"I can have somebody go out and get it," Garfield offered.

"Not yet," Seaforth said. "Let's talk a little longer."

"About what?" Taco asked.

"About who you are," Seaforth said, "and what you do."

"My name is Taco," he said, "and I steal."

"But you must be able to do more than steal," Seaforth said. "For instance, can you work with cattle?"

"Cattle? Oh, you want to know if I am a *vaquero*. No, no, I am afraid not. I do not know anything about cows."

"Can you ride? Shoot?"

"Oh, sí, I can do both of those things." Taco raised his eyebrows. "Ah, you would like to recruit me into your gang?"

"We're not a gang," Seaforth said. "I'm Major Seaforth, and my men are Seaforth's Raiders. Have you heard of us?"

"Oh, sí, sí, I have," Taco said. "You have a reputation as a *muy malo* man."

"Muy malo?" Seaforth asked.

"A bad man," Garfield said.

"Sí," Taco said, "I do not mean to offend you, but—"

"No, no," Seaforth said, "they're right. I am a bad man. You would do well to remember that."

"Sí, señor, I will. But . . . if you are trying to recruit me . . ." He smiled broadly and spread his arms. ". . . I accept."

"Nobody's trying to recruit you—" Garfield started.

"Wait, Gar," Seaforth said. "We can always use a good man, right? Let's not be hasty."

Garfield gave Seaforth a puzzled look, but remained silent.

"And you are a good man, right, Taco?" Seaforth asked.

"Oh, sí, señor," Taco said. *"Muy bien."*

"See, there you go," Seaforth said to Garfield, then looked at Taco again, his face growing stern. "But first we'll wait for our other two men to get here. They were with us when we tried to take that herd. Let's see if either one of them remembers you."

"Herd, señor?"

"Don't worry about it, my friend," Seaforth said, waving to the bartender. "Have another beer."

J AKE, DUNDEE, AND Curly approached the town on foot, having left their horses several hundred yards away. Dundee had his saddlebags over his shoulder, one with dynamite in it, the other with fuses and blasting caps.

As they reached the last building Jake peered around it and had a good view of the main street. He could see both saloons, even though they were a full street apart.

"Get that dynamite ready to throw, Dundee," Jake said.

"Right."

Dundee crouched down, took the saddlebags off his shoulder, and opened both. Curly got as far from his friend as he could, while remaining under cover.

"Relax," Dundee told his friend, "I know what I'm doin'."

"You wanna put some distance between you and your friend?" Jake asked Curly.

"I sure do!"

"Work your way down to that far saloon, see if you can get a look inside from the rear. Then come back and do the same for the closer saloon. And don't take long."

"What do I do if you fellas blow yourselves up?" Curly asked.

"If that happens you're on your own, Curly," Jake said. "You can do whatever you want."

"I'll be back," Curly said, and lit out.

"He better not get spotted," Jake said.

"He won't," Dundee said, sliding fuses into a couple of sticks of dynamite. "How many of these are we gonna need?" he asked.

"Two or three should do it," Jake said. "The only problem is . . ."

"Yeah?"

"You're probably gonna have to toss them in from the front."

"As long as the street's empty, what's the difference?" Dundee asked.

"Okay, then," Jake said. "Get ready. We'll move as soon as Curly gets back."

* * *

GARFIELD FINISHED HIS beer, put the empty mug down on the bar, and headed for the door.

"Where you going, Gar?" Major Seaforth asked.

"Just checking the street again."

"Go back to the bar and relax," the Major said. "We have a guest here who may need some attention."

Taco had been trying his best to appear both puzzled and relaxed, but all the while his mind was racing, looking for a way out of this situation. He knew Big Jake must've been watching through his spyglass, so on one hand he thought all he needed to do was sit and wait for his amigo to make a move to get him out of this mess.

Then again, would Jake think that he could get himself out of this, and simply wait?

"Another beer?" Seaforth asked.

"No, thank you, señor," Taco said. "I was thinking perhaps I could go and get my horse? I would come right back."

"You would, huh?"

"Oh, sí, señor."

"Well," Seaforth said, "you just sit tight. As soon as my other two men get back, we'll know what we're going to do with you—recruit you, or kill you."

WHEN CURLY GOT back he said, "The far saloon is called the Red Cherry Saloon. Why, I don't know. What other colors are cherries?"

"Green," Dundee said.

"Never mind the cherries!" Jake snapped. "How many men in that one?"

"Twelve," Curly said. "They're sittin' around, drinkin'. Looks like they're waitin'."

"And the other saloon?"

"Called the Sunrise," Curly said. "Taco's in there, sittin' with that Major. And the other man is at the bar."

"That's it?" Jake asked.

"Except for the bartender, that's it."

"Bartenders!" Dundee said. "They do one of two things when the shootin' starts. Duck down behind the bar, or bring out a shotgun."

"We'll keep a watch on this one," Jake said. "Now here's what we're gonna do . . . ."

G ARFIELD COULD SEE that Major Seaforth was becoming impatient. This was an oddity, because as long as he'd known him, the man had more patience then Job. Maybe if he walked over to the table and put a bullet in the Mexican's head, it would hurry things along.

He started toward the table, deciding that he'd have his mind made up by the time he got there.

D UNDEE MADE HIS way along the rear of the buildings, then down the alley next to the Red Cherry Saloon. He stopped at the mouth of the alley to check the street. Once he was sure it was still empty, he stepped out with the saddlebags on his shoulder and approached the batwing doors. The men inside were drinking and laughing. He knew if he threw all the dynamite sticks into the saloon, it would kill every one or most of them. But Jake had told him to toss them in one at a time. Up to this point, none of these men had any dealings with Big Jake Motley, and none of them had anything to do with the death of Chance McCandless.

For a man out for revenge, Dundee thought Jake

Motley was still being fairly logical in his thinking.
Vengeance was usually the death of logic, in a man.

But for now, Dundee would do what Jake wanted.

He took out a single stick of dynamite, lit the fuse,
and tossed it over the batwing doors . . .

CHAPTER THIRTY-SIX

GARFIELD WAS REACHING for his gun as he approached the table. The sound of the explosion literally saved Taco's life, for he had decided to blow the little Mex's head clean off.

"What the hell—" Seaforth yelled, standing.

When the second explosion came both Seaforth and Garfield ran for the door. Seaforth took a moment to turn to the bartender and say, "Point your shotgun at him. If he's not here when I get back, you won't be either."

He followed Garfield out.

The bartender brought a shotgun out from beneath the bar and pointed it at Taco.

"Señor," Taco said, "you do not want to do that."

"You're right, I don't," the man said. "But I will."

"Drop it!"

Both the bartender and Taco turned toward the voice.

* * *

JAKE AND CURLY made their way to the rear of the Sunrise Saloon. There was a flimsy back door that they forced easily, and entered. They found themselves in a back storeroom; a doorway was across from them. When they reached it and looked through it, they saw the interior of the saloon.

Jake resisted moving with the sound of the first explosion, but when the second one came, and Seaforth and Garfield ran out, he stepped through the door with his gun out.

"Drop it!" he told the bartender.

The bartender looked like he was about to cry.

"Mister, I can't," he said. "The Major will kill me."

Curly moved in next to Jake, pointed his gun at the man, and said, "I'll kill you if you don't!"

"I—I'll kill the Mex first," he stammered.

"Wait!" Jake said. He moved farther into the room. "I have an idea," he said to the bartender.

"What?" the man asked, and his shotgun lowered an inch.

Jake raised his gun and shot the man in the shoulder. The shotgun discharged harmlessly into the floor. The bartender sank from sight.

Jake walked around the bar and looked down at the man, who was holding his shoulder.

"There," he said, "now Seaforth can't say you didn't try."

The bartender looked up at him, grimaced, and said, "Th-thanks."

There was a third explosion and Jake said, "Okay, that's it. No more dynamite. Let's go!"

Taco sprang from his seat and followed Curly through the door to the storeroom. Jake backed his way to the door, covering them, then turned and ran.

All three hurried out the back door and out of town, hoping that Dundee was doing the same.

WHEN GARFIELD AND Seaforth exited the saloon they stopped and looked around, seeking the source of the noise. They saw a man down the street, standing in front of the Red Cherry Saloon.

"There!" Seaforth said, and they started running.

They had almost reached him when the man turned and saw them.

"Kill him!" Seaforth shouted, drawing his gun. Garfield did the same.

DUNDEE ENJOYED BOTH explosions.

The laughter from inside the saloon turned to cries of pain and surprise. He might have tossed the dynamite farther into the saloon than Jake suggested, thereby injuring or killing some of the raiders. He'd apologize to Jake for that, later. Meanwhile, he might have reduced the threat.

He turned and saw two men running toward him, recognized Major Seaforth. He knew Jake wanted to kill the man himself, but he still lit the fuse on the third stick of dynamite and threw it at the two men. It landed in front of them and exploded . . .

AS THE STICK of dynamite came toward them Garfield acted quickly. He turned, grabbed Seaforth around the waist, and took them both to the ground. The dynamite exploded, sending up a geyser of wood and dirt. When the cloud began to clear Garfield got to his feet, and helped Seaforth to stand.

"Where is he?" Seaforth demanded.

The man who had thrown the dynamite was nowhere to be seen.

"Gone," Garfield said.

"Check inside the saloon," Seaforth said. "I'm going back to that Mexican. He knows something."

They split up. Garfield ran to the Red Cherry while Seaforth headed back to the Sunrise.

JAKE, CURLY, AND Taco ran back to their horses, hoping to find Dundee there.

"He'll be here," Curly said.

"I'm gonna take Taco to his horse," Jake said. "You wait for Dundee. We'll meet you below that rise. Then we'll put some distance between us and here and regroup."

"Got it," Curly said.

Jake mounted up, reached down to pull Taco up behind him. As he did so they saw Dundee running toward them.

"What happened?" Jake asked.

"I tossed the third stick at Seaforth and his man, and got out of there."

"Did you kill Seaforth?"

"I doubt it," Dundee said, "but I gave him an earache."

He and Curly mounted up, and they all rode to where Taco had left his horse.

SEAFORTH ENTERED THE Sunrise Saloon and saw that it was empty. He could see where a shotgun blast had struck the floor. Then he heard a groan from behind the bar. When he went to look he saw the bartender on the floor, bleeding from the shoulder.

"I'm sorry, Major," the man said. "I tried."

"Who was it?"

"Two men."

"What'd they look like?"

"One was older, one younger. The older one shot me."

"Motley!"

Seaforth turned as Garfield came running through the doors.

"How are the men?"

"Two dead, four injured. Where's that Mexican?"

"Gone," Seaforth said. "Big Jake and another man were here. They shot the bartender."

Garfield walked to the bar and peered over it at the injured man.

"They can't have gone far," he said.

"By the time we saddle up, they will," Seaforth said. "Let's see how many men we have who can ride. We can mount up and track them."

"And what about Sequoia and Walker?"

"We'll leave some injured men behind to tell them what's happening," Major Seaforth said. "Then they can ride out and join us."

"How are they going to know where we are?"

"Don't worry," Seaforth said. "That breed will track us down."

CHAPTER THIRTY-SEVEN

SINCE THEY RODE out together they didn't bother going back to the base of the rise they had been using to observe the town. Instead, they rode for some time until Jake felt they had put enough distance between themselves and Three Rivers, then stopped to rest the horses and take stock of their situation.

"Did you kill anyone?" Jake asked Dundee.

"I don't know for sure," Dundee answered honestly. "I may have thrown those sticks of dynamite deeper into the saloon than I intended."

"We'll have to figure some of the men were injured," Jake said.

"That's for sure," Dundee said.

"And maybe even Seaforth and his *segundo*," Jake added.

"I don't think so," Dundee said. "His man moved pretty fast to get him to safety."

"Okay, then," Jake said, "if a third of the men in the Red Cherry were injured, that leaves ten men comin' after us."

"What do you want to do, señor?" Taco asked.

"What I'd like to do is get Seaforth away from his men so I can kill 'im," Jake said.

"How do we do that?" Curly asked.

"The only way I can think of is to split up," Jake said. "That way he'll have to split his forces to track us."

"But he won't know which tracks are yours," Curly said.

"And I won't know which tracks he follows," Jake added.

"If we choose the place where we split up," Taco said, "and you watch, you will see what tracks he picks."

"And then I can track him."

"So where do we do this?" Dundee asked. "And what do we do with the rest of the dynamite?"

"Okay," Jake started slowly, "this is what I'd like to happen. I want to isolate him as much as I can, and make this a him-or-me situation. After that, you fellas can do whatever you want with his raiders, and use all the dynamite you want."

Dundee and Curly looked at each other.

"This could be fun," Dundee said.

Taco looked at Jake.

"Only men this young would think of this as fun, señor."

"You and me, we know better, Taco," Jake said. "Come on, let's find a likely place to split up."

SEAFORTH RODE TO the livery on his horse and met his men out front, led by Garfield. All told, there were now eight of them. When they joined back up with Walker and Sequoia, they'd be ten.

"Two of our men are dead, and two are injured," Seaforth said. "We are going to catch the people responsible and make them pay. And we will not be returning to town until that is done."

He had told Garfield to make sure each man had enough water and beef jerky to sustain him for some time, as they would not be returning for supplies. They had coffee and a coffeepot, in case they had to camp overnight. Seaforth expected running Jake Motley and his men down to take more than a day. He just wished he had Sequoia with him to read sign. Without the breed, he was going to have to rely on Garfield.

Seaforth looked at Garfield and nodded.

"Let's move out!" Garfield shouted.

Garfield trotted his horse up to ride alongside Seaforth.

"Where do we go first?" Seaforth asked.

"I want to take a look where that Mex, Taco, said he left his horse," Garfield said. "We might pick up some tracks from there."

"We'd better," Seaforth said.

"I'll do the best I can, Sea," Garfield said. "I'm no half-breed."

They rode around to the rear of the livery, then followed the directions Taco had given them to his horse—if he was telling the truth. As it turned out, he was. Garfield found the place where Taco had tied his horse, then dismounted to study the ground.

"Well?" Seaforth demanded.

"I'd say once they picked him up from town, they brought him here to his horse." He stood up and faced Seaforth. "I'm seeing four horses, here."

"Four," Seaforth demanded. "Less than he had last time."

Garfield walked to his horse and mounted up.

"Shouldn't be hard to follow the trail left by four horses," he said to Seaforth. "And we're only a couple of hours behind them."

"Yeah, yeah," Seaforth said, "just lead the way."

As he followed Garfield he still wished Sequoia would come back. He depended on Garfield as his second in command, but the breed was his tracker.

S EAFORTH AND HIS raiders only rode for twenty minutes before they saw two riders coming toward them at a gallop.

"Who's that?" Seaforth demanded of Garfield.

"It's Sequoia," Garfield said. "And Walker."

Seaforth called a halt to his column of raiders and they waited for the riders to reach them. They reined in their horses in front of Seaforth and Garfield.

"What brings you back?" Garfield said.

"The breed said he heard explosions," Walker said. "I didn't hear nothin'."

"Dynamite," Sequoia said.

"You got that right," Seaforth said. "It was Motley and three of his men."

"What happened?" Walker asked.

"We'll tell you on the way," Seaforth said. "Sequoia, we're following the trail of four men, according to Garfield."

Garfield pointed and Sequoia took a look.

"He is right," the breed said. "Four horses."

"You take the lead, then," Seaforth said.

"Whatever you say, boss," Sequoia said.

J AKE AND HIS men came to a three-pronged fork. It wasn't a road, per se, but each path had definitely been well traveled and led into some South Texas brush country.

"This should be it, señor," Taco said. He looked around. "You can watch from those rocks."

"We can't have each of you take a path," Jake said.

"Why not?" Dundee asked. "That'll split their force into three."

"They're gonna have to wonder where the fourth horse is," Jake reasoned. "I'll have to ride a ways with one of you, and then double back."

"Ride with me, señor," Taco said, not wanting his friend to go off on his own.

"Okay," Jake said, "and hopefully, Seaforth himself will follow two of us, figuring I'd keep a man with me."

"Why would he figure that?" Curly asked.

"Because I'm old," Jake said. "Maybe I can catch him riding with only two other men."

"You're not gonna take on three men by yourself," Dundee said. "And he'll probably take most of the men with him. He's no fool."

"Dundee, if you get three men following you, you can handle them with the dynamite, right?"

"Definitely," Dundee said. "It would probably only take one stick."

"Okay, after you blow them to hell, double back and give Curly a hand."

"And you?"

"I'll have Taco with me," Jake said. "You help Curly with the men who follow him, Taco and I will handle the rest."

"You better save some of that dynamite," Curly said.

"Don't worry," Dundee said, "there's plenty."

"Let's go," Jake said. "We've probably got a couple of hours on them. Plenty of time for me to double back and the rest of you to take cover and wait."

"So we can ambush 'em?" Curly said.

Jake looked at him. "You can do whatever the hell you like, as long as I get Seaforth."

* * *

SEQUOIA REINED IN as they reached the three-pronged fork.

"They have split up here," he said, pointing to the ground.

"We'll have to do the same," Garfield said.

"No," Seaforth said.

"Why not?" Garfield asked.

"Sequoia," Seaforth asked, "which way is the Mex's horse going?"

Sequoia studied the tracks. After they had told him about the Mexican, he had been able to isolate the tracks of the man's horse. Luckily, he had a distinctive shoe on one hoof, for some reason.

"There," he said. "With the two riders."

"Then Big Jake's riding with him," Seaforth said.

"Why would he do that?" Walker asked.

"That Mex was a calm customer," Seaforth said. "And he's no kid. I think those two have been together for a while. And I think they're together now."

"So what do you want to do?"

"Send two men after each of those tracks," Seaforth said, pointing to the single tracks. "The rest of us are going to follow these two." He looked at the breed. "Sequoia, take the lead."

FROM THE ROCKS above, Jake watched, hoping that they had figured it right, and the raiders would split into equal forces.

To his dismay, Seaforth sent two after Dundee, and two men after Curly. He then took a force of six after his and Taco's tracks. Only Taco was now alone.

"Shit!" he swore.

If they caught up to Taco, his Mexican friend wouldn't have a chance against six men. Right now Jake wished he had some of Dundee's dynamite in his own saddlebags.

He hurried to his horse and mounted up, still not sure what he was going to do.

CHAPTER THIRTY-EIGHT

FOR THE MOMENT Jake could do nothing but follow the six riders.

He rode down from his position in the rocks and started trailing them. He couldn't afford to move close enough to see them, because they might see him as well. He simply stayed on their trail, riding over their fresh sign. Eventually, they were going to get to the spot where he veered off from Taco and doubled back. At that point they would have to decide whether to follow the tracks of the single horse moving forward, or the one that was doubling back. Or—and Jake would have preferred this—they would split up. If three of them followed the trail he left when doubling back, they would soon realize he had been watching them. But by that time maybe he and Taco could take care of the three who had continued on. He wondered what Seaforth would do, though. Continue on or double back?

Okay, maybe this decision of the raiders to have six

men follow his and Taco's trail wouldn't turn out to be so bad, after all.

T HE RAIDERS RODE in a triangle formation, Sequoia in the lead, Seaforth and Garfield behind him, and the other three men behind them. Seaforth was much more confident, now that he had his breed scout riding point, that they would catch up to Motley. He would show "Big" Jake Motley who was truly big.

They rode for several miles before Sequoia stopped, holding up a hand for them to stop behind him.

"What is it?" Seaforth called to him.

Sequoia turned his horse and rode back to Seaforth and Garfield.

"They have split up again," he said.

"Dammit!" Seaforth said. "Which one is Motley?"

"One is the horse we have been following, assuming it is the Mexican's," Sequoia said. "The other could be Jake Motley's."

"But?" Garfield said.

The breed looked at him.

"But we are only assuming the first horse is being ridden by the Mexican. These could be two different men."

"No," Seaforth said. "It was the Mexican's horse, and the other one is Motley."

"So what do we do now?" Garfield asked.

"Maybe," Sequoia said, "they switched horses."

"You mean Motley could be riding the Mexican's horse?" Seaforth asked.

"Yes."

"No."

"Why not?" Garfield asked.

"Because Motley wants me to find him," the Major said. "Or, he wants to find me. Either way, he's not trying to get away from me."

"So what do you want to do?" Garfield asked. "Split up again, too?"

"No," Seaforth said. "Forget about the Mexican. We're all going to follow Motley back."

"What about the others?" Garfield asked. "They're still following Motley's other men."

"We can't change that now," Seaforth said. "But we're not following that Mex anymore." He looked at Sequoia. "We're following the other trail, the one leading back."

"As you wish," Sequoia said.

"Take the lead again."

Sequoia nodded.

As they headed back, following the trail of the single horse, it was not on a road, or a path. At times they had to skirt around trees, and rock formations, and Sequoia had to relocate the trail so they could continue. It was slower going . . .

W HEN JAKE REACHED the point where he and Taco had split up he saw that all six men had veered off and followed his trail back. That was actually a good thing. It meant Taco was safe, and the six men had no idea where they were going. Then he heard something from up ahead and before he could decide whether to take cover or not, he saw Taco riding back toward him.

"What are you doin' here?" he demanded.

"I had the feeling, señor, that they were not following me any longer."

"You're right," Jake said, "but you should've kept goin'."

"No, señor," Taco said, "I knew I should ride back."

"Yeah, yeah, you stubborn Mex."

"What should we do now?"

"Well," Jake said, "the only reason I can see for them to all follow one trail is because they think it's me."

"But . . . it *was* you."

"I know," Jake said. "That breed scout must be with them. He knows what he's doin'."

"Well," Taco said, "they will not follow your trail back to the three-way fork, where they split up. What then?"

"I think I may play with them a bit," Jake said. "Try to get inside their heads."

"What would you like me to do, señor?" Taco asked.

"Go and find Dundee and Curly. I want to know if they're safe."

"Where shall I take them?" Taco asked.

"Back to the three forks," Jake said. "Seaforth and his raiders should be gone by then."

"Gone where?"

"Hopefully," Jake said, "chasin' another false trail. I'll see you later."

"*Vaya con dios*, señor," Taco said.

Jake turned his horse and started after Seaforth's Raiders, who thought they were following him.

S EQUOIA HELD UP his hand for them to stop.

"What's wrong?" Seaforth called.

The breed turned in his saddle and said, "We're here." He pointed.

Seaforth hadn't recognized the spot, as they were coming at it from a different angle.

"So he led us right back here," he said.

"Yes," Sequoia said.

"But why?" Garfield asked.

Sequoia looked around, then up, and pointed.

"Those rocks," he said. "He either is, or was, watching us from there."

"And if he is," Garfield said, "he just saw you point at him."

Sequoia lowered his arm and did not answer.

"Let's circle around those rocks," Seaforth said. "Garfield, you take two men that way; Sequoia, Walker and I will go that way. If he is up there, we might be able to surround him."

"It's worth a try," Garfield said. He waved at two of the men to follow him, then rode to the left.

"Sequoia, take the lead," Seaforth said.

"As you wish."

They started riding the opposite way.

J AKE FOLLOWED THE tracks left by the six men, but it was obvious they were going to follow his trail all the way back to the three-way fork. He decided to try to circle them and get there first.

Thanks to the surefooted sorrel, he did so, reaching the fork ahead of the raiders. He set himself up to watch.

S EAFORTH, SEQUOIA, AND Walker got halfway around the rock formation and met up with Garfield and his men coming from the other side.

"Anything?" Seaforth asked.

"No."

They all looked up.

"It's obvious he'd have to go up and come down this way, but on foot," Seaforth said. "That means his horse would have to be here somewhere." He looked at the breed. "See if you can find it."

Sequoia nodded and turned his horse.

"I suppose you want me to go up there," Garfield said.

"No," Seaforth said, "you and I will stay down here. Send Walker and the other men up."

"And if Motley's there?" Garfield asked.

"I don't want them to kill him," Seaforth said. "Just bring him down here."

Garfield looked over to where Walker was waiting with the other two men.

"I'll tell them."

J AKE SAW SEAFORTH and five of his men—the breed and *segundo* included—come out of the trees. They had a discussion, and then the breed pointed up. After that the riders began to surround the rock formation.

He continued to watch.

Walker and his men started up the hill to reach the top of the rock formation. As they approached the top they drew their guns, but were unable to spread out. They had no choice but to approach the plateau single file.

Walker was first to the top, stepped up and sprang to one side, allowing the next man to follow. In seconds all four men were on top with their guns out.

There was no Big Jake Motley.

J AKE WAS GLAD he had not taken up his former position high on those rocks. If he had, they'd have him now. But instead, he remained in the trees and watched as they surrounded his former hiding place. By now, they knew he wasn't there.

He turned, mounted his horse, and began to leave his new trail for them to follow.

"He was there," Walker said. "There are scuff marks on the rock."

"Are you sure?" Seaforth asked.

"I know enough about reading sign to see that," Walker said.

"It's true," Clark, one of the other men, said. "I saw them, too."

Seaforth looked at Garfield, to see if his second in command was satisfied with the report of his men. Garfield nodded. And at that moment, they heard a horse, and Sequoia returned.

"So?"

"I found where he must've left his horse last time," the breed said. "But nothing now."

"He's playing with us," Walker said, "like a cat with a mouse."

"Yes," Seaforth said, "but it's time for the mouse to become the cat."

CHAPTER THIRTY-NINE

JAKE MADE SURE his trail was easy to follow.

In spite of the fact that he was in front of Seaforth and his men, he finally felt that he was actively hunting the man who killed Chance McCandless. He'd had many jobs as a young man, before finally getting his own ranch, but bounty hunter had never been one of them. He had hunted for food, and on several occasions hunted predators who were victimizing his stock, but he had never hunted for sport or enjoyment. And he never knew what it felt like to hunt a man, until now. And while he would certainly take no joy in killing Major Seaforth Bailey, he thought that he would take a certain amount of satisfaction in catching him. After all, he had promised his friend at his gravesite that he would avenge him. That was a promise he fully intended to keep.

While laying down his trail he wished that he had heard some explosions. It would have meant that Dundee had accomplished his task, and the explosions might play on the mind of Major Seaforth. But either Dundee hadn't carried out his mission, or he had and it happened too far away for the sound to carry. He fervently hoped it was the latter.

As for Curly, he would have to succeed at his appointed task with his rifle, and certainly that would happen too far away to hear.

But with six men on his trail, Jake once again wished he had a few sticks of Dundee's dynamite in his saddlebags. All he had was his pistol and a rifle, and he had never been the marksman Chance had been.

He still wasn't sure how he was going to separate Seaforth from his five men. Perhaps he'd even have to wait for Taco, Dundee, and Curly to rejoin him before taking them on. Until then he'd have to lead them on a merry chase.

S EQUOIA HAD RIDDEN up ahead of Seaforth, Garfield, and the others. His orders were to follow the trail and, if he happened to catch up to Jake Motley, not to engage him or kill him. But the breed had other plans.

Sequoia didn't like Teddy Garfield, and wanted to supplant him as Major Seaforth's *segundo*. In order to do that he was going to have to prove his worth. So he fully intended to catch up to this Big Jake Motley, capture him, and turn him over to the Major for his pleasure. After all, he was a hunter, and Motley was a rancher and no match for him.

He pushed his pony harder as the sign on the ground became fresher and fresher. In addition to his other advantages—youth and experience being the main two—there was no way the rancher's horse could be a match for his mustang.

J AKE MOTLEY KNEW good horseflesh.
     That was the reason he had chosen the sorrel.

The animal was built for stamina, which was an attribute he preferred over speed.

So when he heard the horse coming up behind him, he knew he would never be able to outrun it. But it was the sound of only one horse. He believed the rider had to be Seaforth's half-breed scout coming up on him. And from having watched the man, he knew he was riding a mustang.

He started to look for a likely place to wait and face the man.

S EQUOIA KNEW HE must be gaining on Motley. He took his rifle from his scabbard so that he'd be ready when he saw him. His intention was to shoot the man's horse out from under him. After all, the animal would be the biggest target.

As he rode he alternated keeping his eyes ahead of him and on the ground. In doing that, he thought he would not lose sight of the tracks, and would spot Motley ahead of him. But suddenly, as he looked down, the tracks were gone. He reined in and stared ahead, but did not see Big Jake Motley. He thought he might have to ride back and hope he could pick up the trail again. But first he looked in every direction, and that's when he saw Jake Motley's sorrel off to his right, standing among some Brazilian bluewoods. Those kinds of trees did not grow tall, were often brushy, and formed thickets that were dense enough to hide a man.

Sequoia had to make a decision.

J AKE MOTLEY MIGHT have been a rancher for most of his life but he had spent some time in his youth as a soldier. He had some knowledge of strategy and had already outsmarted Seaforth once, in order to keep his herd. Of course, he had been aided by the man's own arrogance.

In the war Jake had a superior officer who believed in the power of misdirection. "If you don't think you can outsmart an opponent," the officer had once told him, "then misdirect him."

Jake didn't know if he could outsmart the breed, so he decided to take his old commanding officer's advice.

SEQUOIA WATCHED THE sorrel.
    The horse was standing stock-still, occasionally nibbling on some brush or looking around. It was enough, however, to hold the breed's attention long enough for Jake to rise up from his prone position.

But he should have known better. How could a fifty-five-year-old rancher sneak up on a half-breed twenty years younger than he was?

There was one shot, and the bullet struck Jake in the left shoulder. He staggered back, the gun in his hand, feeling so much the fool as he fell onto his back. However, as he landed he reflexively pulled the trigger of his pistol, discharging a single bullet that seemed to have a mind of its own . . .

SEQUOIA KNEW THE trick.
    Motley thought he would sneak up behind him while the breed was staring at his horse, standing off in the brush. But no white man—especially not a broken-down rancher—could sneak up behind Sequoia. He heard the brush rustling as soon as the man moved. He held his rifle with one hand, pointed it behind him underneath his arm, and almost without looking—he took a quick glance over his shoulder—pulled the trigger once.

He had not intended to kill Jake Motley, but this appeared to be a kill-or-be-killed situation. And this under-the-arm shot with his rifle was one that was well practiced. So he wasn't surprised when the bullet hit Jake Motley in the shoulder.

He was, however, momentarily surprised when Motley's pistol fired a bullet that struck Sequoia right in the back of the head.

It was a short-lived surprise . . .

J AKE THOUGHT HE was dead.

He was lying on his back on the ground, and there was sure to be a follow-up shot to the one that had just hit him. Jesus, the breed had fired almost without looking. How could he have hoped to sneak up on a man like that?

But there was no second shot.

Jake pushed himself to a seated position and examined his wound. It appeared the bullet had gone through. There was blood, and pain, but apparently no deadly damage. All he had to do was stop the bleeding.

He took a bandanna from his pocket, wadded it up, and stuck it inside his shirt against the wound. Luckily—or unluckily—he had been shot before, and knew when he was seriously wounded, and when he wasn't.

Picking up his gun from the ground, he got to his feet, and saw the man lying on the ground ahead of him. The mustang he had fallen from was standing still.

He walked over to the man, pointing his gun ahead of him, but as he reached him he saw there was no need. His wild shot as he fell had struck the man in the back of the head and taken part of his face off. But still he could see it was the half-breed scout.

Jake had made a major error in judgment, and by

blind, stupid luck had come out of it alive. But he couldn't count on that kind of luck the rest of the way. He was going to have to do a lot more thinking, and planning.

If Dundee and Curly had taken care of their men, that left five he would have to deal with. But first, he had to decide what he wanted to do with the breed's body.

First he searched it, looking for something useful. In the end, he took only his rifle. An extra gun would come in handy.

Next, he decided to leave the body out in the open so they would be able to see it. Maybe the breed's death would unnerve them.

WHERE'S SEQUOIA?" SEAFORTH complained. "He should've been back by now to report."

"Something must've happened," Garfield said.

"Really? You think Big Jake Motley did something to him?" Seaforth asked.

"I don't think he could," Garfield said. "He's just a rancher. Maybe something else . . . his horse might've stepped into a chuckhole and thrown him . . ."

"Not that mustang," Seaforth said. "That's the most surefooted horse I've ever seen."

"Well, I think that's more likely than Motley overpowering him," Garfield said.

They turned and looked behind them at Walker and the other two men, who were sitting their horses, impatiently waiting for instructions.

"Okay," Seaforth said, "we'll just have to keep moving. Hopefully we'll find him, or he'll find us."

"You know," Garfield said, "I've never thought he was as good as he thinks he is. If that old-timer managed to get the best of him—"

"Never mind," Seaforth said. "Let's just ride."

* * *

WHAT THE—" SEAFORTH said.
He reined in and raised his hand to stop the others.

"Jesus," Garfield said.

Up ahead was Sequoia's mustang, standing still near a thicket of trees, with Sequoia in the saddle. Only he was sitting very unnaturally.

"Is he tied up?" Garfield asked.

"There's one way to find out," Seaforth said.

Garfield looked at him.

"Go take a look."

Garfield turned in his saddle.

"Walker," he said, "go take a look."

Walker rode up to where Seaforth and Garfield were.

"Is he tied in his saddle?" Walker asked.

"That's what you and Gar are going to find out," Seaforth said. "Go!"

CHAPTER FORTY

JAKE SETTLED UPON the idea of tying the breed's body in his saddle. But he had to hurry. There were still five of them, and he still needed to tend to his own wound so that it wouldn't get worse.

He struggled to get the breed into his saddle and almost gave up at one point, but finally got him situated. He hoped the mustang wouldn't wander away, so instead of simply grounding the reins, he tied them to one of the nearby bushes.

That done, he mounted the sorrel and continued to ride north, getting as far away as he could before Seaforth and his men reached that point. He'd have to wait to tend to his wound, trying to find a more permanent solution to his bleeding.

SEAFORTH WATCHED AS Garfield and Walker approached the breed's horse.

Garfield stayed alert, in case Jake Motley was watching and waiting for a chance to take a shot.

"Oh, Jesus," Walker said, "half his face is gone. Is that him?"

"It's him," Garfield said, "after he took a bullet to the back of the head."

"Ambushed?"

"Looks like it," Garfield said, "only I can't see how that rancher could've ambushed this half-breed. Sequoia could hear a fly's wings flapping."

As they reached him they each went to one side.

"Is he dead?" Seaforth called.

Garfield waved his assent, then looked around again.

"Check that thicket over there," he told Walker.

"If he's in there he'll blow my head off before I get to him."

"I'll keep watch," Garfield said. "Go!"

Walker turned his horse and rode toward the thicket, waiting to see the muzzle flash of a rifle. But as he reached it he realized there was nobody hiding there.

He turned in his saddle and waved at Garfield, then turned his horse and rode back.

"What do we do with him?" he asked.

"Bury him," Garfield said.

JAKE SLOWED HIS horse when he felt darkness growing around him. He needed to stop and dismount before he fell off.

Choosing another thicket of bluewoods to use for cover, he knew they wouldn't offer much in the way of protection if any shooting started. But at the moment they hid his horse and him from sight.

He grabbed the extra shirt from his saddlebags, took it with him to a seated position where he was out of sight but could look through the thicket to see if anyone was coming. Tearing the shirt into strips, he managed to fashion a more solid dressing for his wound, which would hopefully stop the bleeding rather than just stanch the flow.

He had some water, wishing he had a bottle of whiskey with him. After pouring water into his hat for the sorrel to drink, he remounted, feeling slightly stronger. But he wasn't in any condition to face five men, so he needed to find a place where he could spend the night, get some rest, and start again in the morning.

SEAFORTH TOLD GARFIELD, "You can leave two men behind to bury the breed. Then they can catch up."

"It'd go faster if we all dug," Garfield said. "Motley can't get that far ahead of us."

"What makes you think that?"

He handed Seaforth Sequoia's rifle.

"One shot's been fired," he said. "I've got to believe he nicked Motley. So the rancher might be riding with a bullet in him."

"But Sequoia was shot in the back of the head."

"Still, I don't think that rancher could've ambushed him," Garfield said. "I didn't like the breed all that much, but I have to admit he was better than that."

Seaforth looked at the sky and sighed. There was no doubt that they were going to have to camp for the night, at some point.

"Okay," he said, "but make it fast. Get him in the ground and let's move."

Seaforth watched while the other four men dug a grave, wrapped Sequoia in a blanket, and lowered him in. That done, they all mounted up again.

"We don't have Sequoia to lead the way anymore," Garfield said.

"Walker, can you read sign?" Seaforth asked.

"I can," the man said.

"Then take point," Seaforth said.

"Yes, sir."

"We're not going to catch up to him today," Garfield said.

"I know that!" Seaforth snapped. "We'll camp soon, but let's get a few more miles under us. Maybe while we're camped the others will catch up to us."

"If they caught up to those other two," Garfield said.

They still didn't know for sure if they were actually on Big Jake Motley's trail, or following one of his men. If it wasn't Motley, Garfield knew that Seaforth was not going to be a happy man.

He hadn't been happy since he ran out of licorice.

J AKE FOUND A dry creek he thought he could camp in and be out of sight. It wouldn't hide his horse, but there was nothing he could do about that.

He could have used some hot food, but he dared not light a fire. For all he knew, Seaforth wasn't letting his men camp for the night. If they were still moving, they were going to catch up to him. That meant he could rest, but he could not sleep.

He had a supper of beef jerky and water, then settled in to try to let his body mend overnight. The wound certainly would not heal, but if it didn't bleed anymore that would be more than he could hope for.

B LOOD," WALKER SAID.

"Where?" Seaforth asked.

Walker pointed.

"There, on the ground," Walker said. "He's ridin' and bleedin'."

Seaforth looked at Garfield.

"You were right. Sequoia put a bullet in him." He looked at Walker. "Good job. Now keep going."

After another hour Walker turned and rode back to the others.

"He's stopped bleedin'," he told them. "I don't see any more blood on the ground."

Seaforth looked at the sky, sighed heavily.

"All right," he said, "we'll camp for the night." He pointed to the other two men. "You two gather wood and get the fire going. We'll have coffee, but we're only eating beef jerky."

"Yes, sir," they said.

"Walker, see to the horses."

"Yessir."

Seaforth and Garfield found a couple of rocks to sit on, watched the men as they set up camp.

"If he's got a bullet in him, we'll catch up to him tomorrow," Seaforth said.

"We better get an early start," Garfield said. "Depending on how bad his wound is, he's liable to sleep longer than he wants to."

"He can sleep as long as he wants," Seaforth said, "but he better not die on me. If we find Big Jake Motley and he's dead, I'll dig that breed up and kill him again."

Garfield knew he meant it.

JAKE WAS HOPING he wouldn't grow feverish during the night. If he did it would drain all the strength from him. He needed to greet the rising sun with some renewed vigor. Without it, he knew he was probably done. There would be no way he could get out of this Texas brush without getting caught by Seaforth and his men.

He was going to be relying heavily on the sorrel to keep him ahead of Seaforth's Raiders until he could come up with a plan. This hunt for Chance McCandless's killer was not going the way he had envisioned.

* * *

GARFIELD COULD HEAR Seaforth tossing and turning in his bedroll. Chasing Motley was starting to
get under his skin. The other three men were splitting
a watch—two hours each—and then they'd all have
some coffee and get moving. But Garfield knew he was
going to have to sleep. He had to be the one who was
rested. Seaforth, when he didn't sleep well and was out
of licorice, was short-tempered and jumpy, and that
was not going to help them catch Jake Motley. At least
Garfield didn't have to smell that sweet candy anymore.

And if they caught up to the rider they were following and it *wasn't* Motley, he didn't know how Seaforth
would react. That would probably be even worse than
if they found Motley dead.

SEAFORTH HOPED HIS second in command was getting
a good night's sleep, because he sure as hell wasn't.
He needed to find this rancher tomorrow and get rid
of him.

He was feeling the loss of his scout, Sequoia. Other
than Garfield, the breed had ridden with him the longest. Now they were going to have to do the best they
could with Walker at point. But the man had impressed
him when he found the drops of blood on the ground.

Seaforth rolled onto his left side, desperately seeking some sleep. This all had to end tomorrow with him
putting a bullet in Jake Motley's heart. That was the
only ending Seaforth Bailey was going to accept.

CHAPTER FORTY-ONE

BIG JAKE WOKE the next morning, had some water and beef jerky, and tried not to think about a hot cup of coffee. He had left the sorrel saddled all night, just in case he needed to make a fast getaway. Now he watered the animal before mounting up.

In the saddle he sat for a moment, took a deep breath, and tried to assess his condition. His left shoulder was sore, but the bleeding had stopped. The movement of his right side was not impaired. He picked up his rifle, lifted it, and aimed. The stock pressed to his right shoulder, which was natural, and he would normally hold the barrel with his left hand. It was painful, but he could do it. He put the rifle back in the scabbard. He was going to have to utilize his left hand and arm during the course of the day, just to keep it from stiffening up. His ability to use his pistol had not been affected.

Now it was time to see how much or little riding affected his wound.

* * *

MAJOR SEAFORTH WOKE to the smell of coffee. As he approached the fire Garfield turned and handed him a steaming cup.

"Thanks."

"The men wanted to make some bacon," Garfield said. "I told them no. They're getting the horses saddled."

Walker came over at that point.

"The horses are saddled."

Major Seaforth dumped the remainder of his coffee on the fire.

"Kill that fire and let's get going," he said.

"Yes, sir," Walker said. He took their cups, started kicking the fire to death.

Seaforth and Garfield walked over to the horses, which were being held by the other two men. The Major never could remember their names, but it didn't matter. They were just his Raiders and they did what he told them to do.

Walker came over and joined them.

"Walker, you take point again," Major Seaforth told him.

"Yessir."

"Mount up!" Garfield told the other two men while he and Seaforth did the same. "Today, this ends."

DUNDEE HAD QUICKLY dispatched his two pursuers with two sticks of dynamite, simply by lying in wait rather than running. Once that was done, he had ridden hell-bent-for-leather to join Curly and help him with his two. He had come up behind them and, with him and Curly catching them in a cross fire, eliminated them. That done, they began to ride back to the fork to figure out what to do next. Along the way they encountered Taco, coming toward them.

"What's goin' on?" Dundee asked. "We each only had two after us."

"They did not split into equal forces," Taco said. "There are six tracking Big Jake right now."

"Then he's in trouble," Curly said.

"Perhaps I should have said, he is tracking them." Taco explained how Jake had doubled back and gotten behind them.

"Still," Dundee said, "he's gonna need help."

"In that case," Taco said, "we should ride."

But as it got later they had to camp, and get some rest. Hopefully, Jake as well as Seaforth's Raiders had also camped.

They had spent the night, and in the morning all emptied the remnants of their cups onto the fire and used their boots to further extinguish it.

"Where do we go now?" Curly asked as they mounted up.

"We should head back to the fork, and go from there," Taco said. "I should be able to tell by the tracks who is tracking who."

"That's not really gonna matter," Dundee said. "We gotta get to Jake before he decides to take on six raiders by himself."

They each spurred their mount into a gallop.

JAKE DIDN'T LIKE the idea of an ambush, but he felt things might be getting to that point. If he could take out two of them before they knew what was happening, then the odds would be whittled down to three-to-one. Also, from a solid position, he had two rifles and a pistol to put to use.

He had his own Peacemaker revolver, and the 1876

Winchester, which held fifteen heavy-duty rounds. The rifle he had taken from the breed was a Winchester '73, which also held fifteen rounds, but of a lighter load. His '76 had a twenty-six-inch barrel, the '73 a twenty-three-inch. Both could be fired accurately at one hundred yards—if he was a good enough shot. Since he was not the marksman Chance McCandless had been, he might have to fire quickly, loosing as many rounds as possible to do as much damage as he could. But with thirty rounds at his disposal—.45-70s from his and .44-40s from the breed's—and six shots from his Peacemaker, he felt sure he would be effective.

As he rode he kept his eye out for a likely position, one that would afford him cover, and them none. With them out in the open, he might even be able to take three before they turned and ran. With any luck, one of them would be Seaforth, in which case he would be done and to hell with the rest of the raiders.

"THE TRAIL'S GETTIN' fresher," Walker said to Seaforth. "We're closin' in. If he's wounded he can't ride that fast. We should have him soon."

Seaforth looked at Garfield.

"You ride drag," he said. "I'm going to ride ahead with Walker. Keep the others ahead of you. I want to make sure they don't run if shooting starts."

"Do you think that's wise?" Garfield asked. "I mean, you riding point?"

"I want the first shot at him," Seaforth said. "As soon as we see him, I'm taking him right out of the saddle. I may not be as good a shot as you, but I'm good enough for this." He touched the stock of his Winchester '73, which he had provided for all his men. He considered it the finest rifle ever made.

"Okay, then," Garfield said. "Have it your way."

"I always do," Seaforth said.

I T WAS LATE afternoon when Big Jake broke from the Texas brush. The trail was more open ahead, with no thicket to speak of. All he needed was the right rock formation for cover, and he would be ready.

The longer he rode and withstood the ache in his left shoulder, the less offensive ambush became to him. After all, they had fired from a distance to kill Chance. In the end a coward should be killed by a coward's bullet—which did not always have to be fired by a coward.

W HEN TACO, DUNDEE, and Curly reached the fork, the two young men had to wait for the Mexican to examine the ground and read the sign.

"When they left here, they were tracking him," he said finally.

"Great," Curly said.

"Six of 'em?" Dundee asked.

"Sí, all six."

"He hasn't gotten to any of them yet," Curly said.

"That could be good news," Dundee said.

"How do you figure?" Curly asked

"It could mean they ain't got to him yet either," Dundee said.

"Either way," Taco said, "we must hurry."

With Taco to read the sign for them, they were able to travel at a brisk pace. After a few hours, Taco called their progress to a halt.

"What is it?" Dundee asked.

Taco pointed.

"A fresh grave."

Once he pointed, Dundee and Curly saw it. They dismounted and walked to it. Close up, they confirmed that it was, indeed, a grave.

"Aw, crap," Curly said. "You think it's Jake?"

"The only way to be sure is to dig it up and have a look," Dundee said.

"No," Taco said.

"Why not?" Dundee asked.

"If it is Señor Jake," Taco said, "I do not think Major Seaforth would have buried him, do you?"

Dundee looked at Curly.

"He has a point."

"So then Jake got one of them," Curly said.

"Sí."

"That's good," Dundee said. "We're down to five."

"Also, I believe Señor Jake is leading them somewhere," Taco said.

"Where?" Curly asked.

"I do not know, but I believe we will soon break from this brush country into the open."

"Where there's no cover?" Dundee asked.

"There is always cover, Señor Dundee," Taco said. "You just have to find it. And Señor Jake will."

They continued to ride.

A S MAJOR SEAFORTH's Raiders broke from the brush they stopped.

"What's going on?" Garfield asked, riding up to join Walker and Seaforth.

"We're gonna be out in the open from here on," Walker said.

"So is Motley," Seaforth said. "And without that brush to hinder us, we can ride faster than he can with a bullet in him." He looked at Garfield. "He's worried," he said, indicating Walker.

"That's not what he's getting paid to do," Garfield observed.

"Right you are." Seaforth looked at Walker. "Go ahead, lead on."

Walker took a deep breath, let it out, and spurred his horse into a trot. The others followed, with Seaforth riding just behind him.

J AKE FOUND HIS SPOT.
It was an outcropping of rocks that he could not only hide his horse behind, but climb up with relative ease, considering his wound and the fact that he was carrying two rifles and a canteen. Once he got to the top, he lay down on his belly, set the canteen and rifles down next to him.

He had no idea how long it would be before the raiders showed up. In fact, he didn't even know if they would. It was possible they had given up the chase, but considering Seaforth's arrogance, he didn't think that was likely. So he was committed now, and had no choice but to wait it out. Every so often he would pick up one of the rifles and sight down the barrel, flex his arm to be sure he'd be able to extend it when the time came. He would take a sip of water every so often, trying to keep the sun from drying him out. But if this took long enough, and he ran out of water, he would have to consider packing it in, moving on, and finding another location—and some water.

E VERY SO OFTEN they would come to a dry creek or gully they thought might afford Jake Motley some cover. Each time, Seaforth would send Walker on ahead to check. Each time, Walker waited for the impact of a bullet, which never came. He rode back and reported no one was hiding there, and they continued on.

As late afternoon came Garfield could see that Major Seaforth's patience had begun to wear paper-thin. This had to end soon, either with Jake Motley's death, or by giving up the entire idea of killing him. This was Seaforth Bailey's personal vendetta, and it had already cost many lives, including that of Sequoia, who was a valuable member of the raiders.

As far as Teddy Garfield was concerned, the price was becoming too high. Seaforth was getting to the point where he'd do anything to accomplish his mission, and that wasn't sitting well with his *segundo* anymore.

On the other hand, Seaforth also knew he had paid a high price to this point, and to him that made it imperative that they succeed. To admit failure and turn back would mean all of the dead raiders had died for no reason. Or worse, they had died because of his personal vanity.

CHAPTER FORTY-TWO

JAKE HEARD THEM before he saw them.

Five men on horseback, pushing their mounts, could be heard from a distance. The dust cloud they were generating could also be seen. Doubly warned of their approach, Jake was ready with his Winchester '76, sighting along the barrel and waiting . . .

EARLIER, GARFIELD HAD decided to finally try to take some sort of control. He rode up alongside Seaforth.

"I think it's time for you to drop back," he said.

"What?"

"Ride drag with me, Sea," Garfield said. "If you're riding point, he could take you out with the first shot."

"From ambush?" Seaforth said. "He's not going to ambush us, Gar. Not Big Jake Motley. That old codger's got too much integrity."

"Humor me, Sea," Garfield said. "Keep me company in the rear for a while."

"You're serious?"

"Dead serious."

Seaforth turned to Walker.

"You stay on point," he said, "I'm going to drop back for a while."

"Yessir."

Garfield and Seaforth slowed down until they were riding behind Walker and the other two men . . .

JAKE SPOTTED THE five men in the distance and, momentarily, had second thoughts about the ambush. He could've just let them ride by, and then head south again and forget all about the matter. By the time they realized they'd lost him, he would be far enough away for it to be all over and would never again encounter Seaforth's Raiders.

But they would still be out there, wreaking havoc on their little part of Texas, unpunished for the shooting of Chance McCandless.

The moment passed . . .

I DON'T LIKE THIS, Garfield said.

"What?" Seaforth asked.

"We're too vulnerable," Garfield said, scanning the horizon ahead of them. "Every so often there's a place he could hide."

"Hide?" Seaforth said.

"He could hide himself and ambush us," Garfield complained, "or he could hide himself and let us ride by, double back again. Then we'd never catch him."

"Not that old man," Seaforth said. "He's not going to give up. He's not going to hide, or ambush us. He's going to want to kill me face-to-face."

"He may have started out wanting that, but he's not going to get it to be just him and you. The odds are going to be against him every time. I'm telling you, he'll have to change his tactics."

"Tactics?" Seaforth said. "You make it sound like we're going up against a soldier, not a rancher."

"Face it, Sea," Garfield said. "The man's outsmarted us twice. First with the herd, and then back in town, with the dynamite."

"I won't face that!" Seaforth snapped. "And if you're going to keep talking that way, I'll go back and ride up front with Walker."

Only, as he urged his horse on faster, the first shot came, and there was no more Walker . . .

JAKE LET THEM get inside a hundred yards . . . seventy-five yards . . . fifty yards . . . in fact, he allowed them to almost draw abreast of his position and then started to fire his Winchester as fast as he could lever fresh rounds into the chamber.

The lead man went down under the first volley. His horse screamed as the rider fell to the dirt. The two men behind him froze just long enough for Jake to fire another volley into them. Forty-five-70 slugs tore into their chests, yanking them both from their horses. The animals reared and twirled, unsure of which way to run off. As Jake set down his rifle and picked up the second, the three riderless horses turned and finally decided to head back—and right into the other two riders.

As their own mounts collided with the panicky horses, both Garfield and Seaforth were knocked from their saddles. They both landed on the dirt hard, but the next volley of shots passed over their heads. Falling from their horses had saved their lives.

* * *

JAKE SAW THE collision, realized his shots had missed the two men who were now on the ground. He recognized one of them as Seaforth.

While they scrabbled around on the ground looking for some kind of cover, he reloaded both rifles. By the time he was ready, one of them had shot one of the horses, and they were now crouching behind the carcass.

AN AMBUSH!" GARFIELD said. "He'd never ambush us, right?"

"Jesus!" Seaforth said. "You shot my horse."

"We needed the cover," Garfield said. "And, it kept him from running off with the others, so we've got this." He reached over and pulled Seaforth's rifle from its scabbard.

"One rifle," Seaforth said. "It sounds like he's got a dozen."

"He's got two," Garfield said. "Fifteen rounds each, Probably Winchesters."

"You counted?" Seaforth asked.

"I guess so," Garfield said, looking up over the horse. "He's up in those rocks."

"He's gone crazy, ambushin' us like this," Seaforth said.

"You think he's lost his integrity?" Garfield asked. "We tried to steal his herd, killed his friend, and now he's got a bullet in him? That pretty much changes a man, don't you think?"

"Why don't you shut up," Seaforth said, "and figure out a way to get him down from there?"

Garfield looked around. There wasn't much cover for them. Motley had picked a good spot for his ambush. He looked over at the other three men lying on the ground, obviously dead. The only good they would do was if he and Seaforth could reach them and grab their guns. But still, they only had one rifle, and handguns weren't going to do much good in this situation, unless they could get closer.

Which they couldn't do because there was no damn cover!

J AKE WATCHED.
    It was all he could do at the moment. The next move was going to have to be theirs. The other three were dead, the horses were gone, Seaforth and his man probably had one rifle between them. He looked back down at his own horse, to make sure he was still there and hadn't pulled himself loose amid all the shooting. The sorrel looked back up at him calmly.

Jake's shoulder ached from firing the rifle. He levered and pulled the trigger with his right hand, but had to keep the left extended, firing the whole time, and now it was aching. He looked inside his shirt to see if he had started bleeding again. There seemed to be some seepage, but not much.

He hadn't known when he started shooting exactly where Seaforth was. Now he realized the man had been riding drag, and when the riderless horses panicked and ran, they pushed Seaforth back farther. It looked like his and his man's position behind the dead horse was about twenty yards away. Their only logical next move was to try to get to the base of the rocks, where Jake couldn't see them. At that point, they would have him trapped up on top, and they would have his horse.

If they both broke from cover and ran for the rocks at the same time, he might get one of them. If he did, what would the other one do? Grab his horse and ride? Or wait for a chance at him when he came down?

* * *

"Y OU WANT TO what?" Seaforth asked.

"Run for those rocks," Garfield said.

"Right toward him?"

"That's right."

"And what's that going to accomplish?"

"Listen," Garfield said, "you go right, I'll go left. He can't get both of us."

"But of the two of us, which one do you think he'll try for?" Seaforth asked.

"What does that matter?" Garfield asked. "If we're fast enough, he won't get either of us."

"He wants me," Seaforth said, "and you're the one who shot his partner."

"Because you ordered me to," Garfield said. "Besides, he doesn't know who I am."

"You're obviously my *segundo*," Seaforth said.

"But he doesn't know my name," Garfield said. "And I bet if I stand up and walk away, he'll stay where he is and wait for you."

"You would do that?"

"I don't want to," Garfield said. "I want the two of us to take him, bring him down off his perch."

"By running right at him."

"Yes," Garfield said, "with any luck we'll surprise him, and he'll freeze with indecision just long enough."

"Okay, how do you want to play it?" Seaforth asked.

"Handguns," Garfield said, taking his from his belt. "We fire as we run. They may not be as accurate as a rifle, but we might throw some stone chips up into his face. We get to the base of the rocks, where he can't see us, and work our way around. I'll bet his horse is there, and that's where he climbed up from."

"And where he'll have to come down."

"Yes."

"And if he happens to kill one of us?"

"Then the other has a choice," Garfield said. "Take his horse and run, to possibly fight another day, or stand and fight, man-to-man."

Seaforth looked around them, could see no other cover. The only other option would be standing and running back the other way.

"What's the nearest town?" he asked.

"Probably San Antonio," Garfield said, "but too far to walk."

And if a man ran long enough, heading south, eventually he'd be on foot in the Texas brush.

Seaforth looked around again, this time hoping to spy a horse that might not have run off so far. There were none in sight.

No matter how long he waited, or how hard he tried, he could not come up with a viable, alternate plan to what Garfield proposed.

"Well?" Garfield asked. "What's it going to be?"

Seaforth looked at his *segundo* and said, "On the count of three?"

CHAPTER FORTY-THREE

I T WAS TOO quiet.

Jake was sweating, his shoulder was aching, and his vision was getting fuzzy. He had one mouthful of water left in his canteen that he was saving, but he had to drink it now. It was while he was drinking that mouthful, holding the canteen with his right hand, that Seaforth and his man decided to move.

They broke from cover and started for the rocks, one from the right and one from the left. As they ran they fired their pistols. Jake dropped the canteen and it went tumbling down to the ground. He grabbed up his rifle and started to fire, even before he realized the man on the left was Seaforth.

And then they were out of sight, and he didn't know if he had hit either of them.

Damn!

O N THREE, THEY both broke from cover, one running left and one running right, firing their handguns as they ran. Surprisingly, Motley didn't start shooting immediately, but then the shots started coming, landing in the dirt around them. When they reached the base of the rocks, they pressed their backs to them.

"You hit?" Garfield yelled.

"No, you?"

Garfield looked down at himself.

"No. Jesus, he didn't hit either one of us?"

"I guess not."

But when Garfield looked at Seaforth, he saw the blood on his left side.

"Sea, you *were* hit," he said.

"No, I wasn't," Seaforth said, reloading his gun.

"Yeah, you were," Garfield insisted. "Look."

"Huh?" Seaforth looked at him, then at where he was pointing, down at his left side. "Oh, hell!"

He put his left hand down to the blood, then lifted it and looked.

"I'm bleeding."

"Yeah, you are."

Things were changing for Garfield. If Seaforth died, he didn't care about Jake Motley. In fact, he had been trying to make up his mind whether or not to quit Seaforth. After all these years, the man seemed to have lost his edge. Now he had a bullet in him and was bleeding like a stuck pig. As he watched, the blood began to run down the leg of Seaforth's pants, dripping onto his boot. He'd been hit good.

So where they were, Seaforth had a bullet in him, and Motley probably had Sequoia's bullet in him. Garfield suddenly realized he was on his own.

"Gar—"

"I'll go around this way," Garfield said, "and you go that way. After we take care of him, I'll take care of you."

"Gar!" Seaforth called as the man turned and disappeared around the rock. Seaforth turned to do the same, but went down to one knee as his legs failed him.

JAKE COULD HEAR the two men talking at the base of the rocks, but couldn't make out the words. He only hoped that he had wounded at least one of them.

He turned and looked down at his horse, decided to try to get to him and wait for Seaforth and his man to come around. He could end this long ordeal—from the trail drive to now. Plus, he didn't want to take a chance of being trapped on that rock.

He started down, carrying the two rifles. Suddenly his right foot slipped and instead of descending slowly, he slid down on his ass with alarming speed. When he hit the bottom, he immediately knew his shoulder had started to bleed again. Stunned, he tried to regain his composure, but suddenly Seaforth's man was there, looking down at him. He had dropped both rifles when he landed, and now all he had was his holstered handgun, but Seaforth's man already had his gun in hand.

So it would end this way . . .

GARFIELD CAME AROUND the rock just in time to see Jake Motley hit the ground. There were two rifles lying out of his reach, and a gun in his holster. He pointed his gun at the fallen man.

But he didn't pull the trigger.

"Major Seaforth's around the front of this hunk of rock," he said. "You both have a bullet in you. You're on equal terms. And I'm taking my leave of the whole situation."

He smiled and waved, sprang onto the sorrel's saddle.

"Good luck, Big Jake."

He laid his heels to the sorrel and galloped off.

"Oh, damn," Jake swore. He didn't know what he regretted most, the bullet wound in his shoulder or losing that sorrel.

He crawled over to the rifles and grabbed his. He had no way of knowing how much truth was in what Seaforth's man had said, but he had to find out.

He staggered to his feet and, leaning against the rock, started working his way to the front.

S EAFORTH TRIED TO get to his feet, leaning against the rock, but his legs buckled again and he was back on his knees. He had dropped his rifle, and now in haste drew his pistol from his belt, not knowing where Garfield or Jake Motley was.

"Gar!" he shouted.

He moved from his knees to a seated position, his left hand pressed to the wound to try to stop the flow, and his right holding his pistol. He kept looking left and right, not knowing from which side Jake Motley would appear. Or would there be a shot? Gar killing Big Jake? Jake killing Gar? Who would come around and find him sitting there in a spreading pool of his own blood? Goddamn Jake Motley, this was all his fault. All he had to do was give up that goddamned herd.

Then he heard someone scraping along the rock, and turned to see Big Jake Motley come around from the right side, where Garfield had disappeared.

Big Jake was staggering, bleeding from a wound in his shoulder.

"Ah," Seaforth said, "we're even."

"That's what your man said."

"Have a seat, then," Seaforth said, "and let's see who bleeds to death first."

* * *

B IG JAKE HAD made his way slowly around the rock, and when he came to the front he saw Major Seaforth sitting there in a puddle of blood.

And when Seaforth said, ". . . let's see who bleeds to death first," Jake pointed his gun at the man and said, "You win!"

B UT YOU'RE KILLING the wrong man," Seaforth said. Jake slid down onto his butt, but kept the gun trained on Seaforth.

"How's that?"

"Where's Garfield?"

"Is that your *segundo*?"

"That's him, Teddy Garfield," Seaforth said. "I didn't hear a shot between you."

"That's because he told me you were hit, got on my horse, and left."

"Well, that's too bad, then," Seaforth said. "There went your opportunity."

"To do what?"

"To kill the man who shot your friend off his horse."

"That was you," Jake said, gesturing with his gun.

Seaforth also had a pistol in his hand, Jake saw, but didn't seem to have the strength to lift it.

"No," Seaforth said, "I could never have made that shot. It was Gar who did it. He can shoot the wings off a fly. It was an easy shot for him."

Jake's finger tightened on the trigger. He felt blood flowing from his shoulder, down his arm, just as the blood flowed down Seaforth's leg.

"Are you tellin' me the truth?" he demanded.

Seaforth laughed weakly.

"At this point why lie?" he asked. "Okay, you've put

a bullet in me, and I'll probably die, but you missed the man you've really been after all this time."

Jake believed the man. But he pulled the trigger, anyway. That fella Garfield might have made the shot, but Jake was sure Seaforth had told him to do it. So they had both killed Chance McCandless.

His bullet went into Seaforth's temple and knocked him over.

Jake knew he had to live. He still had Chance's killer to track down. All he needed was to close his eyes and get some rest, first.

He keeled over onto his side and lay there, a mirror image of Major Seaforth Bailey.

CHAPTER FORTY-FOUR

W HEN JAKE WOKE it was dark, and there was a fire
going.

"What the hell . . ." he choked out.

"He's awake!" Curly shouted.

Taco and Dundee came running over. Taco lifted
Jake's head and put a canteen to his mouth.

"Drink, señor," he said. "When we found you we
thought you were both dead."

Jake swallowed some water, then said, "Very nearly."

Taco set his head back down.

"Sit me up," Jake said.

"You should stay down—" Dundee started, but Jake
cut him off.

"Sit me up, dammit!"

Dundee and Curly both helped him into a seated position. Jake felt something against his back and leaned.

"Where are we?" he asked.

"Right where we found you," Dundee said. "But
we're on the other side of the rock. Seaforth's in front,
dead. We left him there."

"We figure you got up on top and ambushed 'em," Curly said.

"Not proud of it, but yeah," Jake said.

"We count five," Dundee said. "Including Seaforth himself. So you got 'im."

"There was a sixth," Jake said. "His *segundo*, Teddy Garfield."

"What happened to him?" Dundee asked.

"Got on my horse and lit out. Said he was leavin' me and Seaforth on equal terms, each with a bullet in us. Had me under his gun, but instead of killin' me he rode off."

"Why would he do that?"

"Said he'd had enough."

"Perhaps it was true," Taco said.

"Maybe it was, but I can't let him go."

"Because of the horse?" Dundee asked. "We got you another one. Found it wandering around out there."

"No, not the horse," Jake said. "He's actually the man who killed Chance."

"I thought it was Seaforth," Dundee said.

"It was both," Jake said, "but Garfield's the one who actually took the shot."

"How the hell do you know that?" Curly asked.

"Seaforth told me."

"And you believed 'im?" Dundee asked.

"I did," Jake said. "He was dying, he had no reason to lie. And the man left 'im."

"Señor," Taco said, "perhaps he simply did not want this Garfield to get away with leaving him."

"No," Jake said, "I believed him. Still do. I gotta go after him."

"You're pretty stove up, Jake," Dundee said. "You were bleedin' when we found ya."

"Did you patch me up?"

"Taco did," Dundee said, "pretty good, too."

"The bullet went right through, señor," Taco said. "The wound looks clean."

"Then I'll be ready to ride in the mornin'," Jake said. "You boys take care of the others who were trailin' you?"

"All dead, Jake," Dundee said.

"Taco, I'll need you to track this varmint for me."

"Sí, señor," the Mexican said. "Absolutamente."

"And what about us?" Dundee asked.

"You boys have done your part," Jake said. "You're finished."

"What if we don't wanna be finished?" Dundee asked.

"What if we wanna see it through to the end?" Curly asked.

"Then I'll say thank you in advance," Jake said.

"Señor, you should lie down and get some rest. I will wake you to eat. You must regain your strength."

"Ya, you're right, Taco," Jake said. Dundee and Curly both helped him lie on his healthy side.

They woke him two hours later to feed him some beans and coffee, and then let him drift off to sleep again, this time for the night.

WHADAYA THINK, TACO?" Dundee asked later. "You known him the longest."

"I believe Señor Jake knows what he is doing," Taco said. "If he says this *hijo de puta*, Garfield, killed Señor Chance, then I believe him."

"*Hijo de* . . . what?" Curly asked.

"You would say . . . sonofabitch, señor."

"Oh, yeah."

"And he'll keep chasin' 'im?" Dundee asked.

"Oh, sí, señor," Taco said. "Until one or both of them are dead."

"Okay, then," Dundee said. "I guess that's it."

"You think he's gonna be able to ride in the mornin'?" Curly asked.

"I think he will ride," Taco said, "if he is able, or no."

IN THE MORNING they saddled the horses before waking Jake.

When he did wake they let him gather himself and get to his feet on his own, then sat him at the fire with a pan of bacon and beans and a cup of coffee.

"Where'd you get this stuff?" Jake asked.

"We had it in our saddlebags," Dundee said. "Curly had the beans, I had the bacon."

"How come I didn't know till now?"

"Well," Dundee said, "after we got it, you started runnin' cold camps."

"But now it don't make a difference," Curly said.

"And you need the nourishment, señor," Taco added.

Jake wolfed down the plate and ate another one, then had more coffee.

"Can you ride?" Dundee asked.

"I'll ride," Jake said. "What am I ridin'?"

"One of them raiders had a steeldust. We found it wanderin' around."

"Any good?"

"It'll do," Dundee said.

Taco and Dundee broke camp while Curly saddled the horses. They walked the steeldust over to Jake, then helped him up into the saddle.

"This saddle is shit," Jake said.

"The good news is," Dundee said, "there's money in the saddlebags. Enough to buy a new saddle first chance we get."

"Must've been his share from some job they pulled," Curly said.

"Might even be enough for a new horse." Dundee laughed.

"I don't want a new horse," Jake said. "I want that sorrel."

"What was in your saddlebags?" Dundee asked.

"Nothin' important. Just the usual."

"Not your money?" Dundee asked.

"I carry my money on me, not in my saddlebags."

"Good thought," Curly said.

Taco came walking over to them.

"I have the trail, señor. I recognize the tracks left by your horse."

"Good," Jake said. "Let's get movin.'"

They all mounted up.

W HAT'S THE NEAREST town?" Dundee asked, after they had ridden only an hour.

"San Antonio," Taco said.

"That's a big place," Curly said. "Would he go there?"

"Why not?" Jake asked. "Big place, lots of people to hide among."

"Maybe he is not hiding," Taco said.

They were riding just behind him, and he spoke over his shoulder.

"Whadaya mean?" Dundee asked.

"He might think that both Seaforth and Señor Jake are dead," Taco said. "Or that Señor Jake killed Seaforth, and would not be coming after him."

"Or the other way around," Dundee said.

"No," Jake said.

They all looked at him.

"He was sure Seaforth was dying," Jake said. "He could have thought I might be, but he must've been sure I'd kill Seaforth, or he'd die before I got to him."

"So you don't think he's hidin'?" Curly asked.

"No," Jake said, "I think he's just ridin'."

"He is going in the direction of San Antonio," Taco said. "But there will be other towns along the way."

"Smaller ones," Dundee said. "It would be easier to find him in one of them."

"If we catch up to him before he reached San Antonio," Jake said.

"That'll depend on how long he stops at one of the smaller ones," Dundee said. "For a meal and a beer, no good. But if he spends the night, maybe buys a whore . . ."

"Then let's hope he wants to satisfy all his urges," Jake said.

THEY CAMPED THE first night, and once again Taco made a meal of beans and coffee. Jake ached from riding, but didn't let on. He ate, and then turned in, lying on his bedroll on his right side. He fell asleep quickly and didn't hear the others discussing setting up a watch.

"We don't know what this fella, Garfield, is thinkin'," Dundee said. "He could be watchin' his trail, might've picked up the dust we've been sendin' up."

"So you think he'll come back in the dark instead of just increasing his pace?" Curly asked.

"Who knows?" Dundee asked.

"Señores," Taco said, "if I may say?"

"Sure, Taco, go ahead."

"Remembering the way he killed Señor Chance," Taco said, "I believe if and when he realizes we are tracking him, he will fire on us from a distance, hoping to pick us off one by one."

"That makes sense," Dundee said, looking at Curly. "Why take a chance on gettin' close to the four of us?"

"We could still set watches," Curly said. "It wouldn't hurt."

"I agree," Taco said.

"Okay, then," Dundee said. "Three hours each. That way Jake gets nine hours rest."

"He will not like that when he wakes," Taco said, with a smile.

"That'll be too bad," Dundee said. "I'll take the first watch."

"Wake me in three hours," Curly said.

"I will make a pot full of coffee before I turn in," Taco said.

"Good," Dundee said, "we'll need it."

Taco worked on the coffee while Curly went and turned in away from the light of the fire.

"There," Taco said. "That should be enough to get us through the night."

"Get some sleep, amigo," Dundee said.

Taco nodded and went to his bedroll.

Dundee picked up his rifle and sat by the fire, holding it across his knees.

CHAPTER FORTY-FIVE

They camped a second night, and came to a small town called Beckett on the third day. There was no indication that Garfield had stopped there, but they decided to see if a doctor was available. There was, and while Taco took Jake to the office of a Doctor Lyons, Dundee and Curly went to see if they could get some supplies.

"See if you can find me a better saddle," Jake told them. "My ass is killin' me!"

"Right, boss," Dundee said.

In the doctor's office they found a man about Jake's age playing checkers with another, middle-aged man. He stopped when they came in and took Jake right back to his examining room.

"You play?" the man asked Taco.

"Sure."

Taco sat across from the man to set up his black checkers, and saw the sheriff's badge on the man's chest.

"How'd your friend catch that bullet?" the sheriff asked while they played.

"Ambush," Taco lied.

"By who?"

"We're not sure," Taco said, "but we are tracking the man."

"You the tracker?"

"I am."

"And he came here?"

"No," Taco said, "but he passed near here, and we wanted a doctor."

"Doc Lyons's good at his job," the sheriff said. "Your friend's in good hands. King me."

TACO LOST THREE games of checkers to the sheriff by the time Jake and the doctor came out. Jake's arm was in a black sling.

"I've stitched the wound closed," the doctor told Taco, who stood up. "He should spend the next week in bed, but he's explained to me why he can't."

"Anythin' I should know?" the sheriff asked.

"No, Carson," the doctor said.

The sheriff shrugged and set up both sides of the checkerboard for another game.

"Thanks, Doctor," Jake said. "I feel better already."

He and Taco stepped outside.

"Let's find the others and get back on the trail," Jake said.

"Señor, can we stop for a beer?"

"Sure," Jake said. "After we find the others."

"And how about a new shirt, señor?" Taco asked. "That one is very bloody."

THEY SAW DUNDEE's and Curly's horses in front of a saloon, and found them at the bar, having a beer. Jake was already wearing his new clean shirt.

"There they are!" Dundee said as they walked in. "How's the shoulder, Jake?"

"The doc fixed it up. We figured to have a beer and then get back on the trail. Looks like you beat us to it."

"Bartender!" Curly yelled. "Beers for my friends."

When the barman put them down Taco grabbed his and drained half of it gratefully. Jake had a feeling Dundee and Curly were on more than their second.

"Let's finish these and get goin'," he said, sipping his. "Did you find me a new saddle?"

"Not in this town," Curly said. "The one you've got is actually better than anythin' we saw here."

"Fine," Jake said. "I'll make do."

"Jake," Dundee said, "don't you think you oughta take at least one night in a real bed?"

"I wanna get this over with, Dundee," Jake said. "I'm thinkin' if we keep goin' we'll catch up to him in San Antonio. But if you fellas want a night in a hotel bed, don't let me stop you."

"No," Dundee said, putting his beer down, "we're with ya, Jake. Finish your beer and we'll get goin'."

"We bought some more beans and coffee," Curly said.

"So we're set."

"What happened at the doc's?" Dundee asked.

"Taco played checkers with the local sheriff while the sawbones patched me up," Jake said.

"The law?" Curly said, looking at Taco. "What did he have to say?"

"'King me,'" Taco said, "a lot."

THEY FINISHED THEIR beers, mounted up, and rode out of Beckett, with Jake in much better shape. When they camped that night he sat at the fire with them, ate beans, and took a two-hour watch. The next day they bypassed an even smaller town than Beckett, because the trail left by Jake's sorrel went right past it.

That night when they camped Jake took the time to clean his rifle and pistol, making sure they were in good working order. He figured they would make San Antonio the next day, and there would sure as hell be more gunplay.

"We're gonna lose the trail as we ride in," Dundee said. "The streets of San Antone are pretty busy."

"Taco'll do his best," Jake said. "All we need to know is if he rode into town."

"And then just where do we start lookin' for him?" Curly asked.

"Hotels," Jake said, "liveries, saloons . . . and whorehouses."

"You think he's got hisself a destination in mind?" Dundee asked.

"Seems to me he made a split-second decision back there," Jake said.

"And that was?" Curly asked.

"That Seaforth Bailey wasn't the man he thought he was," Jake said, "and he sure as hell wasn't worth dyin' for. But now I think he's driftin'."

"And not runnin'," Dundee said.

"If he thought he was gonna hafta run, he woulda killed me," Jake said.

"I still don't understand why he didn't," Dundee said, shaking his head.

"Well," Jake said, "maybe when we catch up to 'im you can ask 'im . . . before I kill 'im."

As they had expected, the sorrel's trail led right into San Antonio. And as Dundee had predicted, there it was gobbled up by the tracks left by other horses, mules, oxen, and wagons.

They rode down Commerce Street, which ran parallel to the San Antonio River. The street was lined with shops, saloons, cafés, and hotels. San Antonio's infamy stemmed from the fact that the Battle of the Alamo took place outside of town in 1836, when 189 men, barricaded in the Alamo Mission, fought for independence from Mexico against 5,000 of Santa Ana's men, who defeated them and killed them all. But this was of no interest or concern to Jake and the others as they entered town. Their only concern was finding the man Seaforth had called Teddy Garfield.

They stopped at a livery to put up their horses, and questioned the hostler about strangers arriving over the past couple of days. Of course, it was too much to ask that Garfield might have boarded his horse at the same place.

They left the livery and stopped at the nearest hotel, called the River House.

They got three rooms, one for Jake, one for Taco, and one for Dundee and Curly. As they went up the stairs to the second floor Curly asked. "What if he didn't stop?"

They hesitated halfway up, the other three turning to look at him.

"I mean, what if he came here, had a meal and a beer, maybe a poke, and then kept goin'?"

"If he did that," Jake said, "this hunt is gonna take a lot longer. But I'm thinkin' now that he's on his own, without Seaforth, without the raiders, he's gonna wanna set a spell and figure out his next move."

"I hope you're right," Curly said.

As they started back up the stairs, Jake was hoping he was right, too.

A FTER THEY LEFT their gear in their rooms, they all went down to the hotel dining room, where they had steak dinners. While eating, Jake explained that he thought they should split up.

"We'll cover more ground that way," he explained. "If we don't locate him tonight, we'll keep lookin' tomorrow. If we don't find him then, we'll have to figure our next move."

"The only problem with that is," Dundee said, "you're the only one who knows what he looks like."

"I know what he looks like," Taco said. "I saw him when they had me in Three Rivers."

"Hey, that's right," Dundee said. "So you and Jake both saw him."

"Okay," Jake said, "we'll split into twos, then. Taco, you take Dundee, and Curly, you come with me. I could describe him to you, but there's bound to be a dozen men in this town who look like him."

"That sounds like a plan," Dundee said.

"And if you boys see him," Jake said, to Taco and Dundee, "don't approach 'im. Don't let him know he's been spotted. Just come and find me and Curly."

"And then we'll take 'im?" Curly asked.

"And then I'll take 'im," Jake said. "I owe this to Chance, and I'm gonna do it myself. Is that understood?"

Dundee shrugged.

"As long as it's man-to-man, I don't have a problem with that," he said. "My only problem was when he had the backin' of the raiders."

"Sí, señor," Taco said. "Mano a mano it shall be."

"You bet it will," Jake said.

CHAPTER FORTY-SIX

They left the hotel and split up, deciding Jake and Curly would take liveries and hotels while Taco and Dundee searched saloons and whorehouses.

"Why do they get the saloons and whorehouses?" Curly complained.

"Because Taco doesn't get drunk, and he's got a wife in Mexico."

"Really? A wife? He never mentioned her."

"He doesn't like to talk about it," Jake said. "She has a big family, which is why he tries to stay away as often as he can."

"Well, Dundee likes to drink and whore," Curly said.

"That's why I sent him with Taco," Jake said. "That little Mex will keep him on the right track."

"And you'll do the same for me?" Curly asked.

"That's right," Jake said. "You two are young men, with the urges of young men."

"Well," Curly said, "we can control ourselves until this is all over."

Jake patted Curly on the shoulder and said, "That's good to hear."

J AKE AND CURLY went to three liveries, and six hotels, without finding any sign of Teddy Garfield. As it started to get dark, Jake decided they should return to their hotel and see if Taco and Dundee were there.

"Wait," Curly said. "What about that place?"

Jake looked in the direction Curly was pointing. Because it was dark the city's lights had been ignited, and the hotels and saloons that were still open were not well lit. The one they were looking at in particular was almost incandescent.

"That looks like the kind of place anybody visitin' this town would want to go to."

"Taco and Dundee are supposed to be checking saloons," Jake pointed out, "but let's take a look, anyway."

As they approached they saw a sign up on top of the two-story building that read the Crockett Saloon, Casino, and Show Palace.

The word "casino" came from the Italian word for house, *casa*. Casino meant "little house."

When they got to the front entrance they could hear the music from inside, and the sound of men yelling. As they entered they saw girls dancing on a stage in front of the huge, brightly lit room. Crystal chandeliers hanging from the ceiling added to the brightness as they reflected the light from the large hanging lamps.

"This place is pretty modern!" Curly shouted.

"Yeah," Jake called back, "the lamps look electric."

There seemed to be dozens of tables set up with customers, men who were shouting at the girls onstage as they kicked up their heels and hiked up their skirts.

Off to the left was a long bar with men leaning

against it, holding their drinks and watching the action onstage. Off to the right was a doorway with a red sign above it that read casino.

Jake studied the men at the bar, saw that none of them was Garfield. He could have been sitting at a table, watching the girls dance, but there didn't seem to be any tables occupied by a lone man, and Jake doubted Garfield had been in San Antonio long enough to make friends. Of course, he could have come there to meet up with somebody, but Jake doubted he'd had the time to set that up.

"Let's go in the casino," he said, putting his mouth near Curly's ear. "It'll be quieter."

Curly nodded, and they walked to the door under the red sign. It was an open doorway, but already it seemed quieter.

Jake looked around, saw every gaming table possible, with roulette, blackjack, faro, poker, dice. He could hear the chips on the tables, and the sound of the white ball bouncing around on the roulette wheel.

He started to walk around the room, with Curly following, staying near the wall as he looked at table after table.

"Sonofabitch," he breathed. He stopped walking and Curly almost ran into him.

"What?" the younger man asked.

"That blackjack table, with the girl dealin'," Jake said.

"A girl dealer," Curly said. "What's next?"

"Not the girl," Jake said. "The man on the second seat from the left."

"Is that him?" Curly asked.

"That's him," Jake said. "That's Garfield."

It was the man who'd had him under his gun, and hadn't pulled the trigger. Instead, he'd left him there to have it out with Seaforth.

"So whadda we do?" Curly asked. "You wanna walk over there and shoot 'im?"

"We do that, we end up in jail," Jake said. "I want 'im, but I don't wanna go to jail for it."

"Well," Curly said, "we could walk up to him, stick a gun in his back, and walk him outside."

"Somebody'll see us," Jake said, "or he'll force a shoot-up in here, where innocent people could get hurt."

"So whadaya wanna do?"

"What we've been doin'," Jake said. "Follow him. You stay here and follow him out."

"Where are you gonna be?"

"Outside," Jake said. "I don't wanna take a chance of him seein' me."

"Got it," Curly said. "I'll see you outside."

"Right." Jake started to walk away.

"How long are we gonna wait?" Curly asked quickly.

"As long as it takes," Jake said.

J AKE CONSIDERED WAITING in the saloon and show palace for Garfield to come out, but he hadn't noticed if there was another way out of the casino. So instead, he went out to the street. The front of the Alamo was well lit, and there was indeed another door farther down for the casino. Jake crossed the street and found a darkened doorway from where he could wait and watch.

The street was fairly busy, even though it was after hours and all the shops were closed. But there were enough saloons to keep men walking on the boardwalk and crossing the streets. Occasionally someone would ride in, in search of fun or frolic. There was a group of horses in front of the show palace.

Jake realized if one of the horses belonged to Garfield, they would lose him if he mounted up—unless Jake stole a horse and followed him. But hopefully, the man was a walk away from whatever hotel he was staying in.

He'd been dead serious when he told Curly they would wait as long as it took. It was a good two hours before Garfield appeared in front of the door of the casino. He was cooperative enough to pause and light a cigarette, adding illumination to his face, so Jake could properly identify him.

He could have shot the man from hiding, but then Garfield wouldn't know what hit him. And he wanted the man to know who was killing him, and why.

As he feared, Garfield started walking toward a group of horses that were tied to a hitching post. Jake was not going to be able to follow him to wherever he was staying. He was going to have to move now.

He stepped from his doorway and crossed the street as Garfield reached the horses and began to reach for one. That was when Jake saw the sorrel in their midst. At the same time, Curly came out the casino door, and several men exited the show palace, which meant there would be witnesses.

That was a good thing.

Jake moved his pistol from his holster to his belt before stepping into the street.

CHAPTER FORTY-SEVEN

"GARFIELD! HOLD IT right there!"

Jake's voice was loud enough to attract the attention of the men who had just left the palace. The three of them stopped and stared.

Garfield stopped and turned toward the voice. When he saw Jake he stiffened momentarily, then seemed to relax.

"I don't believe it," he said. "Is that you, Big Jake?"

"It's me."

Garfield was standing in the bright light given off by the show palace. Jake was in the shadows in the street. He could see Garfield's gun also tucked into his belt.

Jake knew that a gun battle between two men usually resulted in an exchange of fire with most of the lead landing harmlessly in a wall, or breaking some glass and bottles in a saloon, or occasionally hitting an innocent bystander before one of the men finally struck home with a shot. The days of civilized duels, with men standing back to back, taking ten paces, and then exchanging a single shot, were long gone.

This threatened to be a mess, but at least there were only the three men watching, and Curly, who had come down from the casino doors.

"You kill Seaforth?" Garfield asked.

"I did. I put a hole in him. But not before he told me it was you who shot my friend."

"On his order," Garfield said. "Did he tell you that?"

"It don't matter," Jake said. "You put a bullet in my friend's chest."

Garfield grinned.

"And it was a helluva shot, wasn't it?"

Jake didn't answer.

"And what about you, Big Jake?' Garfield asked. "How's your shoulder?"

"Fine," Jake said. "Got it seen to good and proper by a sawbones."

"Hmm," Garfield said, "guess that's why you're looking better than the last time I saw you." The man looked around. "You alone? Or you got backing?"

"This is between you and me, Garfield," Jake said. "Nobody else."

"Then I'm not going to get one in the back?"

"Only if you run from me, like a coward."

"And what are you planning here, Jake?" Garfield asked. "A dime novel shoot-out in the street?"

One of the three men stuck his head back in the palace door, shouted, and more people began to appear. Now there were plenty of witnesses to this fight being fair.

Curly leaned against a post to watch, his hand on the gun in his belt. Jake hoped the young man would be able to resist getting involved.

"This ain't a dime novel, Garfield," Jake said. "This is real life."

"That it is, Big Jake, that it is," Garfield said, "and in real life, you don't have a prayer against me."

"I tell you what, Garfield," Jake said. "I'm gonna figure that since you're such a good shot with a rifle, you probably can't hit a thing with a handgun."

"Is that the way you figure it?"

There was enough light for Jake to notice Garfield's eyes suddenly darting about, and he realized he'd struck a nerve. It had been a guess, but it turned out to be a good one.

"I tell you what, Big Jake," Garfield said. "I'll give you a chance to walk away from this and forget the whole thing. How's that?"

"I'm afraid I can't do that, Garfield," Jake said. "I've got too much invested in this, already. And too many men have died."

"Well then, fill your hand, Big Jake."

They both drew their pistols from their belts, and later witnesses would comment that it was hard to choose who was slower, since they had both pretty much fumbled their weapons out.

They each pulled their triggers over and over again, hoping at least one shot would strike home. The men standing in front of the show palace scattered, as many of Jake's shots went wild. Glass broke, at least one horse cried out in pain while the others yanked at their reins, pulling them loose from the hitching posts, where their riders had carelessly looped them as they rushed to get inside.

The horses bolted, some of them running between Jake and Garfield.

Garfield could have stepped away from the horses before drawing his gun, but his intention actually was to use them as cover. Big Jake's guess was right; Garfield was a genius with a rifle, and a dolt with a handgun.

As all the horses scattered in fear, the only one who stood his ground was the sorrel.

The horses ran off, the onlookers ducked back into

the palace, and it was suddenly quiet enough for the sound of both guns' hammers falling on empty chambers to be heard.

Jake had to reload.

Garfield dropped his handgun into the street and lunged to pluck his rifle from the sorrel's back.

"Jake!"

He turned toward his name and saw Curly standing there, holding his gun.

"Catch!"

As Curly tossed his pistol in the air Jake dropped his and reached out to catch it, knowing he had a fifty-fifty chance of actually grabbing it as it flipped end over end toward him.

Amazingly, the grips landed right in his hand. As he turned to point the weapon at Garfield, the man also turned, bringing his rifle to bear on Jake.

Jake had fired six shots wildly and missed Garfield completely. But this time he pulled the trigger once, and the bullet struck Teddy Garfield right in the chest. All the strength went out of the man's arms before he could pull the trigger of his rifle, which then dropped from his limp hands. He fell onto his face in the street, dead.

"Stand right there!" Jake heard a voice behind him say. "Drop the gun."

Jake did, and raised his hands.

"Law?"

"That's right."

The speaker came around in front of him, holding his gun, and wearing a sheriff's badge.

"There's a story here, Sheriff," Jake said, "and I wanna tell it to you."

"You'll get your chance," the lawman said.

The witnesses came back out from the palace now that the shooting had stopped, and Curly came walking over to where Jake and the sheriff were standing.

"It was a fair fight, Sheriff," Curly said.

"The kid's right, Sheriff," one of the onlookers called out. "We saw it. That feller on the ground called for the other feller to fill his hand."

The other onlookers began to nod their heads.

"Well," the sheriff said, staring at Jake from beneath bushy white eyebrows that matched his mustache, "that may be, but it looks to me like we got some property damage to take care of."

The sheriff picked up Curly's gun from the ground and stuck it in his belt.

"Let's take a walk, mister," he said to Jake.

As the sheriff marched Jake off to his office, Curly grabbed Jake's gun from the dirt and stuck it in his belt.

The onlookers were now gathering around Garfield's body, taking a closer look.

CHAPTER FORTY-EIGHT

By MORNING JAKE had told the sheriff his story, from driving the herd to Dodge City to tracking Garfield to San Antonio.

Garfield's body had been removed from the street, where a large crowd had eventually gathered, probably made up of the gamblers who had lost their money and had nothing else to do but stare at a dead body, for free.

While Jake was in the sheriff's office, telling his story and answering questions, Curly had reclaimed his sorrel from in front of the Alamo, and had then gone and found Taco and Dundee to tell them what happened.

The three of them were outside the sheriff's office when the door opened and Jake staggered out.

"So no jail time?" Dundee asked.

"No," Jake said, "I just had to pay the city for the lamps I shot out, and pay the show palace for the windows I broke."

"You did fire a lot of shots," Curly said.

"Typical gunfight, huh?" Dundee asked.

"I also had to pay the vet's bill for the horse I nicked," Jake said, with a yawn.

"Sounds like a lot of your money is gonna end up stayin' here in San Antone," Dundee said.

"The money does not matter," Taco said. "You did what you set out to do, Big Jake. Señor Chance has been avenged."

"Yes, he has," Jake said, yawning again.

"You had better get some sleep, señor," Taco said.

"You got that right, old friend," Jake said. "The sheriff wants me out of town first thing tomorrow mornin'."

"At least he's givin' you today," Curly said.

"I told him I needed to get some rest, and then to find my sorrel."

"He's in the livery, Big Jake," Curly said. "I grabbed him last night."

"Thanks for that, Curly."

"So it's all over?" Dundee asked. "You don't mind if we spend some time in a saloon today?"

"Like Taco, says," Jake replied. "I did what I set out to do. You boys are on your own now. Saloon, gambling hall, whorehouse, whatever you want. Go do it. I'm gonna get some shut-eye."

"And after that, señor?" Taco asked. "Where will you be going now that you no longer have a ranch?"

"Taco, my amigo," Jake said, "I don't have any idea."

They watched Big Jake Motley walk off.

Ready to find
your next great read?

Let us help.

Visit prh.com/nextread